ACCLAIM FOR ROBIN LEE HATCHER

"In *Cross My Heart*, book two of her Legacy of Faith series, author Robin Lee Hatcher continues to delve into the powerful influence of a spiritual family heritage. She weaves together two touching stories that examine life choices and their consequences. Utilizing a dual-time plot set against World War II and present day, Hatcher writes with realism and compassion about how hope and healing can grow from our deepest wounds."

—Beth K. Vogt, Christy Award–winning author

"In this seamless time slip novel, Hatcher provides inspiration in each character's growing relationship with the Lord, and prompts readers to reflect on their own journey. This story of loss and redemption is sure to win the hearts of contemporary and historic romance fans alike."

—*Hope by the Book* on *Who I Am with You*

"This [is] a lovely story of love and loss and forgiveness."

—*The Parkersburg News & Sentinel* on *Who I Am with You*

"Best-selling inspirational romance star Hatcher weaves a story of love and identity lost and found . . . The characters are authentic, the butterflies of anticipation are persistent, and the protagonists' deferred attraction is thrillingly palpable; you cannot help but hold your breath until they realize it too."

—*Booklist* review on *Who I Am with You*

"Hatcher's moving novel is rich in healing and hope, and realistically portrays the tough introspection that sometimes comes with being hurt."

—*Publishers Weekly* on *Who I Am with You*

"Tender and heartwarming, Robin Lee Hatcher's *Who I Am with You* is a faith-filled story about the power of forgiveness, second chances, and unconditional love. A true delight for lovers of romantic inspirational fiction, this story will not only make you swoon, it will remind you of God's goodness and grace."

—Courtney Walsh, *New York Times* and *USA TODAY* bestselling author

"Whenever I want to fall in love again, I pick up a Robin Lee Hatcher novel."

—Francine Rivers, *New York Times* bestselling author

"Hatcher's richly layered novels pull me in like a warm embrace, and I never want to leave. I own and love every one of this master storyteller's novels. Highly recommended!"

—Colleen Coble, *USA TODAY* bestselling author

"Engaging and humorous, Hatcher's storytelling will warm readers' hearts . . . A wonderfully delightful read."

—*RT Book Reviews*, 4 stars, on *You're Gonna Love Me*

"Hatcher has written a contemporary romance novel that is a heart-warming story about love, faith, regret, and second chances."

—*CBA Market* on *You're Gonna Love Me*

"Hatcher (*Another Chance to Love You*) creates a joyous, faith-infused tale of recovery and reconciliation."

—*Publishers Weekly* on *You're Gonna Love Me*

"*You're Gonna Love Me* is a gentle romance that offers hope for second chances. Author Robin Lee Hatcher has a gift for welcoming readers into fictional close-knit communities fortified with love and trust. With each turn of the page, I relaxed into the quiet rhythm of Hatcher's storytelling, where she deftly examines the heart's desires of her characters set against the richly-detailed Idaho setting."

—Beth K. Vogt, Christy Award–winning author

"*You're Gonna Love Me* nourished my spirit as I read about a hero and heroine with realistic struggles, human responses, and honest growth. Robin Lee Hatcher makes me truly want to drive to Idaho and mingle with the locals."

—Hannah Alexander, author of *The Wedding Kiss*

"I didn't think *You'll Think of Me*, the first book in Robin Lee Hatcher's Thunder Creek, Idaho series, could be beat. But she did it again . . . This second chance story will melt your heart and serve as a parable for finding redemption through life's lessons and God's grace. Thunder Creek will always hold a special place in my heart."

—Lenora Worth, author of *Her Lakeside Family*, on *You're Gonna Love Me*

"With two strong, genuine characters that readers will feel compassion for and a heartwarming modern-day plot that inspires, Hatcher's romance is a wonderfully satisfying read."

—*RT Book Reviews*, 4 stars, on *You'll Think of Me*

"A heart-warming story of love, acceptance, and challenge. Highly recommended."

—*CBA Market* on *You'll Think of Me*

"*You'll Think of Me* is like a vacation to small town Idaho where the present collides with the past and it's not clear which will win. The shadows of the past threaten to trap Brooklyn in the past. Can she break free into the freedom to love and find love? The story kept me coming back for just one more page. A perfect read for those who love a romance that is much more as it explores important themes."

—Cara Putman, award–winning author of *Shadowed by Grace* and *Beyond Justice*

"Hatcher is able to unravel emotions within her characters so brilliantly that we sense the transformation taking place within ourselves . . . readers will relish the warmth of . . . the ranchland."

—*RT Book Reviews* on *Keeper of the Stars*

"Hatcher fans will be left smiling and eagerly awaiting her next novel."

—*CBA Retailers + Resources* on *Keeper of the Stars*

"True to the contemporary romance genre, Robin Lee Hatcher's *Keeper of the Stars* will satisfy romance fans and give them a joy ride as they travel the road of pain and forgiveness to reach the happily-ever-after."

—BookTalk at *Fiction 411*

"Robin Lee Hatcher weaves a romance with heart that grabs readers and won't let go. *Whenever You Come Around* pulled me in from the get-go. Charity Anderson, a beautiful, successful author with a deadline and a painful secret, runs into Buck Malone, a handsome, confirmed-bachelor cowboy from her past, and he needs her help. I was captivated, and I guarantee you'll be rooting for them too."

—Sunni Jeffers, award–winning
author of *Heaven's Strain*

"A heartwarming and engaging romance, *Whenever You Come Around* is a splendid read from start to finish!"

—Tamera Alexander, *USA TODAY* bestselling author
of *To Whisper Her Name* and *From a Distance*

"A handsome cowboy, horses, and a hurting heroine make for a winning combination in this newest poignant story by Robin Lee Hatcher. A gently paced but delightful ride, *Whenever You Come Around* will take readers on a journey of healing right along with the characters. Readers will feel at home in Kings Meadow and won't want to leave."

—Jody Hedlund, bestselling author of *Love Unexpected*

"First loves find sweet second chances in Kings Meadow. Heartwarming, romantic, and filled with hope and faith, this is Hatcher at her best!"

—Lisa Wingate, *New York Times* bestselling author of *Before We Were Yours*, on *Whenever You Come Around*

"In *Whenever You Come Around* Hatcher takes a look at the pain of secrets that kill the heart. But love indeed conquers all. Robin Lee Hatcher is the go-to classic romance author."

—Rachel Hauck, award-winning, *New York Times* bestselling author of *The Wedding Dress*

"Robin Lee Hatcher has created an emotionally engaging romance, a story of healing and self-forgiveness wrapped up in a package about small-town life and a cowboy who lives a life honoring God. I want to live in Kings Meadow."

—Sharon Dunn, author of *Cold Case Justice* and *Wilderness Target*, on *Whenever You Come Around*

"*Whenever You Come Around* draws you into the beauty and history of the horse country of Kings Meadow, Idaho. With every turn of the page, Robin Lee Hatcher woos readers with a love story of a modern-day cowboy and a city girl. Buck and Charity rescue each other from the lives they had planned—lives limited by fear. Instead, they discover their unexpected God-ordained happily ever after. A discerning writer, Hatcher handles Charity's past heartbreak with sensitivity and grace."

—Beth K. Vogt, author of *Somebody Like You*, one of *Publishers Weekly*'s Best Books of 2014

"*Whenever You Come Around* is one of Robin Lee Hatcher's pure-romance best, with a heroine waiting for total redemption and a strong hero of great worth. I find myself still smiling long after the final page has been read."

—Hannah Alexander, author of the Hallowed Halls series

"*Whenever You Come Around* is a slow dance of letting go of the past and its very real pain to step into the light of love. It's a story that will wrap around your soul with the hope that no past is so dark and haunted that it can't be forgiven and overcome. It's a love story filled with sweetness, tension, and slow fireworks. Bottom line, it was a romance I couldn't—and didn't want to—put down."

—Cara Putman, award-winning author of *Shadowed by Grace* and *Where Treetops Glisten*

"In *Love Without End,* Robin Lee Hatcher once again takes us to Kings Meadow, Idaho, in a sweeping love story that captures the heart and soul of romance between two people who have every reason not to fall in love. With an interesting backstory interspersed among the contemporary chapters, and well-drawn, relatable secondary characters, Hatcher hits the mark with her warm and inviting love story."

—Martha Rogers, author of the series Winds Across the Prairie and The Homeward Journey

"*Love Without End,* the first book in the new Kings Meadow Romance series, again intertwines two beautiful and heartfelt romances. One in the past and one in the future together make this a special read. I'm so glad Robin wrote a love story for Chet who suffered so much in *A Promise Kept* (January 2014). Kimberly, so wrong for him, becomes so right. Not your run-of-the-mill cowboy romance—enriched with deft writing and deep emotion."

—Lyn Cote, author of *Honor*, Quaker Brides, Book One

"No one writes about the joys and challenges of family life better than Robin Lee Hatcher, and she's at the top of her game with *Love Without End*. This beautiful and deeply moving story will capture your heart as it captured mine."

—Margaret Brownley, *New York Times* bestselling author

"*Love Without End,* Book One in Robin Lee Hatcher's new Kings Meadow series, is a delight from start to finish. The author's skill at depicting the love and challenges of family has never been more evident as she deftly combines two love stories—past and present—to capture readers' hearts and lift their spirits."

—Marta Perry, author of *The Forgiven,*
Keepers of the Promise, Book One

"I always expect excellence when I open a Robin Lee Hatcher novel. She never disappoints. The story here reminds me of a circle without end as Robin takes us through a modern-day romance while looping one character through a WWII tale of love and loss and the resurrection of hope and purpose. *Love Without End* touched my heart and guided me to some wonderful truths of how God's love is a gift and a treasure."

—Donita K. Paul, bestselling author

"A beautiful, heart-touching story of God's amazing grace, and how He can restore and make new that which was lost."

—Francine Rivers, *New York Times*
bestselling author, on *A Promise Kept*

Cross My Heart

ALSO BY ROBIN LEE HATCHER

You're Gonna Love Me

You'll Think of Me

The Heart's Pursuit

A Promise Kept

A Bride for All Seasons

Heart of Gold

Loving Libby

Return to Me

The Perfect Life

Wagered Heart

Whispers from Yesterday

The Forgiving Hour (e-book and audio only)

The Shepherd's Voice (e-book and audio only)

LEGACY OF FAITH SERIES

Who I Am with You

How Sweet It Is (available in 2020)

KINGS MEADOW ROMANCE SERIES

Love Without End

Whenever You Come Around

Keeper of the Stars

WHERE THE HEART LIVES SERIES

Belonging

Betrayal

Beloved

THE SISTERS OF BETHLEHEM SPRINGS SERIES

A Vote of Confidence

Fit to Be Tied

A Matter of Character

COMING TO AMERICA SERIES

Dear Lady

Patterns of Love

In His Arms

Promised to Me

NOVELLAS

I Hope You Dance, included in *Kiss the Bride* and *How to Make a Wedding*

Autumn's Angel, included in *A Bride for All Seasons*

A Love Letter to the Editor, included in *Four Weddings and a Kiss*

Cross My Heart

A LEGACY OF FAITH NOVEL

ROBIN LEE HATCHER

THOMAS NELSON
Since 1798

Cross My Heart

Published in Nashville, Tennessee, by Thomas Nelson. Thomas Nelson is a registered trademark of HarperCollins Christian Publishing, Inc.

Thomas Nelson titles may be purchased in bulk for educational, business, fund-raising, or sales promotional use. For information, please email SpecialMarkets@ThomasNelson.com.

Various people have attributed the quote on page 17 to Edmund Burke. But it is generally considered to be of unverified origin.

Library of Congress Cataloging-in-Publication Data

Names: Hatcher, Robin Lee, author.
Title: Cross my heart / Robin Lee Hatcher.
Description: Nashville, Tennessee : Thomas Nelson, [2019] | Series: A legacy of faith novel
Identifiers: LCCN 2018059440| ISBN 9780785219309 (softcover) | ISBN 9780785219323 (epub)
Subjects: | GSAFD: Love stories. | Christian fiction.
Classification: LCC PS3558.A73574 C76 2019 | DDC 813/.54--dc23 LC record available at https://lccn.loc.gov/2018059440

Printed in the United States of America

19 20 21 22 23 LSC 5 4 3 2 1

To Shayla Jo Paskett, my beautiful granddaughter, for sharing your experience in horse rescues and the training of wild mustangs. I've loved watching you grow over the years into a horsewoman extraordinaire.

To Christi King, for generously sharing your time and expertise about the equine therapy program at Ride for Joy.

Prologue

February

KUNA, IDAHO

Ben Henning showed his cousin Jessica into the kitchen of the old farmhouse. "I'm not really ready for company," he told her as he motioned to one of the chairs.

"I can see that." She smiled as her gaze took in the stacks of boxes in the kitchen, the living room, and down the hallway.

"Want some coffee? It's fresh made."

"No, thanks. I don't plan to stay long. I know you're busy with moving and all. Besides, I need to get back to Mom's house before it's time to feed Hope again. She's growing so fast, and she's always hungry."

Ben settled onto a chair opposite Jessica. "How old is she now?"

"Almost six months."

"Can't hardly believe that."

"Me either." Jessica leaned toward the tote she'd set on the floor next to her chair. A moment later she drew out a large book. "This is Andrew Henning's Bible." She slid it across the table to him. "I brought it for you."

"For me?" The leather cover was worn and cracked, the outside edges curled. He ran a hand gently over the book that had once belonged to his great-great-grandfather. The man who had owned this house, this farm, from early in the Great Depression until he was almost seventy.

"For you." Jessica smiled gently. "Great-Grandpa Andrew . . . Well, I guess he was your great-great-grandfather, wasn't he? I always forget that since you and I are close to the same age. Anyway, he gave it to my grandmother before he died, with the instructions that she was to keep it until she felt God tell her to pass it along to another family member. Then that person was to do the same whenever the time came. My mom gave it to me after Grandma Frani's funeral, and now I want you to have it."

Ben opened the front cover, saw that the first page had been torn then mended with tape. Several pages stuck together when he turned them. He pulled them apart, revealing the Henning family tree. His namesake, Benjamin Tandy Henning, was one of the children listed beneath Andrew's and Helen's names. He ran his finger down the list. The change in penmanship told him when someone else had taken over the task of filling in the names of great-grandchildren and great-great-grandchildren.

"Are you sure you're ready to give it up?" he asked. "You haven't had it very long. Your grandmother hasn't even been gone a year."

"I'm sure."

He heard the smile in her answer before he looked up to meet her gaze.

"Ben, when I heard you were moving to the farm to live, I knew God wanted you to have this Bible. I don't know why, but I believe the Lord's got something special in mind for both you and this farm." She leaned toward him. "When my mom gave it to me, she told me to let what I found inside bless me. And it did. What I found helped give me back my faith and restore my hope in the future. And those two changes allowed me to open my heart to love again. I don't know what's in store for you, but I believe God wants to encourage you through His Word and the notes Grandpa Henning made inside that old Bible. I think God wants you to be blessed by it next."

Ben's heart had quickened as Jessica spoke. Just last night he'd believed God had given him a vision for this property. The vision was nebulous at best, but he trusted it would take shape, that God would reveal more in time. His cousin's words seemed to confirm it.

"Thanks, Jessica." He closed the leather cover. "This means a lot to me. More than I can tell you."

She nodded, and he had the feeling she understood even if he couldn't put it into words.

Chapter 1

August

Sitting in his pickup truck, Ben punched the address of the destination into his iPhone. Once the GPS coordinates were set, he tapped the screen to start the map app. "Proceed to the route, then turn left," Siri told him.

That much he'd already known. He put the truck in gear and followed the driveway to the road. Turning as commanded, he couldn't help thinking it would be nice if directions for life were as easy to come by. Just punch in the desired destination, and presto, learn how to get there by proceeding to the route and turning left.

For the past six months, it seemed as if he'd stumbled along, finding his way more by accident than by divine guidance. He'd never lost the belief that God had given him a vision for the farm, but making it happen hadn't been as easy as he'd expected. Counselors had been reluctant to work with him or promise to refer clients. Horsemen had wanted more than he could afford for the right kind of horses. Insurance companies wanted a small fortune to insure. His banker was dubious about him surviving more than a few months.

He'd been frustrated by the number of times he'd thought a door was opening only to have it slam in his face. If this was really God's plan, shouldn't it come together smoothly? When he'd said as much to Grandpa Grant last night, the older man had laughed and told Ben he had a lot to learn. Not exactly what he'd wanted to hear.

Ben hadn't admitted to Grandpa Grant—his mentor, his adviser, his favorite person in the world—that he also believed the Harmony Barn, as he was calling this new endeavor, could be more than just a service to help others. It might be a way for him to finally make amends for what he'd done to his best friend. Maybe the next time Ben tried to reach out to Craig, he wouldn't be shut down. Ben owed the guy, and he wanted to help. If only he'd get the chance—

Siri broke into those darker thoughts, telling him to turn left once again. When he reached the intersection, he did so.

The main roads in this rural county of southwestern Idaho were laid out in perfect square miles. Although the roads might undulate with the rise and fall of the landscape, they ran straight as an arrow, with few exceptions. On Ben's right he passed cornfields that he guessed would be harvested before much longer. Whatever once grew in the field on his left had already been harvested and plowed under. He wondered if Ashley Showalter lived on a farm like one of these.

He hadn't called her in advance of this visit. Maybe he should have made an appointment, but he'd been too excited when the second person in two days had told him Ashley was someone he should talk to about the horses. Perhaps the reason he hadn't called her first was because he didn't want to risk another closed door. He wanted the chance to look her in the eyes and convince her that she should help him.

Sweat trickled along Ashley's spine and down the sides of her face as she carried a board up the ladder. She would rather be inside sipping a cold beverage than outside in this intense August heat. But she expected another horse to arrive today and wanted the new shelter finished before the truck and trailer pulled into her driveway.

The crunch of gravel warned her it might be too late to finish. She looked up, but the silver truck coming slowly toward the shed wasn't pulling a trailer. Great. The last thing she wanted right now was an interruption.

The truck stopped, the door opened, and a man got out, followed by a yellow Lab. Ashley was about to shout a warning about her own dogs, although they were locked inside the house, but the driver moved to the back of the truck and lowered the tailgate. An instant later the Lab jumped into the bed and lay down in the shade cast by the nearest tree.

She watched as the man—thirtyish, tall, blond, and impossibly good-looking—headed for the door of her house without a glance in her direction. Before he reached it, she called to him. "Nobody's in there."

He stopped and turned at the sound of her voice.

Not waiting for him to answer, she went down the ladder. By the time she reached the ground, he was approaching her.

He removed his sunglasses, squinting his blue eyes against

the bright sun, and gave her a brief smile. "Are you Ashley Showalter?"

"I am."

"I'm Ben Henning." He offered his hand.

She acknowledged his introduction with a nod, then shook his hand.

"I was told you might be able to help me."

"Are you looking to buy a horse?"

"Yes and no." He shrugged and smiled again.

Ashley raised her eyebrows, awaiting a better explanation.

"I can probably afford to buy one horse now, if the price is right. But I'm in need of more than one. Or will be eventually."

What exactly did that mean, she wondered.

"I own a farm outside of Kuna." Ben Henning stuck his fingertips in the back pockets of his jeans. "My grandpa raised alfalfa hay on it, and I leased that out this summer. But now I'd like to put the place to use in a different way. I plan to open an equine therapy barn."

Ashley felt a quickening in her chest. She couldn't help it. She believed in equine therapy. Being around horses healed a person's spirit. She knew that firsthand. "Do you know anything about horses, Mr. Henning?"

"Call me Ben, please. As for horses, I'm no rodeo cowboy—" He grinned, showing he wasn't offended by the tone of her question. "But I know the front end of a horse from the back end, and I can saddle and ride one without help."

She relaxed slightly. "Let's go sit in the shade."

"I'd like that, Miss Showalter."

"Ashley."

"Ashley," he echoed.

Something about the way he said her name made her insides shiver. The timbre of his voice was like warm honey. And she wasn't happy with her reaction. Good-looking men with plenty of charm were off-limits. Once burned, twice shy, as the old saying went. And she'd been burned, so all the more reason to stick to business.

Once they were seated on chairs under the covered patio, Ashley gave him her full attention. "Tell me why you want to open an equine therapy barn."

Leaning forward at the waist, forearms resting on his knees, Ben cleared his throat. His expression grew serious. "Do you believe in God, Miss Showalter?"

"Do I—" She drew back in surprise. That had definitely come out of the blue. But Ben waited, watching her. Finally, she said, "Yes, I . . . I do."

"Well, the short answer to your question is God told me that's what I'm supposed to do with the farm. Make it a place where spirits get healed and hope gets restored through the use of horses." He spoke with certainty, a new intensity in his eyes.

"Okay. I like the sound of that. But what makes you so sure . . . God wants you to do it?"

"That's hard to explain. It's just something I feel. In here." He tapped his chest with one hand. "My grandpa would say it was knowing that you know that you know." His smile returned.

"Knowing that you know that you know." It must be nice to be so sure of something. She nodded, encouraging him to continue.

Obliging her, he said, "A number of years ago, I was in counseling myself, and it was recommended that I participate in an equine therapy program. To tell you the truth, I thought it sounded hokey. But by the time I was done with six weeks in the program, I'd changed my mind. It did help me, being with the horses. I don't even understand why. All I know is it helped. I was better because of spending time with Blacky." He chuckled softly as he straightened on the chair. "That was the gelding's name. Anyway, when I inherited my grandfather's farm, I wasn't sure what I would do with it. I'm not a farmer myself. My mom thinks I should sell it."

A shadow passed over his face, and he fell silent.

Feeling a strange need to distract him from whatever had made him frown, she asked, "How large is the farm?"

"Forty acres."

"Wow." What she could do with forty acres. It made her pulse race just to think about it. But she didn't have anyone who would leave her that kind of legacy, and her job as a clerk in a retail store would never earn her enough that she could buy such a place. She was lucky to have her small house and two acres.

"I'm not going to sell the farm," he said emphatically. "I'm going to do something good with it. I don't expect to make a living from it. At least not at the beginning. Maybe never. But if a few hours in the evening or on a weekend could help a kid or a vet or . . . or a guy like me, anybody who's struggling . . ." He let the words drift into silence, his hands absently rubbing the arms of his chair.

She wondered what he meant by "a guy like me." Until that moment, he'd looked so confident and put together. Why had he needed equine therapy? Was he somebody who'd struggled?

"Sorry. I guess I got carried away. It's just that I want this to work out."

"No. You shouldn't apologize for having a passion for something. Especially something that could help others."

"Thanks." With a slight smile of acknowledgment, he leaned back in his chair.

"But I'm not sure why you came to see me."

"I guess I didn't explain that part well, did I? I was told that you know just about everybody around the valley who's involved with horses, including in the rescue network. It seems to me maybe we could help each other. I've done lots of research this summer. I know there are different kinds of therapy programs. The one I participated in was in a remote location in the mountains and had a narrow focus. I've visited one that caters more to kids and adults with disabilities and focuses on riding." He leaned forward, the excitement back in his eyes. "Then there are the places that take in abused horses and ask nothing of them except to let at-risk kids spend time with them, love them, even."

"Broken horses," she whispered, "helping broken people."

"That's it." He pointed at her. "That's it exactly. Broken horses helping broken people. A couple of different people suggested you might be the person I should talk to to help with finding the right horses for my program." He glanced toward the lean-to shelter. "They said your space is limited, so you take in a horse, get it past the crisis, and then find a home for it. Well, I've got lots of space, and I'd like the Harmony Barn to be a permanent home for any rescued horses we acquire."

Her pulse began to race.

"Of course, if we provide a riding program too—and I want to do that—then all the horses can't be abused. Many of the clients will have disabilities of one kind or another, so I'll have to have saddle horses that are well trained and gentle. Perhaps we can buy them. Perhaps we can lease them." He leaned forward again, and his gaze intensified. "Would you be willing to help me find the right horses for our purposes?"

The temptation was to lean toward him too. The temptation was to get so caught up in his ideas and enthusiasm that she forgot to be careful. She resisted it, answering with caution, "I can't say right now. I'd have to see your setup. And I'd want to talk to whatever vet you plan to work with."

For an instant, she saw disappointment in his eyes, and she wondered if he might try to say more in order to convince her. But at last he nodded. "Fair enough. I can arrange to show you around the farm any day next week. You figure out the best day and time for you, and I'll make it happen." His gaze shifted to the shelter a second time. "I interrupted your work. Would you like a hand with that before I go?"

"No, thanks. I'm good." She answered more out of habit than anything. She was used to doing things on her own and had a serious independent streak.

Ben got to his feet. "Well, then, I'll leave you to it." He took a card from his wallet and placed it on the table next to her chair. "Call me when you know your schedule."

"I'll do it." Picking up the card, she rose too.

He paused, eyeing her, then suddenly grinned. "Thanks for listening to my ideas."

"Glad to," she answered, realizing it was true.

Thanksgiving welled up inside of Ben as he drove back to the farm. He'd seen the spark of interest in Ashley Showalter's eyes. She might not have agreed right then, but his gut told him he would hear from her before the week was out. "Thank You, God," he said aloud, beginning to grin like a fool. "Thanks for the open door. Finally, an open door."

The good feeling didn't last. It was chased away by the memory of his mom calling him stupid for holding on to such valuable land instead of selling it.

Ben couldn't remember a time when things had been good between him and his mom. Not even when he was a little kid. She'd resented him. He'd ruined her plans, she'd told him a thousand times. Pregnant at sixteen and a mom at seventeen, Wendy Henning hadn't married the boy who'd fathered Ben. Had she even known who the father was? He'd often wondered, but she'd never said. He only knew she blamed having a kid for every problem in her life, past and present. Probably future too.

Any stability experienced during Ben's childhood had been because of his grandparents, especially his grandfather. Their farm had been a safe haven for him. He'd loved it there as a kid. He loved it there now. But he'd never in his wildest dreams expected Grandpa Grant to give him the farm.

"Sell it," his mom had shouted at him over the phone that morning. "Do you know what that land is worth?" When he'd repeated the same thing he'd said to her every time she brought it up, that he wasn't going to sell, that's when she'd called him stupid—for the umpteenth time—and hung up. It was a scene they'd been playing out for months.

Ben had done plenty of dumb things in his life. Keeping the farm wasn't one of them. He knew that in the deepest part of his soul.

He slowed the truck and turned onto his property, seeing it through the haze of happier memories. He'd spent countless weekends here in his boyhood. And years ago, after his stint in juvie, Ben had lived with his grandparents for a while. That time had given him the roots he'd needed later—too many years later, sadly—to get his life back on track. He could never thank God enough for what he'd found on this farm.

The house was small by anybody's standards. A small kitchen, small living room, small bath, and three small bedrooms on the ground level with an attic room above. His great-grandfather, for whom Ben was named, along with his two brothers, Oscar and Andy, had used that attic bedroom during the thirties and forties. In the decades since, the kitchen had been modernized, and the house was now heated by natural gas rather than wood or coal. And yet whenever Ben stepped through the door, he felt transported back in time. It seemed to him he could hear the voices of his ancestors who'd lived there, even those he'd never known.

He parked the truck beneath the carport, but instead of going into the house, he strode toward the barn. Dusty, his yellow Lab, followed close at his heels. There were no horses or cows in the barn or in nearby pens or pasture, no chickens in the coop. There hadn't been any livestock on the farm since a good five years before his grandfather gave him the place, and Ben looked forward to watching the barnyard come to life again. Horses for the therapy sessions, of course. Maybe a cat or two for the barn and even some chickens in the coop again.

Dusty trotted off, exploring, and when he returned, he had a large stick in his mouth. Ben took the stick and gave it a good throw. The dog raced after it, mindless of the heat of the day. Ben, on the other hand, was ready for a cold drink in the air-conditioned living room.

"Come on, boy. It's too hot to play fetch."

Fifteen minutes later, Ben sat on the sofa, a glass of cold diet soda in his hand. As he sipped the drink, his thoughts returned to Ashley Showalter. He didn't know what he'd expected, but it hadn't been the woman who'd stepped down from that ladder upon his arrival. Her light-brown hair had been caught in a ponytail, but enough strands had pulled loose to give her a delightfully disheveled appearance. Her face had glistened with perspiration. Slender as a reed, she hadn't looked strong enough to carry boards up a ladder or to hammer those same boards together into a shelter. Apparently looks were deceiving.

He sure hoped she would call him soon, because something inside of him said she *was* the right person to help him make the Harmony Barn happen.

Monday, September 4, 1939

Andrew Henning was in the Kuna Feed and Seed when he learned Britain and France had declared war on Germany. He'd been expecting other nations to declare war ever since the Nazis had invaded Poland three days earlier, but when he heard it, it still caught him by surprise.

"Mr. Finkel warned us this'd happen," Andrew's oldest son said. Sixteen years old and several inches taller than his father, Ben wore a conflicted expression, a cross between righteous anger and anticipation. "When the Nazis marched into Austria, he said it wouldn't end there. And then they took Czechoslovakia, and nobody did anything to stop them. Mr. Finkel told us the Nazis wouldn't stop until they overran everything."

"You're right. He warned us."

The Finkels had purchased the property across from the Henning farm three years earlier. Jewish immigrants from Germany, Hirsch and Ida Finkel had often expressed their concerns for what Hitler meant to do in Europe. And it had been happening as the Finkels predicted, step by step.

Ben lowered his voice. "Will America join England and France? Will we go to war, too, Dad? We can't stay out of it now."

"I don't know. I don't know." He reached out, intending to ruffle Ben's hair, the same as he'd done for years. Then he thought better of it and placed his hand on the boy's shoulder instead. Ben was approaching manhood at a rapid rate. If America went to war, he would soon be of age to serve in the military, and given his personality, he would be among the first to volunteer.

"Dad?"

"Hmm?"

"Is there any chance I could go to college?"

The sudden change of topic caused Andrew to frown in confusion, especially this particular topic. From the time Ben had come to live with Andrew and Helen at age nine, the boy had struggled with his schooling. The primary cause was disinterest, not because he wasn't smart enough to excel. And now he wanted to go to college?

Ben's expression was determined. "I want to be a pilot, and I found out yesterday the Army Air Corps Training Center requires a couple of years of college or three years of technical education before a guy can join. I'm gonna have to do one or the other."

Andrew felt his stomach sink when he heard the words "Army Air Corps." He knew exactly what his son would want to do once he became a pilot. And despite the many politicians who preached isolationism, Andrew didn't think Americans could remain aloof to what was happening in Europe. His neighbors had made him aware of too much to believe it. He'd read a quote, attributed to the Irish statesman Edmund Burke, that said, "The only thing necessary for the triumph of evil is that good men should do nothing." It was a statement that kept running through his mind lately. Would he want America to continue to do nothing? Even if doing something meant risking his son?

"Dad?"

He gave his head a shake. "Sorry, Ben. I was thinking of something else. Army Air Corps, huh? Becoming a pilot. You caught me by surprise." He cleared his throat as he tried to focus his thoughts. "College is expensive, and you know we don't have much extra cash, even with the economy improving. You'd have to bring up your grades if you want to go to college, and you'll have to get a job. Not just now but while you're in college. That means going to classes, doing your studies, and holding down work at the same time. It'll be tough. You'll have to want it bad."

"I do want it bad."

"You'll have to be willing to stick with it, no matter what."

"I will."

Andrew believed him. Ben had always been tenacious. In addition, he'd always been protective of others, especially his younger siblings. He cared about people, and he was a boy who kept his word. Boy? No, he wasn't a boy any longer. Not really.

Andrew released a breath. "Then we'll try to figure out how to make it happen. No promises, but we'll do our level best."

"Thanks, Dad. I'll do my part too. I promise."

Silently, Andrew prayed that he wasn't making a bad decision. One that would cost his son his life.

Chapter 2

The following Saturday, Ashley followed the instructions she'd received over the phone from Ben Henning and arrived at his property a little after one o'clock. So much of the farmland in the Treasure Valley had disappeared to urban sprawl, thanks to Boise being among the fastest-growing cities in America. But for now, this farm was what Ashley imagined the entire valley had looked like fifty years before. In fact, it looked like what she would want for herself, if wishes came true in this world.

The small house was white with yellow trim, and a tall weeping willow would shade the west side of it in another hour. The barn was large and sturdy in appearance. It had been painted red at one time, but over the years the boards had been bleached by the weather. Beyond the barn stood a couple of fenced paddocks, and past those the fields were green with alfalfa. Along both sides of the driveway, lava rocks had been used to make low fences. Knowing this area as she did, she suspected she would find more of those rocks around the place.

The yellow Lab that had accompanied Ben last week ran off

the porch and waited for Ashley's truck to roll to a halt. Before she got out of the pickup, Ben appeared in the house's doorway. He waved to her.

"You found it," he called as he, too, came off the porch.

"Not hard. Your directions were clear."

"Good." He looked down at the dog, seated nearby. "This is Dusty."

"Hello, Dusty." She leaned down to pat the Lab's head, and he gave her one of those looks, an invitation to go on petting.

"Come on. I'll show you around."

They turned in unison. Ben's first few strides were longer, but he quickly shortened them to match hers.

What do you know? An honest-to-goodness gentleman. Ashley's mom said gentlemen were a dying breed. It was nice to know she was wrong in this instance.

When they reached the barn, Ben swung the big door open, flooding the interior with sunlight. "There are three stalls in here now." He moved inside. "I thought I could build three more on that side of the barn. So there'd be room for a total of six horses. In time, I'd like to build bigger stables so we can add even more horses."

Ashley followed him inside. It was obvious the barn hadn't been used in a long while. Dust lay in a thick layer on every surface. There wasn't any hay or straw on the floor, only more dust. The workbench was free of tools. The feed boxes inside the stalls stood empty. She put a hand on one of the stall posts and gave it a push. It didn't budge. Not so much as a wiggle.

"Nice and solid." She turned to face Ben. "Ought to work well for your purpose."

He motioned with his head. "Have a look out here."

She followed him. When she'd pulled into the drive, she hadn't seen the round pen or the corral to its right, as they'd both been hidden by the barn.

Ben leaned an arm on the top rail of the corral. "Nice setup, isn't it?"

"Yes, it is." She moved to stand beside him. "You might want to open up more pasture so you won't have to rely so much on hay."

"I thought that too. More pasture, more horses." He smiled that appealingly crooked smile of his. Ashley's mind went suddenly blank, and her stomach tumbled.

A moment later Dusty slipped his head beneath the hand at her side. She was grateful for a reason to look down at the dog. She needed the distraction to get control of herself. She might like what this guy planned to do with this farm. She might even want to help him accomplish it. But that was all she wanted. She wasn't about to be taken in by his—or any other man's—charm.

"I promise you, Ashley, whatever horses come here to stay, they'll have good care." Ben's voice was low and serious.

She drew a breath and looked up. "I believe you."

"So, you'll help me?"

"I think so. Tell me more about what you'll need. The other day you said something about leasing horses?"

Ben turned his back to the corral fence and leaned against it. "Yeah. Some therapy programs lease a horse for a year at a time. Give it a home and food and veterinary care. Whatever it needs. Maybe the owners believe in the program and it's their way to help support it. Or maybe it keeps a family from having to sell a horse when they're going through a rough patch. Anyway, it's a win-win."

"Another way of rescuing horses," she said, more to herself than to him.

"I'm curious. What got you into that? The horse-rescue business, I mean."

"Short answer, my very first horse is the reason. I saved up and bought Gus when I was sixteen. I loved him. But he was older and not up to long, hard trail rides. The kind I wanted to do. So eventually I sold him and bought a younger horse." She frowned. "Later I found out Gus had been mistreated and left to starve. He was a good horse. That shouldn't've happened to him. I want to do what I can to keep it from happening to others. I can't save them all, but I can save one or two at a time. Like you heard, I'm part of a network of people who rescue horses before it's too late. And I'm working on becoming a charitable organization. That way I can accept tax-free donations."

"Seems we both want to be in the rescue business." There was understanding in his blue eyes, giving weight to his words.

"It would seem so."

"I think working together could make us both more successful with our endeavors."

Ben knew Ashley would help him, perhaps even before she realized it herself. Still, he sensed some lingering reluctance as well. He wondered why. He didn't think it had anything to do with the idea itself.

They started walking toward her pickup, Dusty running ahead of them. "I wrote down the information about my vet and the counselor I'll be working with." He pulled the folded three-by-five card from the back pocket of his Levi's. "I told them you might be calling."

"I will." She took the card.

He watched as she got into her truck and drove away. Then, whistling a tune, he went into the house. From the bookshelf he pulled a notebook and set it on the kitchen table. He sat and began to thumb through the pages, stopping occasionally to look at notes he'd written over the past months as his vision for this farm and the equine therapy program had taken shape.

Leaning back in his chair, he remembered telling Ashley that he knew the front end of a horse from the back end. In fact, he'd done plenty of riding with his best friend, Craig Foster, when they were boys. And those hours on horseback had been a time of peace and comfort, long before he experienced the benefits of equine therapy for himself. If only the two of them had kept riding horses instead of doing their best to get into every kind of trouble they could imagine—stealing, smoking, drinking, speeding.

Drinking and speeding.

He closed his eyes, not wanting to remember the sound of grinding metal, not wanting to recall the taste of blood in his mouth and the twisted shape of his friend as they'd lain in the wreckage. But the memories of that awful night were there anyway. Thirteen years and gallons of alcohol hadn't erased them. He doubted he would ever escape them.

He tried to summon some Bible verses, something that reminded him of who he was in Christ, but the dark, familiar whispers pushed them out. He was the reason Craig had spent the last thirteen years in a wheelchair. His stupidity. His recklessness. God had forgiven Ben for what he'd done, but Craig hadn't. And Ben couldn't forgive himself either. Not until he'd done everything possible to make it up to his friend.

His stomach still in knots, he got up and went to the bookshelf again. This time he brought his great-great-grandfather's Bible back to the table. Once there, he ran his hand over the cover before opening it to the title page.

To our beloved son,
Andrew Michael Henning,
on the occasion of his graduation
from the university.
Follow God and you will never lose your way.
Papa and Mama
Kuna, Idaho
May 1929

From the moment his cousin placed this Bible in his hands, Ben had felt a connection with it and with his great-great-grandfather. He couldn't explain it. The feeling was simply there. Sometimes it seemed as if his inspiration for the therapy barn hadn't been able to solidify until this holy book had come into his possession. There was no real reason to think so. No specific verse stood out. Neither did any of Andrew Henning's handwritten notes that Ben had read. And yet he felt the two—the Bible and the inspiration—were linked in some way.

"God, open more doors. Help me know the steps to take next. I need Your guidance."

The prayer seemed to ease some of the tension in his gut. He closed the Bible's cover, his gaze lifting to the clock on the wall, and he realized he was late. With a sigh, he got to his feet and took the keys from a nearby corner table. Before going out the door, he patted Dusty's head. "Stay in where it's cool, boy. I won't be very long."

The drive to the retirement community, a trip Ben made at least once a week, took about twenty minutes. At first he drove through farmland. Crops. Dairy cattle. Horses. But that soon gave way to subdivisions. Upscale subdivisions filled with large homes, private parks, and walking trails. It made Ben wonder where all these people worked. He'd heard there wasn't enough housing for all the people moving into the area. And while growth had served his construction firm well, it saddened him to see the farmland continue to disappear.

When he arrived at his destination, his grandfather stood outside his bungalow, waiting as his overweight black-and-brown dachshund sniffed the front lawn. Grandpa Grant waved as Ben got out of his truck.

"Hey, Grandpa."

"You missed lunch."

"I know. I lost track of the time." He strode toward the older man. "Miss Showalter came to check out the farm."

"And?"

"I think she liked what she saw."

"Good. Good." Grandpa patted Ben's shoulder. "Let's go inside. Come on, Chester."

The dog trotted up the sidewalk to the front door of the house, and the two men followed. After Grandpa opened the door, Chester made a beeline for the water bowl.

"Are you thirsty too?" his grandpa asked Ben.

"No, I'm good. Thanks."

The two men settled in the living room, Ben on the sofa and

his grandfather in his overstuffed chair, his feet up on an ottoman. Ben couldn't remember a time that the chair and footstool hadn't been a fixture in his grandparents' home, although the upholstery had changed a couple of times in Ben's memory. But it was still hard for him to picture his grandfather in a retirement community instead of at the farm.

"Are you happy here, Grandpa?"

The question seemed to puzzle the older man. "Yes, I am. Why do you ask?"

"I don't know. I just wonder if you ever wish you hadn't given me the farm. If you wish you still lived there or . . . or had done something else with it."

Grandpa Grant's expression changed from puzzlement to understanding. "Your mom's been after you again, hasn't she?"

"Yes." Ben never had been able to hide much from his grandfather.

"I'm sorry, son." He sighed. "I pray for the day my daughter's heart will be softened."

Ben found it hard to believe his mom could ever be different from how she was now.

As if his grandfather heard the thought, he said, "God changed you. That was an answer to prayer."

"Nothing is impossible with God," Ben replied softly.

"It's true, son. Remember it. And remember that our prayers never go unanswered, even when things don't turn out the way we expected or wanted."

"Because instead of *yes,* sometimes the answer is *no* and sometimes it's *wait.*" Ben had heard those words from his grandfather more than once over the years. He wished he'd recall them more often, especially when it came to closed doors.

"Indeed."

"Do you think your grandfather would approve of the changes I'm making to the farm? Do you think he'd be pleased to see it used for equine therapy instead of growing crops?"

"I do. Yes." His grandfather's gaze seemed to look into the past. "When I was little, Grandpa Andrew told me that he once resented being forced back to the farm by the Great Depression. Back then, the farm belonged to his in-laws, the Greysons. It went to Grandpa Andrew and Grandma Helen after Frank Greyson died. Grandpa never returned to the business career he studied for and thought he wanted so much. He and Grandma Helen both learned to love the farm, and they raised their five children there." His eyes focused on Ben, and he chuckled as he gave his head a shake. "You know all that. I'm rambling."

"I never tire of hearing it, Grandpa."

"I know, boy. You've always been patient with me."

Tuesday, June 25, 1940

"Andrew?"

He looked up from the newspaper. His wife stood in the entrance to the living room, watching him with concerned eyes.

"You look so worried all the time," Helen said softly. "Is it really so bad? The war in Europe."

"It is."

She entered the room and sat on the arm of his chair. While kissing his forehead, she ran the fingers of one hand through his hair. "We've survived worse times than these."

He nodded but wasn't sure he believed it. Helen trusted in the government to keep them out of the war. But was that a promise that could—or should—be kept? And if it wasn't kept, had they survived the worst? Or was the worst yet to come?

Norway, Denmark, Holland, and France had all fallen to the Nazi regime that year, a year that wasn't yet half over. It had been like the tumbling of dominoes. Only a miracle of God had saved the British armed forces at Dunkirk a few weeks earlier. A miracle of God and a flotilla of private boats and heroic citizens, ferrying over three hundred thousand troops from France to Britain.

His thoughts shifted to Ben. Seventeen and keenly interested in the war news. Seventeen and determined to join the Army Air Corps.

"Andrew?"

"Hmm?"

"I know you're worried about Ben."

He gave her a brief smile. After almost eleven years of marriage, they often understood what the other was thinking or feeling without a word being spoken. And when they did speak, they frequently said the same thing at the same time. It made him love his wife all the more, to experience how aligned they were.

"But if war does come," Helen continued, "would you have to go too?"

"It's doubtful. I'm probably too old for them to want me in the army." He'd turned thirty-five earlier that year. Was that too old to serve? He was in good health. He was strong, although he had a slight catch in one knee that gave him grief now and then. Nothing that made him immobile. "I imagine they'll need me growing food more than they'll need me with a gun."

A soft sigh escaped her, and he knew he'd eased her concerns. Would that he could ease his own as effortlessly.

Chapter 3

Ashley knew the moment she met the mare that the horse would be ideal for equine therapy. The sorrel, fourteen and a half hands high, was calm and gentle. Perhaps even a little on the lazy side. Although thin, she wasn't diseased. Nor was she starving to death, as was too often the case with a rescue.

Ashley stared into the mare's eyes and felt the horse saying, "Yes, I'm the one for the Harmony Barn." Okay, she had some non-horsey acquaintances who would call her nuts if she told them that, but that didn't make the feeling any less true.

When she had a spare moment later that morning, she called Ben Henning. "I've found your first horse."

"Really? That's great. How much?"

"Five hundred. Does that work?"

"Yes, and I'm ready for it. I stocked up on some basic supplies. Whatever the vet recommended that I have on hand. And I've got plenty of hay and grain. When can you bring the horse to the barn?"

"I'm busy the rest of today, and tomorrow I'm scheduled to work during the day. How about tomorrow evening?"

"That'll be perfect. I ought to be home by five, so anytime after that would work for me."

"Okay. I'll see you then." She pressed End and dropped her cell phone into the console of her truck. Then she pulled from the parking space and drove into Boise.

Her mom, Joyce Showalter, waited for her in front of Ashley's favorite restaurant. Actually, it was more of a diner, like the one in the *Happy Days* reruns she'd seen. Ashley's dad had brought her to the Silver Spoon every Saturday when she was little. It had been their special daddy-daughter time. Every Friday at bedtime he'd said, "What do you say we go to the Silver Spoon tomorrow? Just you and me." She'd always answered, "Yes, Daddy! Promise we'll go." And he'd always replied, "Cross my heart." After her dad passed away, Ashley and her mom had started coming here together. Not as frequently, and it had never been quite the same, but Ashley was still thankful for it.

"Hey, Mom." She hopped out of the cab of her truck.

"Hi, honey." Her mom kissed Ashley's cheek. "Was traffic bad?"

"No. Not too bad." It wasn't often they both had a day off in the middle of the week. Ashley's schedule could be all over the place and didn't always coincide with her mom's. "I'm hungry. How 'bout you?"

"Mmm."

They entered the restaurant and were greeted by Carol, a woman who'd waited on them for the past twenty years. Carol didn't own the place, but she often acted as if she did. Ashley adored her.

"Hi, Carol."

"You're lookin' good, kiddo."

"Thanks."

Carol led them to a table and set laminated menus before them. "Be right back with your water."

Perhaps one of the reasons Ashley loved this place so much was its unchangeableness. *Is that a word?* She hoped so because it was what she meant. The Silver Spoon had the same color paint, the same framed photographs on the walls, the same choice of food on the menus, and the same waitress in her blue dress and white apron as when Ashley was a girl and it was her daddy sitting across from her.

"Catch me up, honey," her mom said, not even glancing at the menu. "What's been going on lately?"

"Not a lot to tell. But I did get another rescue horse earlier today. She's not going to stay at my place, though."

What her mom would really like to hear about was a guy in Ashley's life, not another horse. Ashley knew that without being told. But her mom was going to go on being disappointed in that regard. Ashley was gun-shy when it came to men and had no intention of doing anything to change that. Her mom didn't understand Ashley's interest in horses. She tried, but she didn't get it. She thought it should be her daughter's hobby instead of an overriding passion. She didn't understand why Ashley wanted horses to be her life's work.

"Why aren't you taking the new horse to your place?" Her mom tried to sound interested.

"I met a guy who's starting an equine therapy barn, and he wants me to supply the horses for him. I think it's going to be a win-win. Good for his clients and good for my horses."

"Sounds interesting. Tell me about him."

"Who?"

"The guy you said is starting that barn thing."

Ashley needlessly lowered her gaze to the menu—and ignored the request to say more.

Carol returned to the table, order pad in hand. "You two know what you want?"

Glad for the interruption, Ashley ordered a BLT sandwich with fries, a side of ranch dressing, and a Diet Coke. Her mom had her usual chicken salad and iced tea.

"Shoulda known." Carol stuck the pencil behind her ear before dropping the order pad into her apron pocket. Completely retro. Another reason Ashley adored the waitress and the restaurant. All that was missing was for Carol to smack gum.

"What are you smiling about?" her mom asked.

"Nothing. It's just fun to be here with you."

On Tuesday evenings, Ben met with a group of six other men from his church. They ranged in age from twenty-nine to fifty-seven, and most had been meeting together for the past nine years. The men served as an accountability and Bible study group, but time had knitted them into a band of brothers, closer than close friends.

When Ben became one of them, he'd been sober for not quite a year. He'd been looking for something beyond his twelve-step program. He'd wanted something that would strengthen his Christian faith and help him grow into a godly man like his grandpa. He'd found all of that with these men.

At the end of the evening, the group moved from the living room to the kitchen for decaf coffee and something sweet and sticky. Ben sat on one of the high kitchen stools at the raised counter. Their host, Ken Snow, settled onto the matching stool to his right.

"What's the latest on your equine program?" Ken had one of those penetrating gazes that made a person feel seen and heard. It was just one of the things Ben appreciated about this man.

"I'm making headway with the website," he answered. "Todd's given me lots of pointers. And I heard from that gal I told you about last week. She's found the first horse for the barn. She'll deliver it tomorrow night."

"That's great."

"I gotta tell you, Ken. If I could quit doing anything else and concentrate on getting this idea of mine off the ground, I would. Unfortunately, I need to make the money I've got in the bank stretch as long as I can."

Ken shifted. "About that . . . Sue and I talked about supporting your endeavor, and we feel it's what God wants us to do. You can count on us for monthly giving."

Ben stared at his friend, unable to say anything for a few moments. He'd prayed for doors to continue to open, and look what had happened here. He hadn't even asked for donations from friends, yet the Snows planned to support the barn. He shouldn't be surprised, but he was. He blew out a breath. "Thanks, Ken. I . . . I don't even know what to say beyond that."

"We believe in you."

"Thanks," he repeated, hoping he didn't sound choked up or emotional. Although he was both.

Monday, September 30, 1940

Andrew returned to the farm in Kuna after registering with the draft board. The Selective Training and Service Act had been passed by Congress in mid-September, requiring men between the ages of twenty-one and thirty-six to register. Strange how Andrew had feared his oldest son might be headed off to war, yet it was Andrew himself who was subject to the draft that would begin in October.

Instead of going into the house, he walked out into the alfalfa fields. The final cutting of the season would happen in another week or so. Hopefully the rain would hold off until the harvest was done. Right now, there wasn't a single cloud in the sky, but this time of year it was hard to know what to expect. The temperature could hit a hundred or it could dip down to freezing. They could go weeks without rain, or they might get a deluge.

"Penny for your thoughts."

He looked over his shoulder and watched Helen's approach. He'd always loved the way she looked in that lilac-colored dress. But then, she looked pretty in anything.

"How was it?" she asked.

"Nothing much to the registration itself."

"Are you worried about being drafted?"

He squinted up at the blue sky. "I guess I'll have to leave that in God's hands. Not much I can do about it, one way or the other."

Helen slipped her right arm through his left and leaned her head against his shoulder.

"I think it's time we started growing more food for human consumption. Food production could be crucial in the coming years."

"War," she whispered.

He answered by pressing her arm against his side.

"What do you intend to plant?"

"Corn, I think."

"Do we have the equipment we'll need?"

"Mostly. And we'll have plenty of time over the winter to buy whatever we're missing."

She straightened so she could look him in the eye. "Not if you're drafted."

"The draft is only for a year of service."

"That could change."

He leaned over and kissed her forehead. "It could." There was no point lying to her. If the US was pulled into the war, the length of service would undoubtedly change.

She blinked, and he knew she fought tears.

"Even if I'm drafted, the boys will know what to do. And I'll be able to write letters and give advice."

She stood a little straighter, tilting her chin upward in a show of courage. "You're right. The boys and I can handle it. But can we afford to buy new equipment if it's needed?"

"Yes." He smiled, thinking how blessed he was to have her by his side. "We're doing well, Helen. The farm's turned a nice profit the last couple of years. Don't worry."

"I won't. You know best, Andrew."

He said a silent thanks to God, for it hadn't always been that way. She'd doubted him early in their marriage. Doubted that she'd loved him. Doubted he'd been the man she wanted to spend the rest of her life with.

Helen reached up and tenderly laid the flat of her hand against the side of his face, saying with her eyes what she didn't say aloud. That she understood his thoughts. Then she stepped back and turned toward the house. "I'll get back to the kitchen. The children will be home from school soon." She took a couple of steps, then looked at him again. "We'd best talk with them after supper. They need to know what could be ahead."

Andrew nodded.

"I love you," she said.

He reached for her hand, and together they left the fields.

Chapter 4

Although he wouldn't admit it, Ben felt as excited as a kid at Christmas while waiting for Ashley to arrive with the horse. He didn't know a lot about the mare other than that she was a sorrel and sixteen years old. That was it. But he trusted Ashley's judgment. After all, she'd come highly recommended. Although to be honest, he wasn't sure that was the reason for his trust.

It was a quarter after six when the red pickup with the white horse trailer pulled into the yard. Ben waited for Ashley to drive all the way up to the barn. After the truck had come to a full stop, he stepped to the door and opened it for her. "Glad to see you."

She gave him a quizzical look. "Did you think I wasn't coming?"

"No. No, of course not. I'm just eager. Once I've got a horse on the place, it'll feel more real to me."

She laughed softly as she dropped from the cab, her boots raising little dust clouds. "*That* I can understand. Come on. Let's get her unloaded." She headed for the rear of the trailer. Ben followed and watched as Ashley freed the mare's rope and backed her out. Afterward, she walked the horse around in a slow circle so Ben could get a look at her. "She's under fifteen hands. A good size for kids who've never been around horses before. And she's docile." She stopped walking and rested one hand on the mare's neck. "With good feed, she'll probably perk up some, but I don't imagine she'll ever be high energy. She seems to live at a slower pace."

Ben stepped forward and stroked the horse's head. "I like her, Ashley. Looks like I'm getting a good deal."

"You are. I put a saddle on her and rode her a bit. She's got a good way of going. Her mouth's soft, and she's sound."

"Should we put her in the paddock or in a stall in the barn?"

"Let's start with the stall. That way you can control her feed for the first few days."

"Sounds good." He led the way to the barn and opened the door wide.

Ashley took the mare to the first stall and put her inside. Then Ben exchanged places with her, moving around the horse, letting his hand trail over her back and haunches before lifting her hooves one at a time.

"You do know the front end of a horse from the back," Ashley said as she observed him.

He laughed, but his answer was serious. "I avoid telling lies, Miss Showalter. They come back to bite you in the end. I've learned it's better to tell the truth from the start." He straightened, patting the mare's side before stepping toward the gate. "Does she have a name? I forgot to ask."

"Nope. The guy I got her from didn't know what it was. Didn't care either."

Ben shut the gate behind him and stared into the stall at the mare. "Hmm. Any ideas?"

"Naming an animal is kind of a personal thing. It has to fit you as well as her."

"I'll have to give it some thought, then."

Before they left the barn, Ben made sure the mare had water, and Ashley gave him instructions regarding feed. Then the two of them walked to the house. He left her on the porch while he went inside to get the check. When he returned, she stood at the porch railing, staring out over the alfalfa fields to the west.

"It sure is pretty here," she said without looking his way.

"I know."

"It's my dream to own a place something like this one day. I hope there's still land left if I can ever afford to buy."

"Do you own the place you're in now?"

She met his gaze and smiled. "Me and the bank. I got a small inheritance when I turned twenty-three. Something my dad set up before he died. That gave me enough for a down payment and an affordable house payment that fits my salary."

"What do you do?"

She shrugged. "Nothing fancy. Retail sales. Mostly I'm a floor clerk, although I help cover the checkout stands when I'm needed. I've got flexible hours, which I like. What about you?"

"I had my own construction business." He leaned his shoulder against a post. "But I sold it earlier in the summer so I could concentrate on getting the Harmony Barn off the ground. Now I'm doing handyman kinds of things. Like you, it gives me more freedom with my time. And it's a whole lot less stress than having a crew and paying salaries and all that."

She nodded in understanding.

Looking at her, Ben wondered if she had a boyfriend. Probably did. A real-life cowboy would be his guess. He couldn't imagine her with a man who wasn't as involved with horses as she was.

"Well." She stepped back from the railing. "I'd better get home. I've got chores of my own to do before it gets much later."

"Sure." He held out the check to her. "I really appreciate your help. Be sure to call me when you find another horse that might work for us."

"I will."

Ashley was fresh out of the shower, hair wrapped in a towel, when her phone rang. She felt a catch in her chest when she saw who it was. Something had to be wrong for her mom to call at this time of night. "Hey, Mom."

"Are you in bed? Did I wake you?"

"No. I'm still up." She slipped into her bathrobe and sat on the edge of her bed. "What's wrong?"

"It's Dylan."

Ashley's stomach sank. Of course it was Dylan. It was always her brother. "What happened?"

"I got a letter from him today. He's having such a rough time. He's depressed. He feels hopeless. I don't know what to do. They won't let us talk on the phone. They won't let me go up to see him."

"Write back and tell him you love him. That's all you can do."

When Ashley and her mom had met for lunch yesterday, neither of them had brought up Dylan. A pleasant change. For years her little brother had been the focus of almost every conversation they'd had. Dylan's troubles. Dylan's escapades. Dylan's injuries. Dylan's failures.

"It seems unfair," her mom said. "He's so far away from his family."

Frustration coiled in Ashley's stomach. "Unfair? Mom, he broke the law, and not for the first time. He's an addict. He's a multiple offender. He could end up in prison if he doesn't toe the line. He was lucky to be ordered into six months of rehab instead of going to jail."

Her mom choked on a sob.

"I'm sorry." She was sorry. Then again, she wasn't. She drew a slow, deep breath. "I'm not heartless, Mom. But Dylan can't get better if you try to shield him at every turn. He's got to be responsible for his own choices. You need to listen to the counselors. If he gets in trouble again, he won't find a judge so lenient as the one he had this time."

"Lenient?"

Ashley swallowed any further response. It would be a waste of words. Her mom was the queen of enablers when it came to Dylan.

"You're too hard on him."

"No, I don't think so. I want him to be healthy and happy. I want him to be whole, the way he used to be when he was little, before he got into booze and drugs." She drew in a slow breath. "I don't want him to die like one of those movie stars or musicians we read about, mixing prescription drugs and alcohol, and suddenly their bodies give out when they're only in their twenties."

"Oh, Ashley."

"It could happen, Mom. You know I'm right. You saw what he was like the night they arrested him." She heard her mom's muffled sob. "Write him back and encourage him. I'll do the same. We'll tell him we love him and to hang in there, no matter what."

"If only I could see him."

Ashley counted to five before saying, "They've got reasons for their rules."

"I suppose."

"Try not to worry about him. There are people looking out for him. You need to take care of yourself. Now, go to bed and get a good night's sleep."

"Okay, honey. I'll try."

After ending the call, Ashley remained on the side of her bed for a long while, not moving, thinking about her brother. Her first memories of him were when he was two and she was five. Dark haired with big brown eyes and a squealing laugh that could shatter glass. That had been her favorite Dylan. Next she remembered the scared kid on his first day of kindergarten when he wouldn't let go of her hand. After that she recalled the boy sobbing as he lay on his bed after their dad's funeral. All too soon there'd been the teenager stumbling around downstairs after sneaking out to drink with friends. And finally, she remembered the young man as he was led away in cuffs, dark half circles under eyes that seemed empty of life.

Wasn't it strange how she could love and hate her brother at the same time? No, hate was too strong a word. She didn't hate Dylan. But she resented all that he had done to their mom, and she resented the way his addictions had altered her own life too. Sometimes she wished she would never have to see him again, never have to talk to him again, never have to talk *about* him again.

With a sigh, she rose and returned to the bathroom, where she finished getting ready for the night. But once in bed, thoughts of her mom and brother continued to whirl, and even after she fell asleep, they were there, in her troubled dreams.

Wednesday, March 12, 1941

Andrew was returning to the house from the barn when he saw Hirsch Finkel walking toward him, leaning into the brisk March wind while holding on to his hat. Andrew enjoyed visits with his neighbor, but Hirsch wasn't there to talk about farming equipment or the planting season. He was there for another tutoring session with Ben. In Germany, Hirsch Finkel had been a respected professor until the Nazis forbade Jews to teach. Now he was preparing Ben for his first year at Boise Junior College, an endeavor that both of them seemed to enjoy.

Hirsch looked up as he neared the front porch, only then noticing Andrew. "Good day," he said above the wind.

"Good day, Hirsch. Another tutoring session, huh?"

"*Ja*."

"He appreciates your help."

"Your boy is very bright. I do not have to do much."

Andrew knew the older man did more than it sounded, but he let it pass.

"You have seen the newspaper?" Hirsch asked as the two men climbed the steps. "About the Lend-Lease Act."

Andrew opened the front door. "I saw it. God willing, it'll mean Britain and their allies will get the goods and munitions they need to defeat the Nazis."

"God willing," Hirsch echoed softly.

Silently, Andrew said a prayer that the defeat of the Nazis would happen before America was drawn fully into the war, before Ben was old enough to serve, before any of his sons could be called to fight. *Please, God. Stop the aggressors. Stop the deaths. Stop the waste.*

Once inside, both men shucked off their coats and hung them on the rack. Hirsch set his hat on the rack, too, then adjusted his suit jacket. The man might be a farmer in America, but he remained every inch a professor. He wouldn't have thought to come teach Ben while wearing overalls.

"Care for some coffee?"

"Ja. That would be good."

Andrew tipped his head toward the kitchen. "Go ahead and have a seat. I'll let Ben know you're here. Then I'll get you a cup."

As he walked toward the ladder that led to the loft bedroom, Andrew said another silent prayer, expressing thanks once again that he hadn't been drafted the previous fall. If he had been, he never would have been able to save enough to pay for Ben's tuition. Even being there and not off serving in the army, it had been difficult to make it happen. And yet somehow he'd managed it. No, *they* had managed it. The entire Henning family. Everybody, all the way down to five-year-old Andy Jr., had done what they could to cut expenses so that Ben could go to college.

Last night, in the margin of his Bible, beside Deuteronomy 8:18, Andrew had written: *God has given me the power I need to provide for my family. Thank You, Father.* It would be good for him to remember that the promise in that verse had been true during the Great Depression as well as in March 1941. And it would be true in the years to come as well, no matter what they had to face.

He stopped at the ladder and looked up. "Ben, Mr. Finkel is here."

"Be right down, Dad."

As he turned toward the kitchen, Andrew prayed one more time for a quick end to the war. Because as much as he rejoiced that he'd found ways to make a college education available to his oldest boy, he didn't want him using it to enter the Army Air Corps with the world at war.

Chapter 5

Ben sat in his truck, staring at the entrance to the gym. Half an hour before, he'd left a repair job about a block away. He'd been heading for home, but then he'd seen the familiar red vehicle with its large white decal on the back window and had made a sudden turn into the gym's parking lot. It was probably crazy to wait here. In the past five years, Craig had refused every attempt Ben had made to talk to him. He'd disregarded Ben's efforts to reconnect as well as his requests for forgiveness. Calling on the phone got him nowhere other than a few curse words in his ear, followed by a quick hang up.

If he could talk to Craig . . . If he could tell his old friend what had happened to him in recent years—what God had rescued him out of and what God was doing in his life today. If Craig could see what Ben wanted to do with the farm, what good could come from it, perhaps how Craig could benefit from it. But none of that would happen unless Craig would see him, unless Craig would hear him out.

You can't blame him. You were a coward. You bailed on him.

Ben wasn't sure if the voice in his head belonged to the Enemy or to his conscience. Whichever, he tried to push it away. It didn't work. More memories tumbled in, proving the truth of the accusation.

"I *was* a coward," he said aloud. "I *did* bail on him."

After Ben got out of juvie, how many opportunities had he ignored to see his friend? Too many to count. Especially all of those times he could have visited Craig in the hospital. He didn't even know how many surgeries his friend had endured. But Ben hadn't gone to see him, at home or in the hospital. Instead, he'd tried to forget his friend and the accident that had changed both of their lives. Drinking had been his preferred method for forgetting. And after a while, getting drunk had become more important than anything or anyone.

Even now, it surprised him how many people he'd managed to fool through the years. He'd held down jobs and even impressed bosses. He'd managed to keep his grandparents from discovering the truth for a long time. He doubted his mom had seen anything amiss, but then she'd never paid too much attention to him, even when he'd lived at home. Once he was out on his own—as soon as he'd turned eighteen—she hadn't cared what he did with his life. He'd isolated himself and done his drinking in private. At least he hadn't been stupid enough to drive drunk again. That was a mercy.

But eventually the house of cards he'd built had come tumbling down. There hadn't been any hiding the truth from the people closest to him any longer. Or from himself. He was an alcoholic, and his life had spiraled out of control. He'd needed help, and miraculously, he'd received it.

Closing his eyes, he drew in a slow, deep breath. He thanked

God for his grandfather's intervention, for his weeks in a Christ-centered recovery program, for the moment he'd been born again, for the year on the farm that had followed. It was there that he'd learned to live one day at a time, totally dependent upon the Lord. And only after all of that had he tried to contact Craig.

Step 9: making direct amends to persons he'd harmed wherever possible.

His first attempt to see Craig had been thrown back in his face. As had all the attempts that followed.

He opened his eyes again in time to see the automatic doors to the gym open and Craig roll out in his wheelchair. Even from where he was parked, Ben could see the strength in his friend's upper body and the body mass that had been lost in his lower limbs. No one was with Craig, which meant he must be able to maneuver himself into the automobile and then get the wheelchair into it too. Ben had seen examples of the process on the internet, but until now he hadn't known for sure if it was possible for Craig.

Ben reached for the door handle, then stopped, wondering if he was being fair. Craig wouldn't be able to hang up on him or avoid him. He would have to listen, at least long enough for him to get into the car and drive away. Well, maybe he wouldn't listen. But at least he would hear.

"God, am I doing the right thing?" He reached a second time for the handle, and feeling no check in his spirit, he opened the door. "Guide my words, Lord." He walked in the direction of Craig's car, getting there first.

Craig didn't look up until it was too late for him to change directions.

"Hey," Ben said.

It was a second or two before his friend's expression said he'd recognized him. Not because Ben had changed all that much, he suspected, but because Craig hadn't expected to ever see him again. He glowered at Ben but said nothing as he rolled the final distance to the car.

"Craig, will you give me a few minutes?"

"No."

Strange how a single word could strike with such force.

Ben took a step back. "I know I should've been there for you after the accident, and I wasn't. I'll always be sorry for it."

Craig grunted as he opened the car door.

"We were kids. I made a mistake. I was hoping . . . now that we're men—"

"What? That we could put the past behind us? Maybe you can." Craig pounded on his thighs with the heels of his hands. "But I'm stuck in the past."

The bitterness in his friend's voice cut Ben like a knife.

With a practiced motion, Craig hoisted himself into the car. Moments later, he folded the wheelchair and maneuvered it in behind the driver's seat.

"All I want is a chance to talk to you. For us to talk to each other. Will you at least consider it?"

Craig answered by pulling the door closed.

Ben seemed to feel it slam in his chest and took another step backward. But as he watched his old friend drive away, he reminded himself how many doors had been slammed in his face—at least metaphorically—as he'd tried to get his equine therapy program started. But now things had begun to change. Now some doors had opened.

"Nothing is impossible with God."

With fifteen minutes left on her shift, Ashley was refolding towels on a display when movement at the end of the aisle drew her attention. She pasted on a smile, prepared to greet a customer, but the smile faded when she saw Paul Redding.

"Hi, Ashley."

She drew a breath, steeling herself. "Paul."

"I wondered if you still worked here." He smiled. "You never seem to be around when I'm shopping."

It was an untrustworthy smile. She should have recognized that the first time he'd shined it in her direction. Pity she hadn't. It would have saved her a world of hurt.

"You're looking good, Ash."

She hated it when anybody shortened her name like that—and she'd told Paul so in the past. He either didn't remember, or he meant it to be a jab. She supposed it was the latter. "Was there something I can help you find?"

The smile disappeared. "No, thanks."

It occurred to her then that the months since they'd seen each other hadn't been kind to him. His eyes looked tired. His mouth was drawn. True, he remained roguishly handsome, but in other ways he seemed quite changed.

"Well, I won't keep you from your work." He pointed. "Wouldn't want those towels to go unfolded. Important stuff." Then he gave her a much less charming smile before turning and disappearing around the end rack.

Ashley drew in another breath, trying not to feel the insult. She hated that Paul could get to her like that. It hadn't been until she'd broken things off with him that she realized how often he'd made those types of verbal digs. And even then, it had taken awhile to understand the many ways he'd manipulated her throughout their relationship. The many ways she'd *allowed* him to manipulate her. Both with flattery and with words meant to undermine and sting.

She should have seen it long before the night she'd found him drinking with Dylan.

"Ashley?"

She turned at the sound of her coworker's voice.

"You okay?" Shelley asked.

Ashley nodded. "Yes." She folded another towel. "Just finishing up. Almost time for me to head home."

Shelley didn't look convinced but left without saying anything more.

Her thoughts still churning, Ashley headed to the employees' break room at the back of the store. She put her vest in the locker, punched out, then went outside without encountering anybody. Which was to her liking. Her mood was decidedly grim by this time.

Never again, she told herself. She would never make that mistake again. One would think, given a lifetime of experiences with her brother, that she could have seen what was right in front of her face.

Horses and dogs . . . and no men. As long as she had horses and dogs in her life, she could be perfectly happy—and have a lot less stress.

Thanksgiving 1941

A bitter wind pushed Andrew toward the barn to complete his morning chores. Inside the house, Helen and Mother Greyson were up early, preparing for their Thanksgiving dinner. The turkey they'd raised and fattened themselves. Mother Greyson's prize dressing. Corn bread with honey butter. Peas with pearl onions. The corn casserole that Helen always made. And pies. He couldn't forget the pies. Pumpkin and chocolate cream and apple. Delicious odors had filled the house since yesterday.

The Hennings would have a full house for Thanksgiving. Twelve people, including the Finkels and the Morgans, a young couple from church. They would set up a second table in the living room since the one in the kitchen couldn't hold them all. Knowing his family and his friends as he did, he expected a day filled not only with good food but also plenty of laughter.

He could use the laughter and the distraction it would bring with it. There were so many reasons not to laugh these days. The German consulates had been closed by the State Department in June, raising tensions. In August, peacetime military service had been extended from twelve months to thirty months—he thanked God again that his name hadn't come up in last year's draft—and the nine-hundred-thousand-men limit on selectees had been removed. Last month the Nazis had torpedoed and damaged the US destroyer *Kearney*, and less than two weeks later they'd sunk the *Reuben James* with some one hundred lives lost. Both of the ships had been off the coast of Iceland, which suddenly seemed all too close to American soil. He felt the war pressing in upon his home and family and knew he couldn't keep the danger from happening any more than he could stop the Snake River flowing from east to west across Southern Idaho.

God help us.

"Hey, Dad. Wait up."

Startled from his dark thoughts, Andrew stopped and looked over his shoulder, watching as Ben hurried after him, the lights from the house illuminating him from behind. Andrew's heart caught for a moment. He couldn't begin to express how proud he was of the boy. Ben had thrown himself into his college studies and into his part-time job in Boise. And this was the kid who'd wanted to quit school when he was twelve.

"Didn't expect you to be awake yet," Andrew said as his son arrived at his side.

Ben shrugged. "I do a lot of studying early in the morning. I'm used to being up by now."

They moved on.

Inside the barn, out of the wind, it was warmer. The hay, straw, and animals helped. The two milk cows were inside, awaiting them. One of the cows bawled impatiently. Ben went straight to her, taking a bucket and three-legged stool with him. Andrew put hay into the trough in front of the cows, then mimicked Ben with his own bucket and stool. Soon the only sound in the barn was of milk spraying the sides of the buckets. Andrew pressed his head against the cow's warm side and felt himself relax into the rhythm of the milking.

"Dad?"

"Hmm?"

"One of my friends is interested in flying like me. He's going to Canada to join up there. He's not old enough to be a pilot, but he can be part of the aircrew."

Dread coiled in Andrew's gut. "You aren't thinking of doing the same? You haven't even finished one semester of college." He stood and looked over the cow's back. "You could ruin your chance of being a pilot if you give up now."

Was it sound advice any father would give a son, or were they simply words to keep the boy safe at home? He wasn't sure. A little of both, he supposed.

"I won't throw it away, Dad. But I thought you should know what some of the guys my age are doing. We don't think it's right, America ignoring what's happening."

"America isn't ignoring the war. They're trying to stay neutral, if possible. There's a difference."

"How many other nations does Germany have to invade before we do something to stop them? They've taken most of Europe now. Greece, Yugoslavia, and Crete just this year." Ben lowered his gaze to the bucket. "Britain and its allies need our help."

Andrew sank back onto the stool, having no words to dispute his son's assertion. In fact, he agreed with Ben. Andrew didn't think America was doing enough.

What will be enough, God? What will be enough?

Chapter 6

Nicki Day was a wiry woman with short, spiky steel-gray hair and hazel eyes that sparkled behind a pair of turquoise-rimmed glasses. She wore fitted jeans and black boots and carried a cowboy hat in her left hand that she slapped against her thigh at regular intervals. Ben guessed she was in her early sixties, although he supposed she could be even a decade older than that.

"Mr. Henning." She greeted him with an outstretched hand. "Welcome to Shady Lane."

It was an appropriate name for this property tucked away in the foothills north of Boise. An abundance of trees had been planted on the property, including on either side of a long driveway. Irrigation had turned what was naturally a desert covered in sagebrush into a green oasis.

Ben took her hand and shook it. "Thanks for making time to meet with me."

"I'm the one to do the thanking." She motioned with her hand, and they walked together toward a long, wide building painted a dark red. Inside, stalls lined the sides of the stables while an arena filled the center.

Ben released a soft whistle. "This is nice."

"We think so." Nicki's smile brought out more of the wrinkles in her face.

"It dwarfs the barn on my farm."

"We have fifteen horses at present. Nine are boarded. Six of them are ours. We give riding lessons and do horse training as well."

Ben stepped to the nearest stall where a gray horse had thrust its head over the door. He stroked the animal's neck.

"When I heard about your plans, Mr. Henning, I decided I wanted to be a part of it. And I'm sure you'll find a number of volunteers among our boarders and students once we get the word out. Plus my husband and I want to donate three English saddles, along with blankets and other tack. They aren't new, but they're in excellent condition. You can take them with you today."

Surprised, he couldn't speak for a moment. In his mind, he ticked those items off a list of future purchases. "That's very generous of you," he said, recovering himself. "Especially since we're not operating yet."

She shook her head. "I trust Larry's recommendation."

Ben would never be able to repay Larry Dennis for his assistance. Larry was a counselor by profession, the first one to catch Ben's vision for the farm. Now, with Nicki Day's help—another open door—it looked like he would soon have volunteers to help with the riding-program aspect of the Harmony Barn.

Nicki took him down one side of the stables, then across to the other side. She stopped at the third stall from the end. "This is Paisley."

Ben looked into the stall at the black-and-white paint. The horse flicked its ears forward, as if sizing Ben up.

"He's the real reason I asked you here today. We'd like to donate Paisley."

Stunned, Ben looked at the woman, once again struck wordless.

She continued as if she hadn't noticed his reaction. "He's ten years old. Very calm. Three of our grandchildren learned to ride on him, almost before they could walk. Nothing much disturbs Paisley."

"Do you want to sign a lease for a year at a time?"

"We don't want to lease him to you. We're giving him to you. Naturally, we won't transfer papers until your nonprofit status is in place."

"Naturally. That's how I'd want it too. And that shouldn't be much longer. My attorney's getting that all finished up." He looked at the horse again, gratitude swelling his heart. How like God to encourage him in this way after his disappointing encounter with Craig two days earlier.

Ashley stood beside a fence along with nine other volunteers, taking in the small herd of horses in a pasture devoid of grass. How had this been allowed to happen, she wondered as she surveyed the rail-thin animals. Neighbors had to have seen what was going on here. People driving along this country road had an easy view of the pasture and the horses within. It was obvious the animals had been underfed for a long time. Many, many months. Starvation hadn't happened overnight.

The equine rescue network had called Ashley early that morning, soon after Animal Care and Control confirmed the abuse complaint. Most of the volunteers from the network had arrived within half an hour of receiving similar phone calls. No one said a word as they stared at the horses. Sadly, too many of the people with her had seen similar situations before. Anger and sadness swirled inside of her. There was no excuse for this. None at all.

Closing her eyes for a moment, she told herself not to judge others so harshly. Who could say what had befallen the owner? Perhaps he wasn't simply evil, as had been her first thought. Perhaps he was sick. Perhaps he was dying. Perhaps he hadn't been able to let go of the horses he'd once loved even when it had become obvious he could no longer provide for them. She would like to believe there was some logical reason rather than it being plain and simple cruelty. Drawing in a deep breath, she opened her eyes again.

"You been at this long?"

She turned to look at the man who'd spoken. The cowboy's dark face had been leathered by years in the sun, and she couldn't be sure of his age. "A little over a year," she answered.

He shook his head. "Takes the wind out of me, every time."

"Me too."

He glanced up at the sky. "Wasn't that long ago that horse rescue networks didn't even exist. At least that's changed in my lifetime. You'd be too young to remember what it used to be like." He held out a hand. "My name's Rory."

"Hi, Rory." She shook his hand. "I'm Ashley."

"Are you here for transport?"

"No, I've got a little place of my own. I rehome any rescues I take in, once they're well enough. I've got room for two right now."

She thought of Ben's farm, of those forty acres, and wondered how many horses he meant to keep there once everything was up and running.

Behind her, she heard someone call her name. "Looks like I'm up. Nice to meet you, Rory."

"You too."

About an hour later, she found herself driving toward home with two horses in her trailer. Sometimes she was able to turn a rescue around quickly, finding a horse a permanent home in mere days or a week or so. But the horses she'd picked up today needed lots of care before they would be ready for adoption. It would be awhile before they'd be out of danger. They were starved enough that they might still die.

When she pulled into her driveway, she was surprised to see Ben Henning's truck parked near her shed. He was leaning against the tailgate, Dusty once again in the truck bed in the shade.

Silly, the way her heart fluttered at the sight of him.

He waved as he pushed off the tailgate. "I was just about to leave," he said when she'd cut the engine. "Hope you don't mind me dropping by unannounced."

"I don't mind." Which was crazy. She probably should mind.

He opened the truck door for her. "Wanted to share something with you."

"What's that?" She dropped to the ground and moved toward the back of the trailer.

"Somebody donated three English riding saddles and a gelding to my program."

Ashley stopped and turned. "Get outta here."

"Scout's honor." He held up three fingers.

"That's awesome."

Ben moved ahead of her and unlatched the back of the trailer. He kept smiling until he saw the two horses inside.

"Sad, aren't they?" Ashley asked softly.

"Where'd they come from?"

"A small ranch outside of Star. The owner was breeding irresponsibly. Didn't have the funds to feed all of the horses on his land. I don't know if any died before someone finally reported the situation." Tears welled in her eyes as she stepped into the trailer and untied the rope on the first horse. The chestnut mare looked even worse when she was out in the sunshine.

Ben muttered something beneath his breath, his expression clouding. She liked him all the more for his reaction.

He said, "I'll get the other one for you, if that's okay."

"Sure."

The sorrel gelding came out as docilely as the mare had before him. Ashley led the way to the shelters, Ben right behind. Both Remington and Scooter, the palomino mare that had arrived the day Ashley met Ben, thrust their heads over the gates of their enclosures. The chestnut mare went into the first empty enclosure, the gelding into the remaining one.

"What now?" Ben fastened the gate closed.

"The vet's looked at them already. These two didn't have any underlying medical reason for their condition, other than no food. So I'll start by feeding them small amounts of alfalfa hay six times a day. Alfalfa's high in protein and includes electrolytes and phosphorus and magnesium. I'll increase the amount a little each day over the next ten to fourteen days. By then, they should be eating normal amounts."

"Do they get any grain?"

"No. Not yet. Feeding a starved horse can't be hurried. It

can take months for some horses to come all the way out of it. But if they make it past the next couple of weeks, there's a good chance they'll survive."

"You're one brave girl, Ashley Showalter."

The tone of Ben's voice drew her gaze to him. His expression was somber but admiring, and it warmed a place inside of her that had been hurting most of the morning.

"Could I help you? Maybe come do a feeding when you're at work. I can adjust my schedule to my liking."

The offer brought a small smile to her lips. "Really? You would do that?"

"Yes, really."

"Thanks. That would help a lot. My neighbors pitch in when they can, but Bill had surgery last week, so I think Cheryl's got enough on her plate without me asking for favors."

"No need to ask them. Let me know when to come and how to feed the horses, and I'll take care of the rest."

For a moment, Ashley was tempted to pull his head down so she could kiss him on the cheek. But only for a moment. Sanity returned before she could make a fool of herself.

Saturday, November 22, 1941

"You should see her, Ben. She's a real dish."

Andrew stopped in the hallway, listening as Oscar regaled his brother with a description of the girl in question—red hair, green eyes, rosy lips.

"I about flipped my wig when I first saw her. I think maybe I'm fallin' in love."

Andrew's eyes widened at that admission. It was the first he'd heard of the girl, let alone the romantic notions she'd given Oscar.

Ben's voice intruded. "How old are you?"

"You know how old I am."

"Sure, I know. I just wanted to remind you. You don't fall in love at fifteen. You got too much ahead of you. You oughta be thinking about college."

Oscar laughed. "Me? College? Ha!"

Andrew made a bit of noise to announce himself, then strode into the living room as if he hadn't been eavesdropping.

The brothers—both of them as towheaded as the first time Andrew had laid eyes on them outside that soup kitchen in Boise—turned matching blue gazes in his direction.

"Chores done?" Andrew asked, although he knew the answer.

"Yes, sir."

"Good." He went to his favorite chair and sank onto it. "Ben, I'm glad you could stay through the whole weekend. It's been good for the family, having you here with us."

"I've liked it too. And it was good to catch up with Mr. Finkel on Thanksgiving. But I'll have to head back right after church tomorrow. There's some work I need to get done before my Monday morning classes. I thought I'd have time to do it while I was here, but I never got around to it."

Oscar elbowed his older brother in the ribs. "You should be the one thinking about girls," he said softly. "You act as ancient as Dad sometimes."

This time Andrew couldn't pretend he hadn't heard. "Just how *ancient* am I?"

"Sorry." Oscar shot him a sheepish glance.

There was a short silence, then all three of them burst into laughter.

A feeling of gratitude swept over Andrew. He was proud to be these boys' father. Now if he could only keep Ben from running off to Canada and Oscar from making a fool of himself over some girl . . .

Grinning, he reached for his book on the side table.

Chapter 7

Ben parked his truck at the curb and drew a deep breath before getting out of the cab. His eyes went to the house as he reached into the bed for his toolbox. He didn't know if his mom actually had a problem with her kitchen sink or if it was an excuse to get him over to the house so she could berate him about the farm one more time.

He drew a quick breath, hating the negative thoughts that welled in him whenever he dealt with her. It didn't matter that her negativity had come first. He wasn't responsible for her actions, but he was responsible for his own reaction to them.

"Honor your father and mother," the Bible told him. Ben had no father to honor, but he could do his best with his mom. He tried to do his best. Always. He really did. But she sure didn't make it easy for him.

Ben made his way up the walk, rapped on the front door, then opened it when he heard his mom call for him to enter. "I'm in the kitchen," she added.

He found her seated at the table, smoking a cigarette while water pooled on the floor near the cabinet beneath the sink. She hadn't lied about the problem after all. He set his toolbox on the floor.

"How long has this been going on?" He opened the cupboard door.

"I don't know. I noticed it a few days ago, I guess. I've been throwing towels down to soak it up."

"You should have called me right away."

She blew out a stream of smoke before asking, "Would you have answered my call?"

"I answered this one, didn't I?"

She ignored his retort.

"Mom, I always answer unless I'm doing something that requires no interruption."

"That's what I am to you. An interruption."

"Don't. Please. You know that isn't what I meant."

She huffed at him but stayed silent.

He retrieved more towels to mop up the water, then set to work. Fortunately, it wasn't anything major, and he had the leak stopped in a half hour or so. By the time he was done, his mom had chain-smoked her way through a number of cigarettes, glowering at him when he looked her way but keeping her thoughts to herself. Ben knew that wouldn't last.

She broke her silence as he put away his tools. "Have you seen your grandfather lately?"

"Yeah. We were together at church yesterday. As usual."

Another huff.

He sat at the table opposite her. "You ought to join us next Sunday. We could all go out to lunch after the service is over."

"Are you kidding?" Her laughter was harsh. "I haven't let anybody drag me to church since I got pregnant with you."

It was a fact he knew without her telling him.

"How your grandfather roped you into that stupidity I'll never know. Religion's just a lie. A bunch of rules to put you in a box."

He wanted to ask how her life was going without God, but he swallowed the question. It wouldn't help things. Until his mom was ready for her heart to be changed, he could talk himself blue in the face and still get nowhere.

Grandpa Grant had told him of the sweet child Wendy Henning had been, of how she'd loved to crawl up onto his lap and shower him with kisses, of how she'd loved to stand on a stool in the kitchen and bake cookies with her mommy.

"I've never known for certain what derailed her," his grandpa had said. "I wish I knew. I've asked, but if she knows what it was, she hasn't said."

Whatever had gone wrong for Ben's mom during her teen years, he knew without question that it hadn't been the fault of his grandparents. A more loving couple he'd never met.

He frowned. Did he continue to blame his mom for the poor choices he himself had made as a teenager? Probably. Even after all these years. But blaming someone else changed nothing. He had to own the things he'd done. *Own them and don't repeat them.* "*Go and sin no more.*"

"You know what, Mom?" He stood.

"What?"

"I love you. You can say whatever you want about my faith, and it won't change that. I choose to love you, even when you try to make me mad." He rounded the table and leaned down to kiss her cheek. "Let me know if the sink starts leaking again."

"Are you saying you didn't really fix it?"

"No." He stretched out the word. "That's not what I'm saying. Now, I'd better go. I've got another job waiting for me."

"You'd better sit down a minute. There's something I need to tell you."

It was tempting to refuse. Instead, he took the chair opposite her a second time.

"I'm worried about your granddad. I don't think he's been thinking right since Mom died."

"Grandpa? He's as sharp as he's ever been."

She took a drag on her cigarette and blew it out in his direction. "I'm going to see an attorney. Dad needs to be examined, and I think he should be declared . . . incompetent."

"Incompetent? Grandpa?"

"For his own sake. I looked it up on the internet. It'll have to go to court, and doctors will have to examine him. Then they'll decide what's in his best interests. If I'm right, they'd make me his guardian or something so I could manage his affairs."

Ben got to his feet again. "Mom, you can't really mean to do this to him."

"It's for his own good. He's not spending his money right, and the way he's going, he won't have anything left when he gets really old."

Understanding washed through him, and his gut clenched. "This is about the farm. This is because Grandpa gave it to me instead of settling a lot of cash on you."

"You could take care of things. You could keep him from that ordeal." She stubbed out the cigarette in a dirty ashtray. "You could give up on that stupid horse thing of yours, sell the farm, and make sure your grandfather has what he needs."

"And you have what you want. Right?"

"It's up to you."

He picked up his toolbox. "I feel sorry for you, Mom. You know that. You're one of the sorriest people I've ever met, and that's saying something."

She got to her feet, her eyes sparking in anger. "If you think they'd let you be his guardian, you can forget that. They'll look at your record and know you can't look after him."

The words stung more than he wanted them to, but he didn't let her see it. He just shook his head, turned, and left the house.

Ashley had one of those lousy days at work. A customer, furious that a product wasn't in stock, had taken it out on the nearest employee—who happened to be Ashley. She was still mulling over the unpleasant encounter when she pulled into her driveway and, much like what had happened two days before, saw Ben's truck parked near the shed. Her spirit lifted at the sight. She hadn't expected him to be there when she got off work. She stopped her truck and cut the engine, her eyes sweeping the yard until she found him near the farthest enclosure.

"Hey." She closed the door of the truck. "You're still here."

"I guess I lost track of time. I like watching these two eat. I keep imagining them getting stronger." He moved away from the fence. "Hope you don't mind."

"I don't." She pointed toward the house. "Give me a sec while I let out my dogs. Is Dusty with you?"

"Not today."

Ashley's black-and-white border collie, Speed, and brown terrier mix, Jack, barreled out the door when she opened it. The pet door on the opposite side of the house let them into a shaded run with a concrete floor, but they much preferred the freedom of the yard and paddock. When not chasing squirrels, they normally followed somewhere close on her heels.

The dogs let Ashley love on them for a few moments before heading over to Ben, needing to check out the visitor. But a few sniffs told them he wasn't a stranger. They collected pats from him, and then they were off again, burning off their excess energy.

Ben laughed as he watched them. "I need some of what they've got."

"Me too." She motioned to her covered patio. "Would you like something cold to drink?"

"Sure. If I'm not keeping you from anything."

"You aren't. I'd actually like some company while I decompress. It was a rough day at the store."

She went inside to get two bottles of soda from the fridge. When she returned, Ben was seated in one of the Adirondack chairs, Ashley's dogs getting their ears scratched, one on each side of him. She set his soda on the table next to his chair.

"Sorry, Speed," Ben said. "Sorry, Jack." He stopped scratching and picked up the beverage. After taking a few swallows, he looked at Ashley. "Care to tell me about your day? I'm a good listener."

She almost said no, but an instant later she found herself describing the entire disagreeable encounter with the customer. Her upset bubbled up and spilled over. She hadn't known how distressed she was until she detailed the experience, and telling it seemed to upset her even more.

Ben hadn't exaggerated. He *was* a good listener. His eyes, filled with compassion, remained on her face the entire time. He shook his head or smiled sympathetically just when she needed him to do one or the other. Before she knew it, more than half an hour had passed with her talking the entire time. On the heels of that realization came another. She was no longer distressed.

"Thank you," she said.

"I didn't do anything."

"But you did. You let me unload, and it helped a lot."

He shrugged. "I've done my share of unloading on friends over the years. Glad I could do the same for you."

Friends? Yes. Even though they'd only known each other a couple of weeks, Ben had become her friend. She liked him. She felt she could trust him, and she didn't trust men easily.

"Hey, could I pay you back with dinner? Nothing fancy. I planned to make tacos tonight."

"Ashley, you don't have to pay me back."

"Maybe not, but I'd like to do it. You're going out of your way to help feed the horses. Besides, I don't like to cook for myself."

"I get that. I don't like to cook for one either. Seems like a waste of time." He laughed. "But as much as I'd like to accept, I've got to get home. Dusty's been shut up in the house for too long and will be wanting his dinner." He gave her one of his crooked grins. "Can I get a rain check?"

Her pulse did a funny dance. "Definitely. Bring Dusty with you. The dogs can play while we eat. How about tomorrow?"

"Can't do Tuesdays. I've got a men's group I attend."

"Wednesday?" It surprised her how much she wanted him to say yes.

He studied her with those extraordinary eyes of his. It felt as if he could see right inside of her. Finally, he said, "Okay. Wednesday it is. What time do you want me here?"

"Six?"

"Can I bring anything?"

"Nope." She shook her head. "Just Dusty and yourself, Henning." She used his last name, thinking it might make the invitation seem less important to her.

"All right." He drained the last of the soda from the bottle, then pushed up from the chair. "See you then."

Ben's thoughts had been dark after leaving his mom's house earlier in the afternoon. Being with Ashley's horses—feeding them, watching them eat, seeing small signs of recovery—had helped lighten his spirits. But it was seeing Ashley herself that had made him forget his worries, at least for that short interlude. There was something about her that made him want to smile. A lot.

However, it wasn't long after leaving her place that thoughts of his mom's threats returned to plague him. As much as he wanted to keep it to himself, he knew he had to tell his grandfather. It was ludicrous to think Grandpa Grant was incompetent. The older man was surrounded by people who could attest to his soundness of mind, including several physicians. If his mom proceeded, she wouldn't succeed, but it would still be a painful ordeal.

"Please, God, don't let her do this to Grandpa."

He turned into the drive and brought the truck to a stop, his gaze sweeping over the Henning farm, from the house to the chicken coop to the fields of alfalfa to the barn to the paddocks, and he felt a catch in his heart, imagining it sold, perhaps even parceled into lots for a subdivision. He couldn't let that happen to the farm. He *wouldn't* let it happen to his grandfather either.

Sunday, December 7, 1941

It was almost half past noon when Andrew returned from the barn on that Sunday in December. The day was clear and breezy, the temperature a few degrees above average for that time of year. No snow covered the ground, which made him thankful. He removed his coat and hung it on a hook inside the door. Helen, her mother, and Louisa were in the kitchen, chatting about a neighbor's new baby. A ham was in the oven, and delicious odors wafted through the house. He hoped they would be called to dinner soon. He was hungry.

He went into the living room where Ben sat on the floor, college textbooks scattered around him. Having him home so soon after Thanksgiving had been a pleasant surprise. Andrew nodded to Ben before sitting in his chair and reaching to turn on the radio. Normally he didn't listen to the broadcast until after the family finished Sunday dinner, and God alone knew why he did something different today. Too tired to read, he supposed. Classical music came through the speaker, interspersed with a bit of static. He adjusted the tuner, and just as he released knob, the music stopped.

"We interrupt this broadcast to bring you this important bulletin . . . Flash. Washington. The White House announces Japanese attack on Pearl Harbor. Stay tuned for further developments."

It seemed to Andrew that his heart stopped beating. He sat frozen in place, his hand still stretched toward the radio.

"Dad?"

He looked up. Ben now stood before him. Andrew stood, too, and put his arm around his oldest son's shoulders. "We're in it now," he said softly.

"Where's Pearl Harbor?"

"In the Pacific. Hawaii." Andrew only knew this because of Hirsch Finkel. His neighbor kept himself apprised of what was happening around the world and shared the information with Andrew. Because Japan was an ally of Germany and Italy, it was of interest to Hirsch. The former professor had long been convinced the Japanese were a greater threat to the United States than what the news outlets reported.

"Do you think they'll tell us more soon?" Ben asked.

"I don't know, son. I expect they will."

Ben looked toward the kitchen. "Should we tell Mom and Grandma?"

"We'd better. It doesn't seem like something we should keep from them."

Chapter 8

Ashley sat at the small desk, staring at a blank sheet of paper. She'd promised her mom that she would write to Dylan. But other than telling him to hang in there, it was difficult to know what else to say. She chewed on the end of her pen, mulling over her slim options. Finally, she decided that it didn't matter so much what she said as long as she was upbeat about it.

Dear Dylan,

I hope you're doing better since your last letter to Mom. Don't forget that you can write to me too. I don't need to get all my information through her. I like to hear from my little brother without any filter.

I've been working hard around my little "homestead." I've built a couple of new shelters for the horses. The fence around the arena's been fixed. Inside the house, I painted the bathroom. I'm still not much of a housekeeper, but then I don't have people coming inside much.

I picked up a couple of new rescues last weekend. They are in really bad shape, but I hope they will pull through. I think the gelding's doing better than the mare right now, but I've only had them four days.

The most interesting thing that's happened lately is that I'm helping a guy who's starting a horse therapy program. He's still considering all his options, but I think he plans to cater the most to troubled kids and people with developmental problems, as well as to abused horses needing a sanctuary. Anyway, I'm helping him find the right horses for his program. It's really fun to hear him talk about it. He's a super nice guy.

Speed and Jack are both good, in case you were wondering. Work is the same as always. Good days and bad.

I want you to know I'm pulling for you. I know we don't always see eye to eye, and we've had some bad arguments. But I love you. I want you to be well and happy. I hope you'll forgive me if I said anything that's hurt you. Be strong. You can do this. I know you can.

Much love,
Ashley

It was true what Ashley wrote. She did love her brother, and she did want him to be well and happy. She hoped a day would come when they could be close again, the way they'd been when they were kids. Before their dad died and Dylan spiraled out of control.

It was also true that she wasn't much of a housekeeper. In fact, except for vegging in front of the TV some evenings, she would much rather be outside with the horses than dusting, making the bed, mopping floors, cooking, or doing dishes. Perhaps that's why, when she purchased this place, she'd cared much more about the acreage and shed than she had about the one-bedroom house itself. However, following her spontaneous invitation for Ben to have dinner with her, she decided it wouldn't hurt to do a thorough cleaning. No point letting him think her a complete slob.

By the time he knocked on her door on Wednesday evening, her house was tidy, and the taco fixings were ready to go.

"Hope I'm not early," he said when she opened the door. He held a bouquet of flowers in his right hand, and Dusty sat obediently by his left leg.

"You're not early. Come in." She looked down at the dog. "You too, boy."

By the time Ashley closed the door, Speed and Jack had come inside from the dog run. There was a lot of sniffing and tail wagging. Nobody growled, which was a good sign.

"These are for you." Ben held out the flowers.

She smiled as she took the bouquet. "They weren't necessary."

"I don't like to show up empty-handed."

"Your parents raised you to be a gentleman."

He gave his head a brief shake. "If I am one, it's because of my grandparents. Especially my grandpa. My mom . . . raised me alone."

"Really?" She carried the flowers to the sink and found a vase in the cupboard beneath it. "My dad died when I was nine, so my brother and I were raised by our mom too. She never remarried. You were lucky to have your grandparents close. Our only grandparents lived far away when we were little."

"I didn't know you had a brother. Older or younger?"

She arranged the flowers in the vase. "Dylan's three years younger than me."

"Does he live nearby?"

This time she hesitated before answering, "No. He's up in northern Idaho right now." It was the truth without telling the whole truth. Was that respecting Dylan's privacy, or was she protecting herself?

"When I was growing up, I wished I had a brother."

Something in his voice drew her around to meet his gaze, but she couldn't discern a change in his expression. Before she could ask another question, Dusty barked, and Ben turned to speak to the dog. The moment to ask about that wish for a brother was past. Better to let it go, she decided, rather than risk more questions about Dylan.

She turned her attention to food on the stove and in the fridge. Before long, she had all of the taco fixings on the table, and the two of them sat down to eat. "Dig in," she told him. He grinned as he obeyed.

For a short while, neither of them said anything, too busy reaching for various bowls of lettuce, chopped tomatoes, seasoned ground beef, shredded cheese, and salsa. Ben finished filling his taco shells first, but he waited for her before beginning to eat. She picked up her taco, smiled at him, and took her first bite. He smiled back, lowered his eyes for a few moments—although he wasn't looking at his food—then picked up his taco and did the same.

He'd said a silent prayer, she realized. She couldn't remember the last time she'd been around anybody who blessed their food. Years? And even then she couldn't say who it had been. Her family had never been religious, and her own journey toward God had been an unsteady one. Two steps forward, one step back. Mostly it had happened through books. She didn't attend a church. Not yet anyway, although something she'd read made her think it wouldn't hurt her to find one. Something about meeting together with other believers being important for a life of faith as a Christian. Maybe it was time she started looking.

Trying not to be obvious, she set the taco back onto her plate, closed her eyes, and silently thanked God for the food.

Ben noticed when Ashley got lost inside her own thoughts and decided to let it be while they ate. He spent the time watching her, enjoying the way light from a nearby window played across her face. It was such an adorable face too. He didn't suppose anyone would call her beautiful. At least not in a classical sort of way. No, *adorable* seemed the correct adjective. She was simply nice to look at her. Doing so made him feel warm on the inside. He couldn't remember any woman making him feel quite that way before.

After he took the last bite of his meal, he decided it was time to end the silence. Horses seemed the safest subject. He cleared his throat, then asked, "Is the rest of your family involved with horses too?"

She glanced up from her plate, amusement in her eyes, and released a soft laugh. "No. My mom's afraid of them. She's never understood my obsession with horses. That's what she calls it. An obsession."

"How about your brother?"

The smile faded. "No, Dylan never had any interest in horses. None at all." She got up from the table and took her plate to the sink.

Ben got the hint. She didn't want to talk about her brother.

He didn't know why. He didn't *need* to know the reason. After all, he understood the feeling all too well. Talking about his mom made him uncomfortable too. He never knew what to say about her. Obviously, bringing up horses hadn't taken them in as safe a direction as he'd expected. So now what? He stood, picking up his own empty plate. "You cooked. I should do dishes."

"No way." She turned toward him. "That would be a fine way for me to say thanks. Come over and eat, and then you clean up." A hint of her smile had returned.

"Okay. How about we do it together?"

She seemed to consider the suggestion, finally saying, "All right."

"I don't know about you, but I get tired of doing the dishes every single day on my own." He chuckled. "The benefit of being single is the only dirty dishes are the ones I dirty. But the downside is I never get any relief from KP duty."

"KP duty. Were you in the military?"

"No. I thought about joining up after I graduated from high school, but . . ." He let the words trail off. But what? *But I was an out-of-control mess by then.* He didn't really want to say that to her, despite the truth of it.

Filling the sink with warm, sudsy water, she glanced over at him, waiting for him to continue.

He shrugged. "It wasn't to be. So I bummed around for a bit." A polite way of saying he'd let his life spiral completely out of control. "Eventually, I got a construction job and began learning a trade. Of course, I learned a little about farming from my grandparents through the years."

"But you preferred construction to farming?"

"Yeah, I did. I had a decent employer who taught me a lot. I saved up enough to break out on my own right about the time the building business started to come out of its slump. I was one of the fortunate ones."

"Yet you've decided to do something different now."

Ben took a towel and began to dry the clean dishes waiting in the rack. "Yeah. Owning Grandpa's farm changed everything yet again. I mean, if I didn't own that property, I don't know that God would have given me that particular vision."

"You really believe it was God who gave you the idea for equine therapy." She didn't sound skeptical, exactly. Just curious.

"For this particular idea, yes. I do." Which was the reason why he hadn't given up when those first doors closed in his face. Which was why he wouldn't give up now, even if more doors slammed in the future. Which was why he wouldn't back down, even if his mom did something stupid.

Monday, December 8, 1941

On the day after the attack on Pearl Harbor, sixty-two million Americans listened to the president's address to Congress. Among those sixty-two million were the Hennings and the Finkels. All of them together in Andrew's living room, the two families heard President Roosevelt say, "Yesterday, December 7, 1941—a date which will live in infamy—the United States of America was suddenly and deliberately attacked by naval and air forces of the Empire of Japan."

Andrew looked at Ben, who had stayed over at the farm the previous night rather than going to Boise. Ben was eighteen. He was old enough to volunteer for the military. He was a young man, not a boy. Andrew couldn't tell him what to do. Ben could be impulsive, but he was also levelheaded. Still, there was no denying he was enraged by the unprovoked attack by Japan. Would he join a branch of the military now, or would he wait until he could train to become a pilot? Would the draft even allow him to wait? For surely, with the war, the rules would change again.

The president had continued speaking while Andrew's mind wandered. He hoped he hadn't missed anything important.

"No matter how long it may take us to overcome this premeditated invasion," Roosevelt was saying, "the American people in their righteous might will win through to absolute victory. I believe I interpret the will of the Congress and of the people when I assert that we will not only defend ourselves to the uttermost, but will make very certain that this form of treachery shall never endanger us again."

Was it possible to do that, to be certain no one could endanger Americans again? And even if possible, how long would it take to bring about such a result? Andrew met Hirsch's gaze from across the living room. He saw a despair in the older man's eyes that he'd never seen before, and it put a new kind of fear in his heart.

President Roosevelt ended his address by asking the Congress to declare that a state of war now existed between the United States and the Japanese Empire. No one in the Henning living room spoke as Andrew turned off the radio. Even Andy Jr., all of five years old, seemed to understand that only silence was appropriate.

At long last, Hirsch and Ida rose to their feet. "We will go home," Hirsch said.

Andrew stood. "I'm afraid you were right about the Japanese threat."

"Ja." Hirsch looked at Ben and Oscar, sitting on kitchen chairs in the corner, their heads close together. "But I would have liked to be wrong."

Andrew walked with his neighbors to the door and bid them goodbye, watching as they slowly made their way down the drive, their shoulders slumped, as if beneath the weight of the world. He felt a similar weight on his chest as he turned to face his family.

Thursday, December 11, 1941
Four days after the attack on Pearl Harbor, Nazi Germany declared war on the United States.

"Hitler does not understand America," Hirsch said upon learning the news. Whatever despair the older man had felt following the president's radio address had disappeared, replaced with righteous indignation. "He does not know this nation's industrial capacity. And he thinks because it is a nation of different races, because it is not purely Aryan, that it is bourgeois, decadent, inferior, and undisciplined. I am thankful for his ignorance. He will not be ready for your military. He will not be ready for the resolve of your countrymen."

Andrew hoped Hirsch Finkel was as right about this as he'd been about so many other world events over the past three or four years.

Ben took action of his own that day. He enrolled in the Civilian Pilot Training Program and enthusiastically informed his dad of it when he returned to the farm that evening. "I can begin my flight training now and stay in school at the same time. I'll be in the Army Air Forces Enlisted Reserve, and when I graduate, I can go on to train to be a combat pilot." Excitement flashed in his eyes as he spoke.

Andrew didn't hear the news with the same sort of fervor, especially since he knew the words *combat pilot* would strike terror into Helen's heart when she heard them, the same as they had done in his own. Yes, he was proud of his son for wanting to serve his country in its time of need. It would take many men, many sons, to win this war. But this was *his* son, and it was hard not to imagine the worst that could happen to him as a soldier or a combat pilot and to want to protect him from it.

Oscar, on the other hand, was frustrated. "I wish I was older. I could fight. I'm a good shot with a rifle. I'm ready to go right now."

Andrew didn't tell the younger boy that his time might come. He wanted to believe, as many did, that America could whip the Japanese and Nazis in a matter of weeks, that the war would come to an end in no time at all, that before Ben even graduated from junior college peace would have returned to the world.

God willing, those who believed in a swift victory would be right. Andrew was afraid it wouldn't happen quite that way.

Chapter 9

Idahoans loved to flock to the mountains for the last three-day weekend of the summer. Ashley wished she could join them, even if only for one day, especially since she wasn't scheduled to work on Labor Day weekend. But with the two rescue horses to tend to, she needed to remain at home. She settled for riding Remington, her buckskin mare, in the arena at the far end of her property. It wasn't quite the same as riding her horse beside a splashing creek, surrounded by tall pines and rugged mountains, but it brought her joy. Just sitting astride her horse was all she needed to make a day brighter.

It had always been thus. From the moment she'd climbed aboard a pony at the fair when she was five, riding it around in that silly circle, her dad watching from the sidelines, she'd lost her heart to the noble horse. Her childhood bedroom had soon been filled with horses. Stuffed horses. Plastic horses. Paintings of horses. Photographs of horses.

Once Ashley was old enough to earn money babysitting and doing yard work, she'd saved every penny toward the day she could buy her first horse. She'd never spent her earnings on candy or clothes or jewelry. She'd deposited it all into her savings account at the credit union a half mile from their home. She had a tidy sum put away by the time she turned sixteen and was hired to work at a fast-food drive-in. Before the end of that summer, she'd bought Gus.

Trotting Remington around the arena, she smiled at memories of her first horse. The money from her job had gone to pay for Gus's feed and boarding. There hadn't been enough left over to buy a saddle, so she'd ridden the gelding bareback, and she believed those few years without a saddle had made her a better rider. Gus had been her best friend. Being with him had been everything.

Ashley reined in, stopping Remington. Then she let her gaze sweep over her property. The horses in their pens by the shelter. The dogs running along the edge of the arena. The shed and the house. The truck and horse trailer. She couldn't help but wonder how different her life might be today if she hadn't saved up and bought her first horse.

"I wonder what Daddy would think of all this?" she whispered as she patted Remington's neck.

She liked to think her dad would be happy with the way she'd invested her small inheritance. Perhaps he would be disappointed that she hadn't gone on to college after high school, but it hadn't been an option for her at the time. While she'd been a good student, she hadn't been at the top of her class, the type of student that earned free rides to college. Her mom had barely held things together financially, especially after Dylan began getting into trouble, so there hadn't been money to spare for such luxuries as higher education. And the idea of leaving college with thousands and thousands of dollars' worth of debt had terrified

Ashley, especially since she couldn't think of anything she wanted to do besides working with horses.

Perhaps one day.

She turned Remington toward the lean-to shelters and pens. Her thoughts continued to wander as she unsaddled and brushed the buckskin, then fed her and the other three horses. Afterward, as she walked toward the house, her wandering thoughts finally arrived at Ben Henning. A familiar place. He'd been on her mind often in the days since he'd joined her for dinner. To be honest, it bothered her that he hadn't called her since then. Not that he'd had a reason to call. She hadn't needed his help with feedings while she was at work. Her schedule had included several broken shifts that allowed her to take care of the feedings herself. Still . . .

As if in answer to her thoughts, the cell phone buzzed in her pocket. When she removed it, Ben's face smiled back at her from the screen. She'd taken the photo of him on Wednesday as he'd stood beside one of the rescue horses, and she'd attached it to his entry in her contacts. Not that doing so had any special meaning. She tried to do that with everybody in her contacts list.

"Hey, Henning," she answered. "How goes it?"

"Good. How 'bout you?"

"Good too."

"Listen. I wondered if you could spare me a little time later today. I think I've found another horse, but I'd like your opinion before I accept."

"Wow. That'll make three horses already. You're really moving along. Halfway there."

"Only if you agree about the horse."

"A lease?" she asked.

"Yes."

How often would she hear from him once his stable was full? Would he still call her sometimes? It shouldn't matter to her, one way or the other, but somehow it did. She drew a quick breath and said, "Yes, I could take a look today."

"That's terrific. How about I swing by for you about two?"

"Sure. I'll be ready."

They each said goodbye, and Ashley checked the clock on the phone's screen before slipping it into her pocket. She would have plenty of time to eat a quick lunch and take a shower before he came for her.

The owner of the gelding hovered right beyond the paddock gate while Ashley ran her hand over the horse, picked up his hooves, looked him in the face and eyes, watched him walk as she led him back and forth. Ben couldn't read her expression. She seemed intent, but he couldn't tell if her thoughts were positive or negative. When she turned to Ben at last, she gave her head the slightest of shakes. In fact, he wasn't sure that's what he'd seen.

Ashley faced the horse's owner. "Thanks for letting me look him over. We'll let you know."

The owner looked at Ben.

All he could do was repeat Ashley's words. "We'll let you know. Thanks."

Then the two of them left the paddock and walked to Ben's truck.

"What's wrong?" he asked as they both slid onto the seat.

"I could be mistaken, but I think that horse has something

wrong with his hip. My guess is that guy wants you to end up paying for vet treatments."

Ben looked at her in surprise. It had never occurred to him that anyone would want to use a nonprofit program that was meant to help people in such a way, pawning off a less-than-healthy horse in order to avoid paying for care.

Ashley shrugged. "You could call your vet and have him look at the horse, see what he has to say."

"No. I trust your opinion." He started the engine. "I'm disappointed. That's all."

Softly, she said, "People will do that to you. A lot."

Ben cast a glance in her direction, but she was staring out the passenger window. *Who disappointed you, Ashley?* He put the truck in gear and followed the driveway out to the road.

It wasn't long before Ashley broke the silence. "How soon do you hope to be in operation?"

"I'd hoped by the end of September, but that's unrealistic. For a riding program, I need at least one certified instructor plus enough horses in the barn that we can train our volunteers. I've got an instructor's commitment, but not enough horses yet and no trained volunteers." He drew in a breath and let it out slowly. "I'm not sure about starting up just as winter's coming." He glanced at Ashley, then back at the road. "I know diehard horse people like you ride in all kinds of weather. But can the same be true of a therapy program's clientele? Maybe. Maybe not. It's my plan for the riding program to run in six-week cycles with a break in between each one of them. It probably makes sense to wait to open until after the new year. Maybe late February. We usually have some decent weather then."

"Too bad you don't have an indoor arena."

An indoor arena. He hadn't even thought of that before. It wasn't as if he didn't have enough land for it. But he reined in his enthusiasm for the idea almost the moment it began. An arena wouldn't be cheap to put up, no matter the materials used. It would surely be beyond his savings. And borrowing was out of the question. After all, he had no proof that he could make a go of his therapy barn. No financial institution would take a risk on his fledgling nonprofit. Not unless he put up something of worth . . . like the Henning family farm. That he wasn't willing to do. Shoot, his mom would have *him* declared incompetent if he tried to mortgage the farm.

"Hey, did I say something to upset you?" Ashley asked, real concern in her voice.

"No." He glanced her way once again. "Still disappointed about that horse, I guess." It wasn't the full truth, but it wasn't really a lie. And since he wasn't ready to talk about his mom's threats regarding the farm, he would have to leave it there.

Friday, February 20, 1942

Andrew prayed for his nation. He resumed a practice from many years before, going to the barn loft where he could be alone before the throne of God, pleading for His mercies. He prayed when Wake Island fell to the Japanese in December. He prayed when Manila fell to the enemy weeks later, the Philippine forces under General Douglas MacArthur withdrawing to the Bataan peninsula. He prayed as many Americans began to realize that they would not whip the enemy in a matter of weeks, as some had boasted. He prayed they would have the strength to persevere through the months and, he feared, years to come. He prayed and kept on praying for his sons, for his family, for his friends, for his nation.

Ben didn't come home for his mother's birthday. He called to say he had flight training the next day and couldn't leave Boise. He also said something about a visit to the Forty-Second Bombardment Group at Gowen Airfield.

Andrew wondered how long Ben would hold out. Many of his friends—those from his high school years in Kuna, others from his first year at college—had already joined up. Would Ben resist the patriotic urge to join now in order to be able to fly in combat later? Andrew didn't even know what to hope for in that regard.

It was a small birthday party for Helen on that Friday evening in February. Only Andrew, Helen, Mother Greyson, and the four younger kids. Andrew's parents weren't able to come because his dad had a bad cold, and the Finkels stayed home for the Sabbath. There was a cake, baked by Mother Greyson and Louisa, and there were a few simple gifts.

Observing his family, Andrew wondered what would be different by Helen's next birthday. Rationing of tires had begun in December, and the rationing of new cars had begun this month. Other items needed for the war effort would surely follow. Including food. Would there be enough sugar for a cake by next February?

He shook his head, unhappy with the negative spiral of his thoughts. Had God's presence through the Great Depression, the loss of a baby, the troubles in his marriage, and the adoption of three orphaned children not taught him anything? If God could bring the Hennings through all of that, could He not bring them through a war? Had Andrew's heart been unchanged, despite the Lord's faithfulness? Could he not say, "It is well with my soul," no matter the circumstance?

"You're not yourself," Helen said to him as they prepared for bed later that night.

"Sorry." He removed his shirt and draped it over a chair back.

"It's Ben, isn't it?"

"Mostly."

"He's almost nineteen. He's able to make his own decisions."

"Mmm." He remembered himself at the same age. Back then he'd thought he knew everything. He'd thought himself a man. Now, at thirty-seven, he'd learned how little he'd known at nineteen and also realized how little he still knew.

"Darling?" Helen placed her hand on his arm. "Ben's worked so hard for what he wants. He's got a good head on his shoulders, thanks to you. He'll be all right."

Andrew nodded slowly. "I remember the first time I saw him. He was taking care of Oscar and Louisa. Ready to fight for them if he had to." He offered a brief smile to his wife. "He's still ready to fight for them. Just in a different way."

Wordlessly, his wife leaned in and kissed his cheek before she returned to the closet for her nightgown.

"Maybe it would be different if I felt there was something I could do to help. I never served in the military, so I'm not officer material. And I'm beyond the age they want for regular soldiers. Besides, they classified me as III-A. Not that I couldn't fight. I could fight."

Helen turned and stared at him, askance. "Andrew, would you really go off and leave us if your classification was different?"

"No," he admitted. "No, I wouldn't." Two women alone on a farm with four kids who ranged in age from just-turned-six to fifteen. Leaving them would be unthinkable. No, his contribution to the war effort had to be raising as much food as he could squeeze from the land.

"Then don't ever say such a thing again. It frightens me."

"I'm sorry. I shouldn't have said it. I guess I feel . . . ineffective." He shook his head. "Or maybe I'm starting to feel old."

"Andrew Michael Henning." Irritation had entered Helen's voice. "You are *not* old."

A few quick strides carried him to his wife, where he gathered her in a close embrace. "You're right. I'm not old." He kissed her, forcefully at first, then with languid passion. "You keep me young."

Chapter 10

On her first full day off work after the holiday weekend, Ashley drove to Mountain Home to look at some horses on the Richardson ranch. She hoped to find at least one that would be a good fit for the Harmony Barn. When she got out of her pickup, she was greeted by a hot, steady wind blowing across the high desert.

"Hey, Ashley," Ruth Richardson called to her from a nearby corral.

"Hi, Ruth." Ashley walked toward her.

Ruth was closer to Ashley's mom's age than to Ashley's, but that hadn't changed the friendship that had blossomed between them because of horses. Mostly they kept in touch via email and texts since their paths didn't cross all that often. Usually they didn't see each other more than once, occasionally twice, a year. But it always felt like only yesterday.

"It was good to hear from you." Ruth latched the corral gate before giving Ashley a warm hug. "Been too long."

"I know. Seems I'm always running behind with everything."

"How's your mom?"

"Good. Worried about Dylan."

Ruth was one of only a few people who knew what was happening with Ashley's brother. "Naturally," she answered. "I'd be worried, too, if I was his mom."

Guilt twinged in Ashley's chest. Was it a bad sign that she wasn't worried about Dylan? That she thought it a good thing he'd been ordered into rehab, into a place where he couldn't walk out when the going got tough?

Ruth motioned toward a corral closer to the house. "I've got those horses ready for you to look at. I'm glad you called me. Your friend's program sounds like something we'd like to participate in."

"I believe in it." What she meant was she'd started to believe in Ben. A fact that still surprised her.

"That's good enough for me."

They walked together to the corral. Three horses stood inside, flicking their tails at flies. A tall black—about sixteen hands, Ashley estimated—walked to the fence and thrust his head over the top rail, nickering at them.

"That's Thunder." Ruth laughed softly. "Trust me. He's nothing like his name. I thought he might be good when there are larger, heavier clients. I didn't figure they'd all be kids or weigh a hundred and twenty pounds or less."

"How old is he?"

"Fifteen. Gets along with most everybody in the herd, although we've got a mare that likes to pick on him."

Ashley patted the gelding on his muscular neck. She liked the look of him.

Ruth opened the gate, and they stepped inside the corral.

The horse that was closest to them was an Appaloosa gelding. A full hand shorter than Thunder, he had a sturdy build.

"That's Klondike. He's twelve. And the dun is Sundowner. He's thirteen and quiet. Too quiet for most riders. Which might make him perfect for an equine riding program. All three of them are sound and well trained. Recently shod."

Ashley walked around both Klondike and Sundowner, studying them. One at a time, she attached a lead to their halters and led them around the corral, watching the way they moved. She ran her hands over them and lifted their hooves. She trusted Ruth, but habit required that she know each horse for herself.

"Which two is up to you," Ruth said when Ashley stepped to the corral fence again. "Wish we could do more."

Ashley looked at her friend. "Two is generous, Ruth. Really. Ben will be bowled over when I tell him."

"I look forward to meeting him." Ruth's eyes narrowed ever so slightly, as if something had occurred to her.

For some reason, Ashley felt like squirming.

Her friend continued, "How about, instead of you picking up the horses, you let me deliver them? That way I can see where they'll be and get to meet Mr. Henning at the same time."

"Sure. If you want."

"I want."

Ashley felt as if Ruth knew something she didn't, and it bothered her.

"Made up your mind?" Her friend tipped her head toward the horses. "About which two you want?"

Ashley cleared her throat. "Yeah. I think so. I like all three, but I feel like Thunder and Sundowner will be the best fit." She hoped Ben would agree.

"Then those are the two we'll offer. Now, how about something cool to drink."

"Okay."

They left the corral and walked to the house. Ashley waited on the covered patio while Ruth went inside. A few minutes later she returned with two tall glasses of lemonade. By that time Ashley was seated at the patio table.

"So . . ." Ruth sat opposite Ashley. "How many horses have you got on your little place now?"

"Four. My own mare and three rescues." She sipped her lemonade. "One of them is ready to find a home. The other two will need more time. They were part of a big rescue about ten days ago. You probably saw it on the news."

Ruth's eyes darkened. "That place with the thirty starving horses?"

"That's the one. They had to put down some of them. The two I brought home were in bad shape, but I think they're going to make it."

"I don't understand people sometimes."

"Neither do I."

Ruth shook her head as if to dislodge the unpleasant thoughts. "Fortunately, there are more good people than cruel ones. Like this Ben Henning of yours. He sounds like a good one."

"He's hardly mine, Ruth."

Ben rapped on the door of the trailer. It was parked with several others on a half-acre lot not far from the Boise River. Tall cottonwoods towered over the trailers, casting spiderweb-like shadows across the ground. At one time there may have been grass growing around each of the trailers, but now there were only weeds. Rusting barrels stood near a fence that tilted precariously. Old toys, a couple of bent bicycle wheels, and other discards littered any free space.

He rapped again.

"Go away," came a gruff voice from inside.

"Guy. It's Ben Henning." He tried the knob. The door opened. "May I come in?"

"Go away."

The interior was dim, the curtains drawn. Despite the lack of light, Ben could see dishes piled in the kitchen sink and empty liquor bottles on the counter. A movement to his left drew his eyes. Guy Turner was on the built-in sofa.

"I'm coming in, Guy."

He left the door open behind him, hoping to improve the stale smell within. Guy sat up, groaned, then leaned his forehead against his hands. Ben cleared a spot and sat nearby.

"How'd you know?" Guy asked.

"Your sister called me."

"Debbie needs to butt out."

"Maybe. But she knows I'm your sponsor." He waited a few moments before adding, "You should have been the one to call me."

Guy grunted but said nothing.

Over the years of Ben's sobriety, he'd seen plenty of anger and shame, including his own. He'd been sworn at by some men and had listened to the excuses of others. He'd witnessed courage and cowardice, sometimes on the same night, from the same person. He'd sat beside a kid of eighteen and an old man in his eighties, both of them debilitated by booze. He'd been in one home that was more of a mansion and in several hovels similar to the one he was in now.

"What do you want?" Guy said into the lengthening silence.

"To help you."

"I don't want your help. I don't want anybody's help."

"That's evident." Ben stood and went to the nearest window, where he brushed the curtain aside, letting in more daylight. He almost wished he hadn't. It revealed even more of the mess.

"It's useless."

Ben turned around. "There's always hope."

"I'm a lost cause."

"I don't believe in lost causes. I've been where you are now."

Guy lifted his head from his hands at last. His eyes were red rimmed, his complexion pasty white. He hadn't shaved in days.

"There's always hope," Ben repeated.

He thought of the crazy, mixed-up teenager he'd been, of the trouble he'd courted. He thought of the accident that had changed both his life and the life of his friend, neither of them for the better. He'd thought of the way he'd tried to minimize the pain and the guilt with bottles of booze. He'd been a lost cause. His own mother had told him so countless times. And yet there had come the day that he'd grabbed hold of hope. If he could climb out of the pit, so could Guy.

"Let's get you cleaned up." He reached for the other man's arm. "And then I'd like to take you some place where they can help you get sober. If that's what you're ready to do."

Wednesday, May 27, 1942

"You're deep in thought," Helen said as her hand alighted on Andrew's shoulder.

He looked up from the newspaper, open on the kitchen table. Foreign places most Americans had never heard of now appeared in the newspaper on an all-too-frequent basis. Bataan and Corregidor were two of those names. Bataan had fallen to the Japanese in April and Corregidor earlier this month. Men and women killed. Men and women captured. So much loss.

Helen rounded the table and sat opposite him. "Do you suppose there'll come a day when there's good news in the paper again?"

"It'll change. It has to."

Now if either of them could believe it.

At least their youngest two children were oblivious to the war. Frani had lived on horseback ever since discovering the novel *My Friend Flicka*, about a boy and his horse in Wyoming. As for Andy, he was consumed by the new litter of pups that had been born in a corner of the barn a few weeks earlier. What could be wrong with the world as long as there were horses and puppies?

It wasn't the same for the older Henning children. When together, Ben and Oscar talked of little else besides the war. The war and Ben's interest in flight. As for Louisa, not quite sixteen, she was writing letters to a sailor. Not a boy she'd met before. He was the distant cousin of a friend. Just eighteen years old and already serving on a ship in the Pacific.

"Heaven help us," Helen had said the other night, "when she falls for someone she actually knows and can spend time with."

Andrew agreed with his wife. Louisa was a rare beauty with her pale-blond hair and her startling blue eyes. Ben's college friends liked to come home with him for visits, and Andrew hadn't failed to notice that they came more to flirt with Louisa than to spend time with Ben.

Helen brushed hair from her forehead. "I think I'll turn in early. Do you mind?"

"Of course not. It's been a long day."

This spring the Henning family garden had been tripled in size, leaving only a small patch of lawn. Just room enough for the picnic table Andrew had built five years earlier. On lined school paper, Helen had sketched the plans for this new garden, the rows of peas and beans, carrots and onions, peppers and tomatoes, beets and squash, lettuce and kale. As soon as the weather allowed, the planting had begun, with peas and lettuce going into the ground first. Helen tended to the garden daily, in addition to preparing meals and tending to the house and the needs of the children. It was no wonder she wanted to turn in early.

Folding the newspaper and setting it aside, Andrew wondered what his father-in-law would think if he could see everything now. Frank Greyson had passed away before Frani or Andy Jr. were born and before Andrew and Helen adopted the three Tandy orphans. He'd passed away while the country lay in the grip of the Great Depression and while many other farmers had been displaced. He'd died while the world still believed that the Great War had been the war to end all wars. A pity that hadn't proven to be true.

Andrew rose and went into the living room. The room was empty, every member of his family now in their bedrooms, although judging by the sounds coming from upstairs, not all were asleep. He reached for his Bible as he settled onto the chair. He didn't open the book at once. He simply sat, willing himself to be still, willing his mind not to spin off into worry, willing his heart to be turned to the Lord.

At last he turned to the book of Joshua. He'd been reading and studying there for several months. He'd even memorized the ninth verse of the first chapter, repeating the words to himself when he felt overwhelmed by the news of the world. His eyes went there now and he whispered the verse aloud. "'Be strong and of a good courage; be not afraid, neither be thou dismayed: for the LORD thy God is with thee whithersoever thou goest.'"

The story of Joshua had taught him, once again, that he must hold fast to God. He'd rediscovered that loyalty to God required sacrifice. Sometimes great sacrifice. He'd learned afresh that he wanted to finish well, to be faithful, and to trust despite his circumstances.

He recalled now that the stones of remembrance taken from the middle of the Jordan River, the ones the Israelites used to build a memorial to what God had done, had come from the deepest part of the river. He'd made a note in his Bible that he, too, brought his own stones of remembrance from the deepest waters. The places that had been the hardest to cross through had also been the ones where he'd discovered God holding him up. Those were the times worth remembering, the times worth making a memorial of, to tell others about and to glorify God.

Another verse came to mind, and as before, he quoted it aloud: "'And we know that all things work together for good to them that love God, to them who are the called according to his purpose.'"

He quieted himself a second time, closing his eyes. Then he prayed that verse from Romans over his family, trusting that all things would work together for good for them.

Chapter 11

Ben invited Ashley to come to the farm for lunch the next Sunday. Actually, he invited her to join him for church first, but she declined. That didn't surprise him. He'd learned she had no church affiliation. There was a guardedness about Ashley, and he had to wonder if that was why she didn't attend services. Church was about community, about forming relationships, about being vulnerable and known. He suspected something like that didn't come easily for her.

Ruth Richardson, Ashley's friend, had delivered Thunder and Sundowner the previous day. Ben had been as excited to see their arrival as he'd been when the still-as-yet-unnamed sorrel mare arrived weeks ago. Add to that the expectation of Nicki Day's gelding, Paisley, which would be delivered at the end of the week, and he thought it was all too perfect to be believed. With four horses and an instructor—still unpaid but hopefully one day to be on staff—they could begin training volunteers.

Ben was in the barn when he heard a vehicle pull into the yard. He expected it to be Ashley. Instead, when he went outside, he saw his mom getting out of her car. She frowned toward the house, as if it offended her in some way. His gut tightened.

"Mom," he called to her.

She turned to face him, still frowning. "I'm glad you're home. I was afraid you might be with Dad."

"Grandpa went fishing this weekend with friends." He walked toward her.

"Dad and his fish. I never did understand the fun in catching something cold and slimy."

"Fish aren't slimy."

His mom wrinkled her nose in disagreement.

He leaned over and kissed her cheek. "It's nice to have you come out to visit me." He tried to mean it when he said it.

"Well, don't get used to it. You know I hate this place."

"Yeah, Mom. I know." He motioned with his head. "Come see the horses."

"You've got horses already?"

"I told you about—" He broke off. It never worked out the way he wanted when he started reminding her what he'd already told her. "Just come have a look." He turned so that they were both facing the same direction.

Reluctantly, she fell into step beside him. "No chickens, I see."

"Not yet, but I plan to get some."

"Don't do it. They're a pain. Noisy, smelly, dirty. You have to feed them and gather their eggs." She shuddered.

He lowered his voice, hoping to soften the question. "Wasn't there *anything* you liked about growing up on a farm?"

"Nothing. Not a single thing. That's why I got out of here the second I could." That had been on the back of a Harley, as she'd told him more than once.

"Not even horses?" he persisted.

Her nose wrinkled again. "No."

He wished there was at least one thing they both loved about this place. He could have made a long list of his own. Maybe if he could help her admit to having some good memories, she wouldn't be so bent on the sale of the farm. Maybe it would then become more important to her than money. But at least she hadn't brought up that crazy incompetency idea again. Almost two weeks had passed, and she hadn't said anything more about it, not to him or to Grandpa Grant. Ben's warning to his grandfather hadn't seemed to cause the older man much concern, and so Ben tried to have the same attitude about it.

They stopped at the paddock fence. Ben leaned his forearms on the top rail while his mom stayed a short distance behind him. He pretended not to notice as he pointed to each horse, telling her the few facts he knew. "That last one still needs a name." He glanced over his shoulder. "Got any ideas?"

Her disdaining look stopped him from pressing for an answer.

As if coming to his rescue, he saw Ashley's truck pull into the drive and stop.

"Who's that?" his mom asked.

When he'd invited Ashley to come for lunch, he hadn't planned on introducing her to his mom, but he didn't have any other choice now. He stepped into full view and waved to her, answering, "A friend."

Ashley walked toward them, shading her eyes with one hand. "Is the herd getting along?"

"Yeah, they seem to be."

"That's good. You never know. Especially with mares." Ashley's gaze flicked to his mom, then back to him.

"Ashley, this is Wendy Henning." He paused. "My mom."

Ashley's smile was warm and genuine. "Nice to meet you, Mrs. Henning."

"It's *Ms.* Henning. But you can call me Wendy."

Ben cringed at the tone of her voice. "Mom, this is my friend, Ashley Showalter. She's been helping me find the horses I need for the equine program."

"Ahh."

If Ashley noticed his mom's obvious disapproval, she didn't let on. "It's been fun. Your son's got a good heart, Ms. Henning. You must be proud of him."

For once, his mom kept her opinions to herself. But her eyes spoke volumes.

"Are you joining us for lunch?" Ashley asked.

"Lunch? I suppose I could spare the time." His mom looked at him. "If Ben doesn't mind."

Why did he feel like a fly caught in a spider's web? "Sure, Mom. Join us. It's nothing fancy. I made chili and corn bread."

"Your grandpa's favorite."

"Mine too. If you remember." He turned toward the paddock, wishing he hadn't added the last bit. It served no purpose except to try to wound her. Which it wouldn't. *God, help me say the right things. Help me be kind, no matter what.* He inhaled deeply before facing the two women again. "Come on into the house. I don't know about you, but I'm hungry."

In truth, he had no appetite at all.

Ashley pretended she didn't notice the tension in the air. There was no denying that Ben's mom had taken an instant dislike to her. Was it because Ashley had called her *Mrs.* Henning? It seemed a small thing to have offended the woman.

But she cared less about Wendy Henning's reaction to her than she did about Ben's upset over it. He tried to hide it, but she saw it anyway. He always seemed so at ease, so comfortable in his own skin. That wasn't the man who sat opposite her at the kitchen table. She wished she could tell him it was okay.

Wendy took a bite of chili, chewed, swallowed. Then she leaned back in her chair. "I don't suppose you've got a beer in the fridge."

"No, Mom. You know I don't."

"Just thought maybe you'd loosened up a little."

He dropped his gaze while he buttered his corn bread.

Wendy's gaze moved to Ashley. "What about you? You a tee-totaler too?"

"I guess you could call me that. I don't care for the taste of it."

"Beer?"

"Any of it."

"Sheesh. Takes all kinds." Wendy returned to her chili.

There was something hard and brittle about Ben's mom, and Ashley wondered how on earth her son had become such a kind, polite man. Had she always been like this? Ashley remembered him telling her that if he was a gentleman it was because of his grandparents. She'd thought it a way of deflecting a compliment. Now she believed it was true. This woman couldn't have taught him. Not as she was now.

Ashley decided to focus on eating and to avoid more eye contact that might encourage conversation. Whether or not that was a good decision, she couldn't say. The only sounds in the room after that were the clatter of spoons against bowls and the softer ones of chewing.

Suddenly Wendy pushed her bowl away and stood up. "I need a smoke. I'll be outside."

After the door closed behind her, Ben said, "I'm sorry."

"What for?" Ashley stirred the remaining chili in her bowl. "You didn't do anything."

"I was born. That's enough."

She drew back in her chair and looked at him, expecting him to shrug or tell her he was joking. But his expression was serious. He gave his head a shake, then rose and took his and his mom's dishes to the sink. Ashley hesitated a few moments before following him with her own bowl and drinking glass. Wordlessly, she stepped to his side, looking out the window as she did so. His mother leaned against the side of her car, a cigarette in hand. Ashley heard Ben draw a slow, shaky breath, and the sound made her heart ache. She thought it better not to let him know, so she turned and walked to the entrance to the living room.

"I like your place, Henning." She kept her voice light. "It's cute. Did you tell me it's been in your family for a hundred years?"

"Yeah. My great-great-great-grandparents, the Greysons, built the house." Ben joined her. "Their daughter Helen married Andrew Henning. Andrew's and Helen's oldest son was Ben Henning. I'm named for him. He was dad to my grandpa, Grant Henning. And my mom is Grandpa's only child as I'm her only child."

"Your mom grew up on this farm? I assumed she'd married a Henning."

"Nope. My mom's never been married."

"Oh. That's why she didn't like me calling her Mrs."

"To be honest, I don't know if she really cares or if she was being contrary. It's hard to tell with her sometimes."

Did it bother him, Ashley wondered, that his mom had never married? Single women chose to have kids on their own all the time these days. Marriage was often an afterthought, if it happened at all.

"Here. I'll show you the rest of the place." He motioned for her to follow him. "Not much to it, really. There are three bedrooms, none very large, and a bathroom that's just got room to turn around in. And those stairs"—he pointed—"lead up to the attic. Grandpa said it was converted to a bedroom right before or soon after his uncle Andy was born. Sometime before the start of World War II. There weren't stairs at first. Only a ladder."

"It's rare anymore for a house to stay in a family for generations. I'll bet that makes it special to you."

His smile removed some of the tension from his face. "Yeah. It does. When I sit in the living room in the evening, I sometimes think I can hear their voices. Does that make me sound crazy?"

"No." She laughed. "Well, maybe a little."

His laughter joined hers. "I hope it won't scare you away."

"I don't scare that easily."

His smile slowly vanished, and his expression turned serious. His gazed lowered from her eyes to her mouth. For one surprising moment, she thought he might try to kiss her. Her stomach tumbled at the idea, and her breath caught in her chest. Against her will—at least she thought it was against her will—she felt her body start to lean toward him, as if she might welcome his kiss. Would she? How could she? She'd been so determined never to—

"Ben!"

His mom's shout from the front of the house startled them both. He took a quick step back from Ashley and hit the bathroom's doorjamb with his shoulder. When he turned, he nearly tripped over his own feet. Suave, he wasn't. But the actions broke the tension of the moment, allowing her to draw a relieved breath as she watched him walk away.

She waited what she hoped was an appropriate amount of time. Enough that his mom could say whatever it was she wanted to say without doing so in front of Ashley. Then she moved down the short hallway and looked toward the front door. Ben and his mom stood on the porch, deep in conversation. Rather than intrude, she went to the kitchen and proceeded to wash the lunch dishes. She was drying the last pot when she saw Wendy Henning walk to her car, get in, and drive away.

Ben stared at the dust cloud that lingered in the air after his mom's car turned onto the road. Emotionally spent, not to mention embarrassed by her behavior, he wondered why she had to act the way she did. Especially today when all she'd come for was to borrow money. And borrow was a loose term when it came to his mom. He would never see that hundred dollars again, even after she got her paycheck. At least he could be thankful she hadn't made any more threats about the farm.

Raking his hair with one hand, he turned and went inside. He found Ashley in the kitchen. In his absence, she'd done the dishes.

"You didn't have to do that."

She finished folding the dish towel before facing him. "It seemed the thing to do."

"My mom's gone."

"I know. I saw her leave." She glanced over her shoulder at the window.

Ben moved to the table and sat on a chair. "This wasn't the way I envisioned today."

Ashley sat opposite him.

"Mom and I don't always agree." Did she sense the size of that understatement?

"I don't always agree with my mom either."

He doubted they meant the same thing.

"You know what makes me feel better when I've had a disagreement with somebody?" Ashley's smile warmed the kitchen. "I go riding. Let's saddle up a couple of those horses and go for a ride."

The desire to kiss her returned. Lucky for him there was a table between them. Best not to ruin their friendship. "Good idea," he answered. "Let's do it."

Thursday, December 31, 1942

Without telling his parents, Ben took extra college classes in the spring and fall semesters and managed to graduate five months early. As promised when he'd joined the War Training Service, he enlisted in the US Army Air Forces as soon as he had his degree. Before Christmas he left Idaho.

Andrew supposed it was too much to hope that his son would eventually be assigned to Gowen Field in the desert near Boise, a training ground for servicemen flying in B-18 and B-26 bombers. He hoped it nonetheless.

They received their first letter from Ben on the last day of the year.

Dear Mom and Dad,

Don't write to the address on the envelope as I'll be moving to my permanent training center soon. There's a good chance it will be in Utah, although I won't know for certain until it happens.

It took a couple of days on a troop train to get to this camp. It's an interesting bunch of guys I'm with. All different ages. Some are almost as old as you, Dad, and some have got kids. I think it's going to be the hardest on the married guys, but I've noticed they are mostly nicer than the single guys closer to my age.

Mom, we eat good. Three meals a day and the food's not bad. Some complain, but not me. We've got our gear and clothes now. There's a library, bowling alley, and theater here on the post. Not bad.

I've got lots of training ahead of me before I'll be going overseas, including 12 weeks in Officer Candidate School. But what I want most is to get to train to fly bombers. Not sure how far off that is. Feels like I've waited for it forever.

Some guys here don't seem to care much about the families at home. Makes me appreciate you both and Louisa, Oscar, Frani, and Andy all the more. I miss you all. More than I thought I would. I thought it wouldn't feel much different than when I was in Boise and couldn't see you for weeks at a time. But I was wrong. It's plenty different.

Happy New Year to all of you. Hope you get this letter in time for that to mean something.

Will write more soon.

Ben

Chapter 12

Ashley finished reading her brother's letter, then let the two pieces of paper drop to the table, understanding at last what her mom had meant about Dylan's depression. Her heart broke for him at the same time that anger roiled within. Anger at the boy who had served Dylan his first beer. Anger at the dealer who had sold him his first illegal drugs. Anger at the doctor who had written that first prescription for a painkiller and all the other health providers who had continued to write opioid scripts, even when it was obvious to a blind man that Dylan knew how to play the system.

Anger at Dylan for . . . for everything.

She pushed away from the table, rose, and went outside. Speed and Jack rushed by her in search of a squirrel or some other ground creature to bedevil. Ashley ignored the dogs and headed straight for Remington's pen. She slipped between the rails, wrapped her arms around the mare's neck, and pressed her forehead against the sun-warmed coat. It felt welcoming to her. She breathed deeply, waiting for calm to replace anger. It took awhile, but eventually it worked. Being with a horse usually did.

She drew back and looked at Remington. "At least I can trust you."

People failed people. It happened all the time. People even failed the people they loved. A fact of life. Dylan might not ever get sober. He might never do the right thing. He might go on failing their mom. He might go on failing her. He might never be the boy he'd once been or the man she'd hoped he would become.

People failed people. Horses didn't. Horses never lied.

Ashley drew in a long, slow breath and released it. "Is that why I don't let myself have many friends?"

Remington blinked.

It was true. Ashley rarely let someone get emotionally close to her. At first, it had been to avoid embarrassment. During her high school years, she couldn't ask other kids over to her house because she never knew what her brother might do or say or what shape he might be in. It reminded her of that slogan about addiction and secrets. She didn't know it exactly because she'd never been truly involved in Al-Anon. She'd only attended a few meetings with her mom. Not that the meetings had done her mom much good either. But the "secrets" part she remembered, and she knew it was true. She'd kept a lot of them about her brother, about the state of their home life, about the time Dylan had blacked her eye, about the things he'd stolen—stolen from her and their mom as well as from others.

And the one time she'd let someone get closer than most, he'd—

Remington huffed. The sound seemed a confirmation to Ashley's dour thoughts, and she laughed. Better to laugh than to cry.

"I shouldn't let it get to me this way."

The mare huffed again, this time adding a bob of her head.

"And I *do* have friends."

There was Ruth for one . . . and Ben for another. Ben. It was unexpected, the way she'd let him into her life, despite lessons from her past urging her to be cautious. She'd liked him from their very first meeting. Trust had come more reluctantly, but it had come, along with an understanding that a special friendship had blossomed between them.

Why is that?

With another steadying breath, she slipped out of the enclosure.

The certified equine therapy instructor, Emily Cooper, paid her second visit to the Henning farm on Monday evening. The first visit, a few weeks earlier, had solidified her willingness to work with Ben, based on the recommendation of their mutual friend, Larry Dennis. This second visit was a more in-depth facility inspection.

Emily was in her thirties, tall and reed thin with long, straight red hair and a pale complexion. She wore a sleeveless top, skinny jeans, and boots that had seen better days. Like Ashley Showalter, Emily knew her way around horses and tack. Ben hung back and let her do her thing, staying just close enough to answer questions if any were asked. None were. When Emily finished, the two of them walked to the porch. They sat and discussed the timetable for opening the barn, first to the volunteers and then to clients.

"The website will be operational in a couple of days," Ben told her.

"Who's doing it for you?"

"I'm doing it myself, with help from a friend in my men's group."

Emily tipped her head slightly to one side, giving him a close look. "You've got lots of people helping you with the program, don't you?"

He paused to consider her comment, realizing how true it was. Too often he'd focused on the number of refusals he'd received. He needed to get better at focusing on the good news. "Yeah. I do at that."

"It says a lot about you, Ben. I can tell you this: Larry thinks highly of you."

"It's mutual. They don't come any better than Larry."

"Well . . ." She stood. "I'd better get on my way."

He got up from his chair.

She offered her hand. "I'm glad to be a part of the Harmony Barn. I think we're going to do good work together."

"I think you're right, Emily. I think you're right."

She started to walk away, then stopped. "You should think about holding a fund-raiser while the weather's still good. You're set up enough for folks to get a good idea of what you hope to accomplish with the barn."

"I have a couple of donors lined up, but I wasn't planning on holding any fund-raisers until spring. Or at least not until we have our first sessions planned."

"Sooner rather than later, I think. Even before you're holding sessions, you're going to have expenses crop up. There'll be vet bills for sure, and you already know the insurance will be high.

I don't doubt that you'll get the volunteers you need or that the right horses will come your way. But fund-raising is a part of a nonprofit like yours. You might as well get used to it now." She smiled. "If you need me, I'll be glad to help."

As Ben watched Emily Cooper drive away in her pale-blue SUV, his first thought was to call Ashley and tell her about this second meeting with the instructor and Emily's suggestion about the fund-raiser this fall. Ashley would respond with enthusiasm, as usual. She would be ready to jump in and help. She would rejoice with him over how much closer he was to starting the program than he'd been when he first called upon her, asking for help with finding horses. That had been only a month ago, but it felt as if he and Ashley had been friends for years instead of weeks.

Yesterday he'd been tempted to kiss her, which would have changed their relationship from friendship into something else. Not wise. He wasn't in the market for a romantic relationship. He'd steered clear of them since getting sober. He'd seen them derail other guys in the program. He didn't mean to be among them. Besides, all he had to do was imagine an introduction between some nice young woman and his mom to put a damper on any desire for something more serious. Any woman with a lick of sense would run away the minute she met Wendy Henning and felt the barbs of her tongue.

Although, to be fair, Ashley was a nice young woman, and she hadn't been intimidated by his mom. At the memory, a smile tugged the corners of his mouth. She had a backbone, that one, while at the same time she was kind. A nice combination.

He gave his head a shake, trying to dislodge thoughts of Ashley. Better to focus on work. There were plenty of things he needed to get done before he called it a day.

Monday, March 8, 1943

Although Andrew didn't tell Helen, he fell a little bit in love with Greer Garson in *Mrs. Miniver* when they saw the movie in the summer of 1942, so when both the actress and the movie won Academy Awards in March of 1943, he could only think the Academy voters had gotten it right.

Andrew and Helen had begun going to the movies on a somewhat regular basis. Depending upon the film, sometimes the children and Mother Greyson went too. He didn't know about the others, but movies helped to distract him from his concerns for Ben—even the movies that included references to war. Sitting in the dark interior of the theater in Kuna, he could let the stories on the big screen replace reality for a couple of hours. *Casablanca. Random Harvest. Yankee Doodle Dandy. Holiday Inn. The Pride of the Yankees. Road to Morocco.* All those and more had played at the Rialto, and the Hennings had been there to see them.

Andrew was thankful movies weren't rationed the way sugar, canned goods, and coffee were. But he tried not to complain about the things he had to do without. After all, the Hennings were far better off than people who lived in the cities. His family ate well from their own garden and livestock. They had milk from the Jersey cows and eggs from the chickens and meat from the hogs and beef calves. They had fruit and vegetables, fresh in the summer, home canned the rest of the year. Of course, some rationing was not easy to get used to. Gasoline and shoes were the two that came quickly to mind.

Ben still wrote in his letters that the Army Air Forces fed him well. Andrew wondered if his son would tell them if the food was ghastly. He thought not. One thing he didn't doubt: Ben loved the training. He loved flying, and he hoped to be sitting in the cockpit of a bomber, taking out the enemy, before much more time passed. Ben didn't care if he was sent to Africa or to the Pacific. The boy was ready to fight.

The boy . . .

Andrew supposed it was time he stopped thinking of him that way. He would turn twenty soon. He was a pilot and about to become an officer. Ben was a man and a fine one. Andrew and Helen could be proud of him.

May God keep him safe and bring him home to us.

Chapter 13

The intense heat of summer began to ease. There was the hint of fall in the early morning September air. A nice change. Ashley was ready for autumn to arrive in earnest. It was her favorite time of year. Crisp nights and mild days. Perfect for working outside. The entire world seemed to explode with brilliant colors—yellows, golds, oranges, and reds.

Five days after her lunch at Ben's ranch, she was repairing the gate to the paddock when her phone buzzed. She felt a flash of pleasure when Ben's face appeared on the screen. She hadn't realized until that moment how much she'd hoped he would call. Not that she couldn't have been the one to call him. Silly that she hadn't. Friends called friends.

"Hey, Henning," she answered.

"Hey. How are you?"

"Fine. You?"

"Good too. Listen, are you working today?"

"Just around my place. Why?"

"Nicki Day is delivering Paisley this afternoon. Wasn't supposed to be until tomorrow, but something came up and today worked better for her. I was hoping maybe you could be here when she delivers the horse. I know it's an imposition, but I value your opinion."

She smiled. "It's not an imposition. And it isn't like it's that far between our places. I drive about as far to get to the grocery store. What time do you want me there?"

"Come for lunch again."

"You don't have to feed me to get me to come over."

He laughed. The sound was nice in her ear. "I know, but come anyway. Noon. It'll just be sandwiches and chips. Nicki's supposed to be here around one."

"All right."

After finishing her most pressing chores, Ashley took a quick shower. Her hair went into a ponytail. Her only makeup was a bit of eyeshadow and mascara. It was her day off, after all. Then she dressed in a sky-blue T-shirt, jeans, and the requisite boots.

Before leaving the house, she texted Ben.

Ashley: Okay if I bring Speed and Jack?

A reply came quickly.

Ben: Sure. The more the merrier.

"Come on, guys. Road trip."

Her dogs knew those two words better than they knew *sit* or *stay*. They scrambled for the door, waiting impatiently for her to catch up. Laughing, she grabbed her truck keys and hurried to open the door for them before their tails beat holes in the wall.

Ashley arrived at Ben's at ten minutes before the hour. Dusty ran out to the truck as if he knew his new doggie pals were inside the cab, even though this was their first time to visit the farm. Ben stepped onto the porch about the same time Ashley opened her truck door. He wore jeans, a red T-shirt, and that easy grin of his that had become so familiar. The three dogs took off, chasing and tumbling over one another. Ashley laughed at the sight of them.

"Come on up," Ben called. "Lunch is ready. Hope you like cold meat loaf sandwiches."

"Homemade meat loaf?"

"Yeah. It was my dinner last night."

She approached the porch. "Chili and corn bread. Now meat loaf. What else do you cook, Henning? Anything besides ground beef?"

"Actually, yes." He grinned. "My grandmother taught me to cook all kinds of things when I lived here on the farm with her and Grandpa. What some people would call plain food, but good and filling."

She wasn't surprised the teacher hadn't been his mother. Not after meeting her. "How old were you when you lived with them?"

He didn't answer right away. For a while, she thought he might ignore the question. But then he said, "Not until I was in my midtwenties. Actually, I stayed with them quite a bit when I was a teen, but I didn't come to live here until a little over five years ago."

She'd expected a different answer, a younger age.

"I was kind of . . . lost after high school." His face clouded over, until no hint remained of his earlier grin. "No. That's not strong enough. To be honest, I was completely messed up for a long time after high school. I might never have gotten my act together if not for my grandparents. They helped turn me and my life around."

She thought of Dylan. "You were lucky to have them."

"Don't I know it." He cleared his throat. "Come inside. Lunch is waiting."

In the kitchen he took two plates with sandwiches and chips from the counter and carried them to the table. Glasses of ice water were already at their places. They each sat. She waited to pick up her sandwich, knowing he would pause long enough to close his eyes and say a silent prayer. She'd learned that about him from the other times they'd shared a meal. He didn't make her or anyone else join him, but neither did he fail to do it. She closed her eyes and said her own silent thanks. When she opened her eyes, she found him watching her.

"Eat up." He smiled.

The look made her stomach tumble. "Tell me more about your grandparents," she said, trying to ignore her reaction. Then she took her first bite and found the sandwich better than expected. Just the right amount spices in the meat loaf.

"What can I say? The best kind of people."

"When did your grandmother die?"

"A few years go. Cancer. It happened really fast. She was gone three months after she got her diagnosis." His expression was pensive. "A blessing and a curse, I think. For her to go that fast."

Ashley hadn't known any of her grandparents. Her mom's parents had perished in a car accident before she was born. Her dad's parents had come from the East Coast when she was a toddler, not long after Dylan was born, but she didn't remember the visit. They'd returned again for her dad's funeral. Nine-year-old Ashley had been too grief-stricken to remember much about them. After that, they'd sent gifts on birthdays and Christmases and called a couple of times a year. Then her grandmother got sick and died. Ashley rarely heard from her dad's dad anymore.

"You know what," Ben said, drawing her from her thoughts. "You should meet my grandpa. He and I go to church together on Sundays, then we usually go out to eat afterward. Why don't you join us this Sunday?"

This was the second time he'd invited her to church. She didn't feel pressure to accept. Ben probably asked people all the time to go with him. He was that sort of guy. Why not accept? What could it hurt? "Okay," she answered.

"Terrific. I'll swing by to get you about ten."

She nodded, hoping she wouldn't regret her hasty decision.

Nicki Day didn't linger after delivering Paisley. Only long enough to see the gelding make himself at home in one of the paddocks and to ask a few questions that she hadn't asked when Ben first met her. Then she was on her way. After waving her off, Ben returned to the paddock where Ashley stood, watching the new arrival.

"He's a beauty," she said when Ben stepped to her side.

"That's what I thought when I saw him. Still can't believe he's been gifted to the program."

"It's pretty amazing. Does everything in your life happen like this? You know. Good things falling into your lap. You must live right, Henning."

"Ha. Not hardly." Dark memories flashed through his head. "Trust me, anything good that happens to me is due to God's grace, not because I deserve it."

"I'll bet you're being hard on yourself."

"No. I'm not."

"Well, pardon me if I don't believe you. I may have known you only a short while, but all I've seen you do is think of others and how you can turn this place into a sanctuary for hurting people and horses. So I think you deserve whatever good stuff comes your way."

What if she saw Craig in his wheelchair and knew Ben was the reason for it? That would change her mind about the good she thought he deserved. Maybe he ought to tell her more details about the years he'd called "messed up." But he wasn't ready for that conversation. Not yet. Not now.

"Trust me," he said at last. "If not for the grace of God, I wouldn't be here today."

Curiosity flickered in her eyes, but she didn't press the matter.

"There's something else I'd like to talk to you about, Ashley."

"What's that?"

"Emily Cooper, the instructor I told you about. She thought I should do a fund-raiser right away, even before the barn holds its first sessions. She thinks I need to get the Harmony Barn's name out there so people are talking about it. What do you think?"

"I'm no expert, but it makes sense to me. Every nonprofit horse outfit I'm familiar with holds fund-raisers of one kind or another."

"But what could we do?" He looked at the horses grazing in the paddocks, placing his arms on the top rail. "I don't know where to begin."

She was silent for a long while before saying, "I think you ought to have an open house. You should let people see the farm and the horses and the barn." Enthusiasm began to raise her voice. "You should stake out where the arena will be, and put up a sign out near the road. You should have Emily what's-her-name be here to talk to potential volunteers. And that counselor who's going to send you clients can be here to explain the benefits of equine therapy."

"And what do you plan to do?" he asked, grinning as her excitement washed over him.

"Me?" She met his gaze.

"You're a part of it too."

"Then I guess I'll be your wrangler for the event." She returned his smile. "I'll show off the horses."

"We should have a couple of the rescue horses here so people can see what we intend to do for them too." Ben glanced toward the paddocks, then back to Ashley. "What do you think?"

"I think that would be great, Henning." Happiness made her eyes sparkle. "We'll make it happen."

Thursday, May 13, 1943

Ben came home for ten days' leave before shipping overseas. He couldn't give his family details, other than that he would spend some time in England. But soon, Andrew knew, his son would fly bombing missions in some dangerous parts of the world. If the prognosticators were correct, the campaign in Africa was winding down. The Allies had the war on that front almost won. Then the focus would rest upon the invasion of the Continent. Italy or France was Hirsch's guess. "And then on to Germany," the older man had said grimly as he, Ben, and Andrew stared at a map on a wall in the Finkels' home.

Three days after Ben's twentieth birthday, he and Andrew stood at the pasture fence, watching a newborn colt kick up its heels as it scampered around its mother.

"I miss this," Ben said. "The quiet in the evenings. The way the air smells. Watching the animals."

Andrew nodded.

"I miss home."

Andrew wanted to answer but discovered the lump in his throat made it impossible.

His son looked at him. "Thanks, Dad. I don't know if I ever said it, but thanks for taking us in and making us part of your family. Who knows what would've become of us if you hadn't found us that day."

If Andrew wasn't careful, the lump in his throat would turn to tears on his cheeks.

"I love you, Dad. You and Mom. You need to hear that, in case I never come—" Ben broke off abruptly.

It didn't matter. Andrew understood what went unsaid. "Son, I love you too. No father could be prouder than I am of you."

Ben must have felt the same emotions, for he turned away,

clearing his throat. Minutes passed before he spoke again. "Louisa's got quite a crush on that sailor, doesn't she?"

"Samuel Valentine. Yes, she fancies herself in love with him, although they've never met." He almost added that he worried what it would do to her if the boy died, then thought better of it, not wanting to mention that possibility. As if Ben hadn't been referring to the same thing a short while before.

"Maybe you'd better give me his address. I'll write to him and warn him not to hurt my sister."

"Oh, she'd love you for that."

Ben's tone was droll when he answered, "Yeah, wouldn't she?" He ended with a laugh.

Andrew smiled, thankful for a lightening of the mood. For at least a short while, he would rather not remember that young men like Samuel Valentine and Ben Henning were sailing or flying or marching into danger in places all around the world. He would rather not remember that many had died already and many more would die in the months to come.

Chapter 14

Since Ben had never seen Ashley in anything but boots and jeans, he didn't know if she wore a dress on Sunday because she wanted to or if she wore it because she thought it was expected. No matter. She looked adorable in the blue-and-white frock with its round neckline, short sleeves, and flared skirt.

He opened the passenger-side door to his truck and, with a hand beneath her elbow, helped her into the cab. She didn't need his help, of course, but he gave it anyway. She smiled her thanks to him once she was seated.

"Will we pick up your grandfather?" she asked as he pulled out of her driveway.

"No. He'll meet us there in his own car. He likes to go early so that he gets his favorite chair."

She lifted an eyebrow. "Favorite chair?"

"Mmm. We know the exact place we like to sit. Perfect view of both pulpit and screen without a post in the way. You'll see what I mean when we get there."

The look on her face suggested that her only real experience with church was what she'd seen in romantic made-for-TV movies—an old stone church with wooden pews and stained-glass windows, the setting in a small town in an unspecified state. No posts. No stage with musicians playing drums and guitars. No screens showing lyrics. No one dancing or kneeling or raising their arms in worship. All of which she would, almost certainly, experience at Ben's church that morning. He hoped it wouldn't overwhelm her. Instead, he prayed she would feel the Spirit moving throughout the large sanctuary and feel the Father drawing her into a new community.

The parking lot of the church was filling fast by the time they arrived. Ben drove to the end of a row and took the one remaining space. He got out of the cab, then reached behind the driver's seat to retrieve his Bible. Before he could round the front of the truck, Ashley had opened her door. He offered his hand to help her down from the high seat.

They fell into step together as they headed for the entrance. Families, couples, and singles walked in front and behind them. The sounds of conversations and laughter grew louder as they stepped from outside to inside. The large entry hall was filled with clusters of folks.

"Would you like coffee?" He indicated the coffee bar off to his left.

She shook her head.

"That's the bookstore." He motioned with his head to the right, then put his hand onto the small of her back, gently guiding her through the crowd of people on their way to the sanctuary. They had to stop more than once as people spoke to him and he made introductions.

Once they were in the sanctuary and the hubbub died down, she said, "Everybody seems to know you."

He shook his head, smiling. "Not everybody. But this has been my church for quite a few years. They're part of my family now. Not like my grandpa, but I'm close with quite a few. I've served in several different ministries, and you get to know people well when you're serving together."

She said nothing in response. He suspected she didn't understand what he meant. Not yet anyway.

Grandpa Grant waited exactly where Ben had known he would be. The older man's gaze went straight to Ashley as he stood. "This must be your friend, Miss Showalter." He took Ashley's right hand, enfolding it within both of his. "I'm delighted to meet you at last. You're every bit as lovely as Ben said you are."

She blushed, her gaze lowering. It made Ben want to put his arm around her shoulders and draw her close to his side.

"Come," Grandpa said. "Sit here beside me and tell me about the horses you like to rescue. My grandson is impressed with all you do. We talk on the phone or see each other several times a week, and you and your help with the horses have been part of almost every conversation in recent weeks." Grandpa looked at Ben and gave him a mischievous wink.

Stop playing matchmaker, Grandpa.

He knew his grandfather wouldn't heed the look or obey, even if he did manage to read Ben's thought. Grandpa was a romantic. He'd been blissfully happy with Ben's grandmother, Charlotte Henning. The two of them had moved through life in perfect harmony. They truly had become one throughout the course of their marriage.

Ken Snow appeared at Ben's side. Despite his usual warm welcome, it was obvious all he really wanted was to meet

Ashley—the first woman Ben had escorted to church in the years he'd been a member. Before Ben could accomplish the task, Todd Holly had joined Ken. Grandpa Grant noticed them, and it was he who performed the introductions. Ben felt like the proverbial fifth wheel all of a sudden. It made him glad to see the worship team step onto the platform. A short while later, the first notes of a song sounded, and people finished their conversations and moved to their seats.

Ben sat on Ashley's free side as the lights in the sanctuary dimmed. Only the stage was bright now. The praise team—two singers, three guitarists, one drummer, and a fiddler—began to play a favorite song of Ben's. He closed his eyes and purposefully turned his attention from Ashley to worship. It wasn't quite as easy to make the shift as he'd expected. He caught a whiff of a fruity scent. Probably her shampoo. He'd smelled it before when close to her. It made him want to lean to his right and take a deeper breath.

In the last year or two, several different married couples in the church—happily married couples were always the first to try to be matchmakers—had introduced Ben to single women. He'd felt obliged to take the women out to dinner or a movie. But nothing had clicked for him. As a recovering alcoholic, his caution about romantic relationships had been stronger than any mild attraction he might have felt. If he was ever to marry, it would have to be because he felt the way Grandpa had felt for Grandma. Nothing less would do.

He gave his head a shake, realizing how far his thoughts had drifted from worship of the Lord. He glanced to his right. Ashley wasn't singing, but neither did she look uncomfortable. He was glad for that.

Straightening, he closed his eyes again and allowed the music and lyrics to wash over him.

The service was nothing like Ashley had expected. Of course, her only experience with church had been Sunday school with friends when she was a child. But she'd imagined something staid, something old-fashioned and perhaps a little boring. That wasn't her experience that morning. The band was polished, the singers excellent, the song choices upbeat at times and moving at others. During a time of greeting, she met even more people than she had on the way in. Everyone was warm, and their welcomes felt genuine. As for the sermon, the pastor wasn't much older than Ashley herself. Perhaps five years or so. He had a great sense of humor. She'd never expected to laugh during a sermon, but she did, more than once.

Leaving church after the service took time. It seemed Ben and Grant Henning *did* know everyone, despite Ben's earlier denial. It reminded her, for the second time in a week, how few people she'd allowed into her life. She wondered if the Hennings were aware how lucky they were.

"Next time," Ben said, "we'll get help to take care of the dogs and horses. Then we can go up into the mountains for lunch. There's a place outside of Hope Springs that serves amazing food."

Next time?

"Of course, that means we'd better do it soon. Winter arrives early in the mountains. Sometimes Jessica has snow at their place by mid-October."

Next time? "Who's Jessica?"

"My cousin. She and her husband live in Hope Springs. Do you know where that is?"

"Yes. I've ridden some trails up near there."

They got into the truck and pulled out of the lot onto the street, then waited at the curb until Ben's grandfather's car appeared. Ben put the truck into gear and followed the old Buick down the main thoroughfare. Ashley was no expert on cars, but she'd guess the automobile was from the fifties, although it looked almost new with its shiny chrome and sparkling clean condition.

"Mexican food okay?" Ben asked.

"Absolutely."

"Grandpa's got a favorite restaurant in Meridian. Garcia's Cantina. It's kind of a hole-in-the-wall place in a little strip mall. Off the beaten path but really good. We go there a lot."

Ashley searched her mind, trying to think where the restaurant might be located, but drew a blank. When Ben pulled into a parking lot, she knew why. Even with directions, she might have driven right past it. The signage was close to nonexistent. How did new customers discover the place?

Grandpa Grant had found a parking space near the restaurant entrance and waited for them at the front of his car. Approaching him, Ashley realized the older man's grin was identical to his grandson's, as was the warm look in his eyes. Genuine warmth.

"The Garcias will be surprised when Ben and I walk in with you, Ashley. They pity us because we are alone." He offered his arm. "You are good for an old man's ego."

Ben held the door open before them as she and Grant entered

the restaurant side by side. The moment reminded her of those wonderful father-daughter lunches she'd had before her dad died. Those times when she'd felt like a princess.

They were quickly greeted in Spanish and taken to what Ashley guessed was their usual table. There weren't any windows near them, but they were seated across from a bright-colored mural. The painting made her feel festive and happy.

When their server—an attractive woman in her thirties, wearing white and red, her black hair caught back from her face, her dark eyes dancing—appeared, she held a rapid-fire conversation in Spanish with Grant. Despite two years of Spanish in high school, Ashley understood almost nothing the two of them said to each other.

Ben leaned close to her. "Don't feel bad. I can't keep up either. My Spanish is pathetic."

"It's on my bucket list."

"What?"

"To become fluent in Spanish."

"How? One of those audio courses?"

"No, I thought I'd do it at the community college. Maybe take the course online so I can do it at odd times."

He nodded. "Good idea. Maybe I should join you. It would be nice to be as fluent as Grandpa."

"When did he learn?"

"He was a little kid. My great-grandpa was good friends with a José Lopez during the Second World War. The two men served together for a long time, flew a lot of missions together, and I guess one of the things they did in their downtime was José teaching Great-Grandpa Ben Spanish. Years later, my great-grandpa taught my grandpa to speak it. Grandpa was only three or four when those lessons started. He's always liked being multilingual so much that he studied it in both high school and college."

Ashley loved hearing Ben talk about his family. She envied him too—the relationship he had with his grandfather.

"Grandpa tried to interest my mom in learning a second language when she was a girl, but she would have none of it. She didn't want to be anything like her parents, even when she was little. If her parents tried to get her to do something, she wanted the very opposite. She hated being a farmer's daughter. She hated living in Kuna. She hated going to church." Ben frowned. "I've never understood why she is the way she is. Not toward her parents, anyway. I guess I'll die wondering."

Ashley's gaze shifted to Grant Henning, and she felt grateful for his influence on his grandson. Ben could have turned out so very different from the person who'd become her friend.

Sunday, July 4, 1943

Early in the morning on the fourth of July, Andrew walked through the cornfields, feeling a sense of pride over the success of this new crop. Raising corn would do more than bring a tidy profit come the fall. It would help feed people and animals alike. In a time of rationing of all sorts, it felt good to do something to improve conditions. From what little Ben had been able to share in his letters home, food shortages and rationing were much worse in England than they were in America.

And where was Ben now, he wondered as he watched the rising sun pour a golden hue across the top of the cornfields. Bizerte and Tunis had fallen to the Allies in early May, and in the following week the remaining German and Italian forces in North Africa had surrendered, ending the war in that theater. Had Ben been part of that final campaign? And was he even now piloting one of the Allied planes that was bombing Europe?

Andrew's heart ached when he allowed himself to consider all of the innocent Europeans who were in harm's way thanks to the Germans and Italians. The Allies would have specific targets. The pilots were surely doing their best to avoid civilians. All the same, innocents would perish. They always did in war. He'd only been a kid during the First World War, but even a kid could take in some of the horrors reported in the news and talked about by adults.

He stopped and turned, his gaze going to the house, where sunlight had created a halo around it. He thought of the family within its walls. He thanked God for each one of them by name, ending as he always did with Ben. "Keep him safe, Lord. He is in Your hands. They are *all* in Your mighty hands."

Later that day, the Hennings and the Finkels participated in an Independence Day celebration in Kuna following the Sunday-morning church service. In many ways, it was a somber affair. Several local families had been notified of the deaths of husbands or sons in recent weeks. Even though none of those families were present in the town park that day, they remained in the minds and hearts of their friends and neighbors.

The women of Kuna had managed to set out a banquet, despite food rationing. Participants dined on fried chicken and a variety of fresh fruits and vegetables as well as several types of salads. Finally, there were cakes for dessert. Andrew suspected sugar would be in short supply in many homes after all that had gone into those cakes. But, oh, the delight of that frosting melting on his tongue . . . It surprised him how much he enjoyed it. It wasn't as if they hadn't gone without sugar often in recent years. During the worst of the Depression, sugar had been at the bottom of the list of things to buy with their hard-earned money. Yet it seemed even sweeter today. He had no idea why.

"Andrew." Helen leaned close on his right side. "Look."

He followed her gaze in time to see Oscar and a girl step behind a large tree at the opposite end of the park. They didn't reappear on the other side of the tree.

"Who's he with?" he asked.

"Rose Atwater."

"They're friends. They've been friends since they were six."

She cocked an eyebrow at him. "Is that supposed to reassure me?"

"Probably not." He rose from the wooden bench. "I'll take care of it."

Not wanting to draw attention to himself—and therefore to the sixteen-year-olds behind that tree—he didn't rush across the park. Every so often, he stopped and spoke to someone, but he didn't remain long. He seemed aware of every passing second. Away from the tables at last, the conversations behind him softened to a murmur, enough that he clearly heard the girl's giggle.

Uh-oh. His pace quickened a little.

Almost exactly as he'd imagined the scene, he found the teenagers wrapped in each other's arms, their lips pressed together and their eyes closed. Andrew cleared his throat to announce his presence.

Oscar jumped back from Rose as if burned. "Dad."

"Uh-huh."

Rose's cheeks flamed. "Mr. Henning."

"Young lady, I believe you should rejoin your family."

"Yes, sir." She scurried away.

Andrew turned his gaze back to Oscar. "I'm disappointed, son. Rose isn't ready for this, and neither are you."

"We're not kids." Sullen, Oscar looked at the ground as he kicked at a clump of grass.

"Maybe not. But you're not adults either."

"Come on, Dad." The boy looked at him. "It was just a kiss."

Andrew drew a slow breath and let it out. "Believe it or not, I remember what it was like to be your age."

Oscar's eyes said he didn't believe it.

Andrew swallowed the urge to laugh, knowing it wouldn't send the right message. "Come on. Your mom will wonder what's keeping us." He let Oscar lead the way and, with his son's back to him, allowed the smile to come to his lips. After all, he really did remember what it was like to be sixteen.

Chapter 15

The open house for the Harmony Barn happened on the last Saturday in September. It amazed Ben how quickly it came together, once the idea had been planted and shared.

Announcements were sent out to the media, and one of them resulted in an interview with the local newspaper. The article appeared the day before the open house. Still, even with the nice write-up and the colored photographs in the paper, Ben hadn't expected the turnout to be as big as it was. People came from as far away as Ontario in the west to Mountain Home in the east. Thankfully, they had enough volunteers to show off the place and sign up supporters. Ashley spent all of her time that day introducing the horses to curious visitors. Emily Cooper and Larry Dennis were on hand to answer questions about equine therapy.

A couple members of Ben's men's group had made a beautiful sign. Balloons—courtesy of Ben's grandfather—were tied to the new sign as well as to the porch railing of the house, the doors of the barn, and the still-empty chicken coop. To top it off, they were blessed with perfect weather—lots of sunshine with temperatures in the low seventies.

The crowd of visitors had dwindled to only a few stragglers by the time Ben found his grandfather sitting on the porch, a glass of water in one hand.

"A grand day," Grandpa said.

"I'd say so." Ben sank onto the chair next to him.

"Do you know how much was raised?"

"No. I thought I'd leave that to others. I didn't want money to be my focus today. I just wanted to share my vision for the Harmony Barn. Help people know the good we want to do here."

Grandpa chuckled. "Admirable motive, but I'm afraid a nonprofit like this one will require you to focus on funds more often than not."

"Yeah. I know you're right."

Ben looked toward the paddocks and watched as Ashley put feed into a hay box. He hadn't said more than a half dozen words to her today. They'd both been too busy. He would like to talk to her now, to thank her for all of her help.

"Go ahead," Grandpa said. "I'm going to sit here and enjoy the quiet."

Before Ben left the porch, a car pulled into the drive. Rather than head for the paddock, he walked in the direction of the newcomer. He hated to turn anybody away, but the event was over. Even the volunteers had started to go home.

He was halfway there when the driver, a woman, got out of the car. She closed the door and turned, and Ben's heart stuttered in his chest.

"Mrs. Foster?" He took a breath before continuing toward her.

"Hello, Ben."

He hadn't seen Craig's mother in close to a decade. Her face was more careworn. Her hair had more gray in it. But she still looked like the woman who had welcomed him into her home for so many years. Right up until he'd put her son into a wheelchair. After that, she hadn't been as welcoming.

"I saw the article in the paper," she said.

"I'm afraid you missed everything."

"That isn't why I came."

A knot formed in his stomach.

"I'm glad you're doing well, Ben."

"Thanks."

"Is this place about Craig?" To his surprise, she asked the question without rancor, and he sensed she'd made peace with the past. He wished he could claim the same.

"Mrs. Foster, it would mean the world to me if Craig could be helped by what we plan to do here. I won't lie about that."

"He won't come."

"Maybe not. But we'll be here if he changes his mind."

"He said you tried to talk to him."

"Several times. I wanted to tell him what equine therapy did for me."

"He wouldn't listen."

"No. Did he see the article?"

"I don't know. We don't talk often. He has his own place, his own work."

"Mrs. Foster, if I could undo what happened, if it could've been me instead . . ." He let the words fade into silence.

She drew in a slow breath. "Ben, I was wrong to place all the blame on you at the time of the accident, and Craig is wrong to place all the blame on you still. I should have let you know that long ago. You and Craig made a very foolish choice that night. You've both paid for it in different ways." She gave him a sad smile. "I think you've both paid enough. Don't you?" Her gaze swept over the farm. "I hope this place succeeds. And if I can, I'll try to make him change his mind."

Ben's throat was thick with emotion, but he managed to say, "Thanks."

With a nod and a quick squeeze to his arm, she got into her car and started the engine. Ben wasn't sure what he felt as he watched her drive away. He wanted her words to release him from the last of his guilt. He was sure that was what she'd wanted too. God help him. He wished it had worked.

Trent McGrath, the senior pastor of Ben's church, looked up as Ashley walked toward the barn. His grin told her all she needed to know.

"It was a success?" she asked anyway.

"An enormous one." He straightened the stack of paper on the table that had been set up on the sunny side of the barn. "Between pledges and one-time donations, the Harmony Barn is starting off with a bang."

"Does Ben know the results?"

"Not yet, but he's about to." Trent tipped his head, indicating she should look to her left.

She turned as Ben drew near. He didn't look as happy as she'd expected him to after the number of people who'd turned up at the farm today. Even without knowing the financial result, he should have been pleased.

Trent rose from the chair. He took the top two pieces of

paper from the stack and held them toward Ben. "Here's what we took in today in cash and checks. And this one has the list of pledges for the coming year."

Ben took the proffered papers. His eyes scanned them—once, then again—and his expression changed. Not to happiness but to utter shock.

Ashley couldn't help but laugh.

"This is unbelievable," he said at last. "Are you sure?"

Trent laughed too. "I'm sure. The donations came in all sizes. One of them was a bunch of quarters from a little girl's piggybank that she opened right in front of me. There's also a sizable cashier's check in the cash box. The donor wished to remain anonymous."

"I never imagined this."

"I confess I was rather surprised myself. Shouldn't be. We can't outgive God."

"Another open door," Ben said softly, his eyes once again on the papers in his hands.

Trent lifted the cash box onto the table. "It's time for me to get home. I'm turning over my fiduciary responsibility to you. Plan on a trip to the bank on Monday."

"I appreciate your help, Trent."

"Ben, it was a blessing to be a part of this. It truly was. See you tomorrow." The pastor said goodbye to Ashley, then walked to where he'd parked his car earlier in the day.

"Ashley," Ben said, drawing her attention back to him. "Do you know what this means?"

"I'd say it means you're off to a great start."

He set the papers on the table before staring off in the

direction of the alfalfa fields. She could tell he was envisioning something that wasn't there, something that she couldn't see but wished she could.

"I need a barn manager," he said, looking at her again.

"A barn manager?"

"Yes, someone to look after the horses that are here. Someone to find other horses that need to be here. It's a bigger job than I can handle, and with these donations and pledges, I can afford to hire somebody." He took a step closer. "How about it? Will you?"

"Will I—What are you talking about?"

"I need a barn manager," he repeated himself. "You need a place to house more rescue horses and the time to tend to them. You'd be helping me and doing the work you love. Will you be my barn manager?"

Her heart began to race. "Do you mean a paid position?"

He nodded. "Yes. It wouldn't be a huge salary, but I'll bet we could manage to match whatever you make now and get you some health coverage. And if you aren't sure about quitting altogether, maybe you could go part-time at the store and part-time here." He watched her face, obviously trying to gauge her reaction.

She almost couldn't breathe. From the moment she'd first visited this farm, she'd felt as if she belonged here. She'd captured the vision Ben had for the Harmony Barn from day one. Now he wanted her to be a more permanent part of it.

"Come to work for the Harmony Barn, Ashley. You won't regret it."

Passion filled his eyes. A passion for making the Harmony Barn all that he wanted it to be. A passion for helping others. A passion for doing what God had called him to do. A passion she found hard to resist.

"Come on." His eyes pleaded with her. "Say yes."

How could she refuse him when he was offering to make her own dreams come true? More room for rescues. More time to be with the horses, to work with the horses. Perhaps there were reasons—good reasons—for her to refuse, but she couldn't think of a single one. "All right," she answered softly. "I'll do it."

Relief burst across his face, followed instantly by that appealing grin of his. "Great. When can you start?"

She matched his smile with one of her own. "I'll have to give the store two weeks' notice."

He pulled out his phone and opened to the calendar app. She watched him as he typed something. "How about you start on Monday, October 14?" He looked over his shoulder toward the paddocks. "You can leave those two rescue horses here. I can tend to them until you start."

"Thanks."

"If you've got time to spare, could you stay awhile and help me map out some changes I want to get started on right away? Stuff I thought would have to wait. Chances are I can get quite a bit of volunteer labor from guys at church to help with the construction. But I think you'll know what I need to ask for more than I would."

"Sure. I've got the time."

There was that grin again, and it sent her heart racing a second time. Only for a different reason. One she wasn't yet ready to examine.

Wednesday, September 15, 1943

Helen found Andrew near the chicken coop, replacing some of the wire. "Honey, we have a letter from Ben!"

He immediately dropped his hammer and came to meet her. Letters never came often enough. The wait seemed even more interminable after a major offensive. Less than two weeks earlier, the Allies had invaded Italy. American bombers had played a part in the invasion, of course, which made it difficult for them not to wonder if Ben was all right.

Helen held out the V-Mail. "You read it. Read it aloud."

Without looking, he knew the letter had to have been written prior to the latest offensive. Hearing from Ben now wasn't any guarantee that he was fine. But Andrew kept that thought to himself. It was better to hope than to fear. He opened the letter and read it to Helen, as requested.

Dear Mom and Dad,

I hope this letter finds you both well. Tell my brothers and sisters that I'd love to get letters from each one of them. Even as much as you two write to me, it never feels like I get enough news from home.

I'm based in England for now. Can't tell you where exactly. My posting could change at any time. It all depends upon what happens next on the Continent. Even if I knew, I couldn't tell you where I'll be going. I suppose you know as much as I do a lot of the time. The generals and admirals don't ask the opinions of those of us in the ranks. They make the decisions, and we obey. Mostly that's okay by me. But sometimes it rankles a bit. You know the way I am. Sometimes I pull against the reins, like old Belle used to do when she was sick and tired of us kids riding her. Remember?

When I'm not flying, I spend a lot of time thinking about all of you and the farm. Sometimes I wish I could walk into a pasture and throw my leg over a horse and ride like crazy across a green field. No bridle. No saddle. Just letting the horse take me where it wants.

It's real pretty here where I am. Different from the farm. They get more rain in England than we get in Idaho. Lots more rain. And it doesn't get as hot as it can get at home. But like I said, it's pretty. We're not near a woods. The landing fields have to be flat and open. But they've got them here. Again, different from the forests in the mountains of Idaho. Not as rocky or arid as ours. I remember Mom telling us the stories of Robin Hood when we were younger, and sometimes I find myself waiting for a glimpse of some guy dressed in forest green, carrying a bow and quiver of arrows. Good thing I don't tell the guys that. I'd never live it down.

Listening to the other men when we're all lying around the barracks, I've learned how lucky I am to have you for my parents and for the kind of childhood you gave us. Some of these guys come from really lousy places. Dads who are drunks. Moms who don't care what the kids do. One guy eats like the food's going to disappear before he can fill his hollow leg. He never had enough to eat at home when he was a kid. He doesn't care what he finds in the mess. He's ready to eat it just for the sake of being full.

Thanks for the Bible you gave me before I left home. I'm reading it lots and finding comfort in it. Some of the guys here don't ever think about God, don't ever think about where they'll go if their plane goes down and they die. I'm not very good about sharing what I believe, but I'm trying to be better about it.

Again, without you being examples to me and teaching me, I'd be as lost and afraid as so many others.

It's about time for lights out. I'll end this letter so I can mail it tomorrow. Give my love to everybody, including Mr. and Mrs. Finkel. Tell Mr. Finkel that I hope to be leaving Hitler a calling card before the year is out.

Your son,

Ben

"He's all right," Helen said on a breath.

"He's all right." Andrew folded the letter and offered it back to her.

She took it, pressing it to her breast. "I knew it would be hard," she said in a whisper. "But I never knew it would be this hard."

Sensing she was close to tears—and feeling a lump forming in his own throat—Andrew drew her into his embrace. They stood that way, in silence, for a long, long time.

Chapter 16

After Ben's grandfather and the last of the volunteers left, Ashley followed Ben around the farm once again, seeing it all through his eyes. Not that she hadn't understood what he planned to do, but she hadn't captured his full vision for the place until today.

"If we left those acres for growing hay"—he motioned with his arm—"we'd have enough, even more than enough, to feed the horses we'll keep year round. I figure we can handle at least fifteen horses. Maybe as many as twenty. But that'll be up to you as barn manager. We'll create more paddocks over there." He motioned in a second direction. "We can have that indoor arena now instead of later. It doesn't have to be as large as the outdoor arena. We'll put it there." He pointed again.

She wondered if he realized he'd said "we" and "our"—as if she were an equal partner rather than the newly hired barn manager. An equal partner or . . . or something else.

Do I want it to be something else between us? Her pulse quickened, and her stomach tumbled. *Do I want him to mean something else?* Perhaps she did, even though she knew she shouldn't. *Should I?*

"Sorry." He tried to wipe the smile from his face but failed. "I'm a little giddy. That's what Grandma called it. Everything I wanted and imagined is falling into place. It's hard to take in."

"I feel a little giddy myself, listening to you. Maybe we should pinch each other to make sure we aren't dreaming."

They laughed in unison. Her stomach tumbled a second time, and she found it difficult to breathe. When her phone vibrated in the pocket of her jeans, she almost ignored it, wanting to keep laughing with Ben, wanting to keep smiling at each other, wanting to keep feeling breathless and giddy. But common sense returned, and she looked to see who was calling. Rather than a phone call, it was a text message.

Mom: Dylan missing from rehab. Police looking for him now.

Her gut tightened, and the happiness of the day evaporated. "Dylan, you idiot," she whispered.

"Ashley?"

She looked up. Ben's smile was gone, too, and he watched her with concerned eyes.

"What's wrong?"

"It's my brother. He . . . He's in trouble."

Ben didn't ask what kind of trouble, and Ashley appreciated it. She didn't want to explain.

"Do you need to go?"

"I'd better. My mom's worried."

"Sure. Go. We'll have lots of time to lay out the plans. But let me know you're okay." He hesitated only a moment before adding, "And Ashley, I'm here if you need me."

His words brought tears to her eyes. "Thanks." She hurried to the truck and got into the cab. Before turning the key in the ignition, she replied to her mom's text.

Ashley: On my way to your house. Be there fast as possible.

She dropped her phone into the console. When she looked up, she saw Ben standing near the front porch of the house, watching her. Their gazes met, and he lifted his hand. She felt his caring, even at a distance. Tears came again, and she blinked them away before pulling out of his barnyard.

Ben waited until the dust caused by Ashley's departure settled back onto the driveway. Only then did he turn on his heel and go into the house. He was concerned for her, of course, but at the same time he was disappointed for himself. He'd hoped to have her company for another hour or two. He'd hoped she might even stay for dinner. They both deserved time to relax after such a hectic day.

"The books," he muttered when he saw them on his kitchen table. He'd meant to share a couple of books with Ashley. Then again, she might not have any time to read if her brother was in trouble.

He frowned, wondering what that meant. What sort of trouble? Injured? Sick? Something else? Whatever it was, the news had rattled Ashley. The color had drained from her face as she'd read the message on her phone.

Ben said a silent prayer for her, as well as for her brother and their mother. He might not know the nature of the problem, but God did. When he was finished, he looked around the room. A clock ticked. The refrigerator whirred. The sounds seemed to exacerbate the emptiness he'd felt since watching Ashley drive away. The feeling was more than a little disconcerting.

He'd always felt comfortable here, first when he'd stayed with his grandparents, later when the farm had become his and he'd moved in on his own. He'd never minded being alone.

All the same, he minded it now. He wished he'd offered to accompany Ashley to her mom's house. Maybe he could have been some kind of help to them. Emotional support if nothing else. He took his phone from his pocket, almost put it away again, then opened the app and typed in a text.

Ben: If I can help, let me know. Praying for you.

He hit Send and let the message *whoosh* away before he could think better of it.

The silence surrounded him a second time, and now he decided to escape it. He grabbed the keys to his pickup from the side table and headed out of the house. He called for Dusty to join him. Soon enough the pair were on their way to town.

When Ashley arrived at her mom's, she looked at her phone before getting out of the pickup. She read Ben's text, and his few words were enough to strengthen her for whatever awaited inside the house.

Ashley: Thanks. I will.

She got out of her truck and hurried to the front door, opening it without ringing the bell or knocking. "Mom?"

"In here."

She followed the voice to the kitchen. "What happened?"

"He left in the night." Her mom's eyes were red from crying. She blew her nose before adding, "They aren't sure how he got out without being seen. It's supposed to be a secure facility."

It didn't surprise Ashley that her brother had found a way out. He was as slippery as an eel.

"The police have a warrant out for him already. If they catch him, he's going to prison."

"I know, Mom."

"I don't think I can bear it if that happens."

"You'll have to bear it. So will he. He knew what the consequences would be if he didn't stay in the program. He's made his choice."

"Ashley . . ."

"I'm sorry, Mom, but it's true."

Her mom began to sob, hiding her face in her hands. Ashley felt both heartbroken and heartless. Heartbroken for her mom. Heartless about her brother.

"I don't want him to have to go to prison," her mom said after a long while. "He isn't a murderer or some desperate criminal. What he does wrong, he does to himself. When you're a mother, you'll understand how I feel. It isn't easy to wish for your child to hit bottom, whatever that means."

"I don't know that I'll ever be a mother."

Her mom wiped her eyes with another tissue. "Of course you'll be a mother. Someday."

Ashley was glad her mom's thoughts had turned away from Dylan, but she wasn't happy that the attention had turned to her.

"You just haven't found the right man yet."

Ben's face flashed in her mind. She shook her head to chase it away.

"You can't live your life expecting everyone to fail you, Ashley."

She hated to admit it, but her mom was right. That had been her attitude and expectation. Until recently. *Until I met Ben.*

Her mom sighed. "Don't let what happened with Paul throw you off men altogether."

"Paul?" Paul hadn't thrown her off men. He'd only confirmed what she'd already known.

"You haven't had a boyfriend since you ended that relationship."

"He wasn't a stand-up kind of guy. I knew it in my gut, but I ignored the warning signs."

Her mom sighed a second time as she lowered her eyes to her hands, now folded in her lap.

Ashley felt like sighing along with her. Because her mom's words had reminded her that it was better if she didn't let others get too close. Her words had reminded Ashley that she was a poor judge of character, that she couldn't spot the obvious to save her soul.

Ben's face returned to her mind once again, and she wondered if she would regret letting him into her life.

Monday, October 25, 1943

"Hey, Dad."

Andrew turned at the sound of Oscar's voice. As his older brother had done at the same age, the boy had shot up a good four inches since turning sixteen in the spring. His blond hair was paler than Ben's, his eyes even bluer. But the two boys still looked a lot alike, enough that it made Andrew's breath catch sometimes when he looked at Oscar—a reminder of the danger Ben was in.

Andrew set the pitchfork aside. "What is it, son?"

"Would you let me take the car to drive over to Rose's? The Atwaters got word that Charlie was killed in action."

A heavy band tightened around Andrew's chest. Charlie Atwater, Rose's older brother, was the same age as Ben. They'd gone through school together. "Does your mother know?"

"Yes, sir. She took the call."

"Let me wash up. I'll drive you over. I'll want to offer any help I can to Peter and Bertha."

Oscar nodded, although his eyes said he was disappointed he couldn't take the car on his own.

Andrew strode to the house, the late afternoon sun warm on his back. Despite it, he felt a chill in his heart. Inside, he found Helen seated at the kitchen table, crying. He knew her thoughts had gone in the same direction as his own—to Ben and the missions he flew over enemy territory. If Charlie Atwater could die despite so many prayers lifted on his behalf, then so could Ben. Not that they hadn't each known it already, but this news made it all the more real.

"I'm going with Oscar," Andrew said as he placed his hand on his wife's shoulder. "Do you want to come along?"

She sniffed before answering, "Not today. All I could do is cry and upset them more. I'll go tomorrow when I'm a little more in control of my emotions." She looked up at him. "Is that terribly selfish of me?"

"No." He kissed her forehead. "It's all right. They'll need lots of support for a good spell to come. Go when you're ready."

"Oh, Andrew. What if—"

"Don't, Helen. Don't do that to yourself. We can't live in the what-ifs. We have to live in the present." *And please, God, let me follow my own advice.*

After another kiss placed on his wife's forehead, he went down the hall to the bathroom. He washed up in the sink, put on a clean shirt, and then he and Oscar were off.

His son was quiet during most of the drive, but when the Atwater house came into view, Oscar said, "I wish I could be part of the fighting. I'd like to shoot the guy who killed Charlie. I want to make those dirty Nazis suffer."

"Son, I understand what you're feeling. But if we live with hate in our hearts, we are the ones who suffer, not the people we hate."

Oscar grunted, his gaze turned out the window.

Andrew pulled into the barnyard of the Atwater farm and cut the engine. They weren't the first to arrive. Several other cars were parked nearby.

"Dad?"

"Hmm."

"If it's not right to hate, how can it be right to go to war? If Christians are supposed to love everybody, then how can we fire weapons and drop bombs and all that? I mean, people are gonna die."

Andrew didn't answer quickly. In truth, he'd pondered similar questions himself since the bombing of Pearl Harbor. "Oscar," he said at long last, "followers of Christ have had to wrestle with such questions for almost two thousand years. Many, like the Quakers, are pacifists, and I do not think they're wrong in their position. Nor do I think those who fight are wrong, assuming the fight is just. In the end, I believe each one of us has to listen to the Holy Spirit and to our own conscience."

"You, then. Would *you* go if you were called? With a clear conscience?"

He paused only a moment this time before answering, "Yes, I would go, and with a clear conscience. Because if those of us who are able don't stand up to evil, if we don't resist tyranny, then many, many more people will needlessly die. Germany and Japan were the aggressors. Now we have to respond and protect."

Oscar's gaze went to the Atwater house, and he gave a grim nod. "Thanks, Dad." Then he opened the door and got out.

Heart heavy, Andrew did the same.

Chapter 17

As usual, Ben and his grandpa went to lunch after church. This time at a popular pancake house. After ordering, Ben took his phone from his pocket and laid it on the table next to his knife and spoon. The screen remained empty of any message notification.

"Why don't you call her?" Grandpa asked.

He met the older man's gaze. "Do you think I should? I don't want to intrude."

"You care about her, Ben. Showing your concern isn't the same as intruding. Or at least it needn't be." Grandpa gave him a searching look. "My boy, I wonder if you realize that you've changed since you met her. You're . . . happier."

"Happier?"

His grandfather took a sip from his water glass, looking as if he was gathering his thoughts before continuing. "Son, you were lost in your troubles for a lot of years. Then, after you got sober, you needed to work your program. You needed to be well grounded in both your sobriety and your faith. And you did that. Since then, you've given of yourself generously in many circumstances to many people. You've sponsored other men in recovery. You've helped in various ministries at the church. And now you're pouring yourself seven days a week into this equine therapy barn and all it entails."

He nodded, not sure where his grandfather was going.

"But you're like a doctor who's on call 24/7. Ben, you *are* allowed to have a life of your own. You are permitted to be happy."

"I *am* happy."

"You can't fall in love if you don't open your heart to the possibility."

"Love?" He drew back in his chair. "Whoa! Are we talking about Ashley again? She's a *friend*, Grandpa."

As if to question his own words, he remembered the moment he'd almost kissed her. He remembered the way he eagerly anticipated the next time he would talk to her, the next time he would see her.

"Friendship is a good place to begin. She's a nice girl, and I can see that the two of you have a lot in common. You enjoy her company. You're at ease with her in a way I haven't seen you with other single women. I just don't want you believing you don't deserve more, that you don't deserve love and a family. God's plans are often more than we expect. We simply have to be open to them."

Ben wondered if his grandfather was right about him. Had he closed himself off from something God might want for him? Then again, wasn't the Christian life one of sacrifice and service to others? Weren't they told to put others first, before self?

"Remember," Grandpa continued, "we can become so busy

doing good things for God that we miss the best things He intends for us."

When Ben returned to the farm an hour and a half later, he took a walk with Dusty, much as he'd done the day before with Ashley. He tried to envision all of the changes he had in mind, but he couldn't quite see them without her at his side. Finally, he quit trying. He pulled out his phone.

Ben: How are you? How's your brother? Is there anything I can do? You remain in my thoughts and prayers.

He waited as the text was sent and saw the notification that it had been delivered. He hoped for an immediate response. It didn't come. After a long while, he slipped the phone back into his pocket and strode to the barn. Maybe some physical labor would take his mind off of Ashley until she responded. He would begin by finishing that last stall in the barn. After that, he would mow the area to the west of the barn and chicken coop where he'd already staked out the site of the new indoor and outdoor arenas.

Ashley stared at the message on her phone.

Ben: How are you? How's your brother? Is there anything I can do? You remain in my thoughts and prayers.

Tears blurred her vision. She wanted to answer Ben, but what could she say? She wasn't ready for him to know about Dylan. Especially since she didn't know if her brother would be found.

Perhaps he'd escaped north and found a way to cross the border into Canada. Perhaps he'd had the help of one of his friends, and now they were hidden in some cabin in a dense forest, far from authorities. And what if, despite everything, he'd found lasting sobriety? Would she want him sent to prison in the midst of that success?

After blinking away the tears, she checked the time. "Mom, I've got to go home. I need to take care of the dogs and horses." She stood. "If you want me to come back afterward, I can."

Her mom's eyes were red rimmed and bleak. "No. You don't have to come back. I'm all right."

"Are you sure?" She stepped over to her mom and kissed the crown of her head.

"I'm sure."

"Then I'll call you later. And of course you know to call me if anything comes up."

Her mom sighed. "I will."

"Try not to worry too much."

Ashley knew it was useless advice. No matter what she said, her mom would worry about Dylan. She'd been worrying about him for years. It was an old, ingrained habit by this time. A well-deserved one.

Taking a deep breath, she left her mom's house. She'd driven a few miles before she realized her eyes were squinted against a throbbing headache. If she had her way, when she got home she'd go straight inside, curl up on her bed, pull a blanket over her head, and stay there until the world righted itself again. But she had responsibilities, and she'd never been one to shirk them.

She finished the chores with her usual efficiency, but at the end, she lingered inside Remington's enclosure. Pressing her forehead against the mare's neck, she breathed in the familiar horsey scent. It soothed her fractured nerves, helped her feel that not everything had gone wrong.

Ben drifted into her thoughts. She envied the serenity that seemed to surround him, like the air he breathed. She envied his quiet strength. Even when he was uncertain about details, he didn't fear the future. So different from her. She wished—

"Ash."

The whispered word almost didn't penetrate her thoughts.

"Ash."

She stepped back from the horse and turned. At first she saw no one, but then she found him, in the shade of the elm tree. "Dylan?"

"Will you let me go inside?"

She shouldn't. She knew she shouldn't. "Are you alone?"

"I'm alone."

"All right. I'm coming." She gave Remington one last pat on the neck, then left the enclosure and strode quickly toward the back door.

Dylan entered the house right on her heels. "Thanks. I was afraid somebody would see me."

"You should be afraid. The police have a warrant out for your arrest. What were you thinking, Dylan?"

Defiance flashed across her brother's face. "I was thinking I wanted out of that hellhole. I had enough."

He was high. She saw it in his eyes, heard it in his voice. A day after running off, he'd managed to get drugs or alcohol or both.

Stiffly, she said, "You can't stay here. They'll be expecting you to come to either Mom or me. They'll be watching. You've got to go."

"I didn't ask to stay. Don't want to. Don't need you looking down your nose at me. But I need some money. Just enough to help me get as far away from Idaho as I can go. They're not going to search far. It's not like I'm a real criminal."

Not a real criminal. Stealing from a doctor's office didn't count in his book. She drew a long, slow breath. "I don't have any money to give you, Dylan."

He swore beneath his breath.

"I really don't have it. I don't keep cash on hand. You know that." He also knew *why* she didn't keep cash on hand. He was the reason. She'd learned that no matter where she hid it, he would find it.

"You can feed those nags out there, but you can't help out your own brother?"

She knew this dance of manipulation and guilt. She'd performed it with Dylan for a lot of years. "I'm sorry. I can't help."

"You mean you won't."

"I *can't*. As in, I'm unable to do it."

For an instant, the rage in her brother's eyes made her wonder if he might strike her. Instead, he took a step back. "If you won't do it, will you ask Mom to help me?"

"Dylan, Mom's tapped out. Do you have any idea how much money she poured into lawyer fees for you? Money she couldn't afford and didn't have."

"Let me ask, then." He held out his hand. "Let me use your phone."

She tried to decide the best thing to do. She wanted to protect her mom. But wasn't that another form of control? She couldn't be her mom's protector any more than she should try to protect and control her brother. "All right." She gave him the phone.

He dialed quickly, waited, then said, "Mom . . . Yeah, it's me . . . No, I'm okay. But I need to borrow some money . . ."

Borrow. Hearing the word made Ashley want to scoff. As if Dylan ever paid anybody back who gave him money.

"Meet me across from McDonald's. The one near your office." He looked at Ashley, as if about to ask a question. He must have figured out what her answer would be. "It'll take me awhile to get there. I've gotta call a friend for a lift."

Should she be ashamed of herself for making her brother find another ride? Was she refusing to help him for his own best interests, or was she being selfish, as he'd implied? It was so hard to know.

Friday, December 31, 1943

Andrew finished his prayers, then opened his eyes and wrote the date in the margin of his Bible. Afterward, he closed the cover before leaning back in the kitchen chair. A sharp wind buffeted the house. Stinging flakes of snow tapped against the window glass in a *rat-a-tat-tat* rhythm.

He tried to remember how many New Year's Eves he'd sat in this kitchen, the last in the household to go to bed. How many times had he been the only family member to see in the new year? Half a dozen, at least. The Hennings weren't much for late-night parties, not even this time of year.

Understatement, he thought with a chuckle.

Tonight, after Helen retired, Andrew had pulled out his Bible and read for more than an hour. He'd returned once again to the book of Joshua, this time in chapter 6, where he'd written the date moments before. After reading about the conquest of Jericho, he'd closed his eyes and envisioned himself marching around Berlin. He'd asked God to give the Allies that city the way He'd given Jericho to the Israelites. He'd asked the Lord to bring the war to an end in the new year. He'd begged Him to keep Ben safe, to give His angels charge over his oldest son.

Now he rose and added fuel to the fire in the wood-burning stove, trying to chase the chill from the room. He thought about going to bed but felt a restlessness that he knew would keep him awake. So he sat down at the table a second time, this time with a pen and paper.

Dear Ben,

It is nearly midnight as I begin this letter. Very soon it will be 1944. I think back to the morning of December 7, 1941. How innocent we were as we returned home from church. That was barely two years ago, but it feels like decades. Your mother and I long for our family to be together again. All of us in one place. Everyone felt your empty place at the dinner table this Christmas, although each tried to hide it in their own way.

Oscar has been struggling with his school studies ever since the death of Charlie Atwater. There is an anger inside of him that worries me and your mother. I understand his wish to join the fight, but the hatred in his heart is pushing out all that is good. He is ready to fight with anyone who disagrees with him, even his closest friends. I think even Rose is beginning to be afraid when she is with him, because his temper seems so volatile.

Grandfather Henning is feeling better at last, although he isn't back to full strength as yet. Not surprising that recovery takes longer at his age (68 on his next birthday). He suggested that Oscar go to stay with him and your grandmother when spring planting begins. Oscar can help with their farm over the summer, and perhaps your grandfather can help your brother find a way to let go of his anger. Something I have failed at.

Louisa continues to write to Samuel Valentine, her sailor friend. She fancies herself very much in love with a young man she has never met. As you know, she is nearly eighteen, and she says that if Samuel gets leave, she is going to find a way to join him in San Francisco or Honolulu or wherever the navy sends him for rest. I don't know how she would afford the fare to get to him, but there will be no way to stop her if she does come up with the money. Your sister is nothing if not determined.

At least I can say that Frani and Andy are causing us no grief. They are in good health, and neither gets into mischief beyond what is normal for children their ages. With Andy about to turn eight, your mother is beginning to feel the day approaching when all of her chicks have flown the nest. That's still a good ten years away at the earliest, but she feels it keenly anyway.

Rationing has been the topic most talked about when people get together here in Kuna. This year it was canned goods, meat, fat, cheese, and shoes. We all wonder what will be rationed in 1944. We are better off than many, so I remind everyone to be grateful rather than complaining.

Salvage drives, the newspaper reports, have collected over 255,000 tons of tin cans, six million tons of wastepaper, and twenty-six million tons of scrap metal. I always hope that what we have salvaged here at home will make a difference for my boy and the men who serve with him.

I am sure I told you that Jewel will foal in late March. Remember when Jewel was born, when you and I waited up through the night with Belle? I suppose it will be Frani or Andy who wait with me this time. Frani, most likely. Her love of horses hasn't dimmed one bit.

Speaking of waiting up through the night, the clock in the living room just announced that the new year has arrived. I will end this letter with wishes for a safe 1944 for you, dear Ben. We are all very proud of you. God bless.

Your father,
Andrew Henning

Chapter 18

It didn't matter how much nail driving or mowing he did. Ben's thoughts returned to Ashley throughout that Sunday afternoon. They were still on her when, after a shower, he settled at the table with Andrew Henning's Bible. Without any particular verse in mind, not even one from that morning's sermon, he flipped from book to book, reading a verse here and a verse there. He had no idea how much time passed before he found himself in the book of Joshua. There, toward the end of that book, he discovered a slip of paper, pushed deep into the gutter. He removed and unfolded it. Bold handwriting filled the page. Handwriting that he recognized from other places in this Bible. The note belonged to Andrew Henning.

> Is my loyalty being tested by setbacks and delays? I am weary, for there is no end in sight. Joshua tells me to hold fast to God. Finish well. The Lord is present. He rewards faithful obedience. See what He did for the people of Israel. He will do the same for the Henning family. A. M. H. February 1945.

He read the words once, then a second time, savoring them. He wondered if Jessica had read this note. Had her grandmother Frani read it before her? Or was Ben the first to see it since the day Andrew had penned the words?

Wait until he showed it to Grandpa Grant.

He turned his attention back to the Bible, intent on finding the passage or passages that had caused his great-great-grandfather to write that note to himself. But the notification sound on his phone interrupted him.

Ashley: I could use a friend. May I come over?

Ben: Yes. Come anytime.

He waited for a response. None came. He could only assume she was already on her way. He refolded Andrew's note and returned it to the gutter of the Bible, tucking it firmly between the pages so it wouldn't be inadvertently lost. Then he said a quick prayer for Ashley, asking that he might be the kind of friend she needed, whatever the reason. Afterward, he went out onto the porch to await her arrival.

It wasn't long before Ashley's truck pulled into his driveway. A moment later she hopped to the ground. As soon as she looked in his direction, he knew she'd been crying. He seemed to feel her pain, and a need to protect her surged in his chest.

"I'm sorry for bothering you," she said as she walked toward him. "I didn't know who else to talk to."

"You're not bothering me, Ashley." He resisted the urge to go to her and gather her in his arms.

"It's about my brother."

"What happened?"

She climbed the few steps to the porch. "It's a long story." Defeat was written on her face.

"I'm a good listener." He motioned toward chairs on the porch. "Let's sit down, and you can tell me about it."

Ashley sank onto the nearest one, her gaze lowered to the porch floor in front of her. Ben waited a few moments before crossing to the chair beside her. Silently, he studied her expression, his heart hurting on her behalf without knowing the reason why.

When she spoke at last, her voice was low. "Dylan started acting out while he was still just a kid. He was six when our dad died, and it was like he lost his compass after that. He couldn't navigate anymore. Mom did her best, but she was never good at discipline and enforcing rules. As Dylan got older, he kept pushing boundaries."

Ben made a soft sound in his throat to let her know he listened.

"I'm not sure when he first started drinking. Maybe when he was twelve. Maybe a little younger. All I know for sure is he was addicted young. He was drunk more often than he was sober in junior high."

Ben's pulse skittered with alarm. He hadn't guessed this was her brother's problem. Should he have suspected because of something she'd said in the past? Had there been a sign that he'd missed?

"Eventually drugs entered the picture too. Prescription drugs that he stole wherever he could, mostly from the parents of friends. Any medicine drawer or cabinet that wasn't carefully watched was fair game to him. Later he faked injuries to get opioids." She drew a slow, deep breath and released it. "He's good at playing the system. Mom always believed him, no matter what."

Ben swallowed any comment he might have made. Especially the one about most addicts being master manipulators. He should know. He'd lived it. He'd been one.

"My brother can be mean when he's using. He got in fights a lot." She rubbed her jaw.

Ben suspected she was remembering a time when Dylan hit her. Anger stirred in his chest. Anger and sorrow. And trepidation over what this might mean for him. For them.

"He started getting in trouble with the law while he was still a juvenile. It got more serious when he became an adult. This last time—" Her voice broke, and she was silent for a while.

Waiting grew harder for Ben. He longed to offer words of advice or comfort or both.

"This last time, he did something that could have put him in prison, but the judge decided to give him one last chance. He ordered him into rehab. A six-month program with a long probation to follow. He wasn't happy, but Mom and I hoped it would work this time."

She sighed. "He left the center the other night. We're not sure how he got out. It's supposed to be secure, although it isn't like a jail. But when they catch him, he'll go to prison. That's guaranteed." She looked at him at last. "He came to my house earlier today. He came to ask for money, although he must have had some because he wasn't sober. I refused to give him anything. So he called Mom. She probably gave him what he wanted." Her voice dropped to a whisper. "She always does."

"I'm sorry, Ashley." It was cold comfort.

"I don't know what to do now. If I tell the police, wouldn't Mom be in trouble for helping him?"

"I'm not a lawyer, but probably not. Not more than a scolding anyway." Ben looked away from Ashley, his gaze sweeping over the barnyard and farmland. He prayed for wisdom. What should he tell her? He understood so much more than she realized. From both sides. "He's got to want to get clean."

"I know."

He drew a long breath, hoping she would understand how much he cared, how much he wanted to help, even while he gave what he thought was the best advice. "Have you tried going to Al-Anon or Celebrate Recovery? They're twelve-step programs for family members of alcoholics. A group like that might help you deal with everything. But you've got to want the help, just like he does."

"I'm not the one who needs help." Irritation had entered her voice. "And I don't have to *deal* with Dylan. Either he disappears because he's escaped, or he gets caught and goes to prison. Regardless, he's gone."

"And you don't think either of those options is something you'll have to deal with?"

Ashley sucked in a breath as she straightened in the chair. Her eyes told him he'd hit a sore spot. He was sorry, but he wouldn't have taken the question back, even if he could. It was a truth she needed to face.

"Look, Ashley. Nobody can tell you exactly what to do. You've got to figure that out on your own. I sure don't have answers. But I know something about what your brother—"

She stood. "I shouldn't have involved you in this. I'd better go."

Ben rose to his feet, wishing he could take her in his arms and simply hold her. But he was certain that would be no more welcome than his advice. She wasn't ready for anything he might have to offer, including his own experiences. He would have to wait until she was.

Ashley fought tears all the way home. She'd expected to feel better after seeing Ben. She didn't. She blamed his suggestion that she attend some of those stupid meetings. She wasn't the one with a problem, and she certainly wasn't an enabler like her mom. Ashley had never lied for her brother or cleaned up after him or bailed him out of trouble.

As if responding to that thought, her mom's ringtone sounded on her phone. Without a word of greeting, she answered, "Did you give him money?"

"No." Her mom's voice caught on a sob. The sound hit Ashley like a truckload of guilt.

She pulled off to the side of the road. "What happened?"

"He had his friend wait for him in the alley. When I didn't have any cash to give him, he . . . he left." The hesitation in her mom's voice told her there'd been an altercation. A bad one.

"Do you need me to come over?"

"No. I'm going to lie down. I'm just . . . tired. I'm so very, very tired."

"Mom . . ."

"It's okay, honey."

Another wave of regret swept over her for the way she'd answered the call. "There must have been a reason you called me besides to say you're going to lie down."

"I . . . I wanted to hear your voice."

"Oh, Mom. I'm sorry. I'm so sorry."

"It's all right. Really."

"Let me know if . . . if you hear anything." She didn't bother to explain what she meant. She didn't need to.

"I will."

After ending the call, Ashley sat in silence for a long while. An occasional vehicle drove past her, but for the most part the road was untraveled. In the field to the right, stalks had begun to dry following the last harvest of sweet corn. She supposed within a few weeks the stalks would disappear beneath the wheels of a combine, and then the ground would be turned under by a plow, readied for planting in the spring. A cycle of life. A farmer could count on it. Plant seeds. Add sunshine and water and time. Harvest. Till. Wait out the winter. Plant seeds again. Trustworthy and sure.

Unlike people.

She drew a deep breath, looked in the side mirror, and pulled back onto the road. It wasn't long before her thoughts returned to Ben. Had it been rude to leave like that? With hardly a word of goodbye? Of course it had. He'd listened to her. When she'd looked at him, she hadn't seen judgment or censure of any kind. He'd behaved like a friend. A good friend. Exactly what she'd wanted him to be. And while his suggestion about twelve-step groups upset her, it wasn't advice she hadn't heard before. In fact, she shouldn't have let it bother her. She supposed he was even right about her having to deal with whatever happened to Dylan.

That realization darkened her mood a second time.

Thursday, February 24, 1944

"Mother! Dad!" Louisa's voice rang through the house.

Helen left the kitchen, drying her hands with a towel, at the same moment Andrew came down the last step from the attic bedroom.

"Samuel's been wounded. They're sending him back to the States. To San Francisco."

Andrew met his wife's concerned gaze.

"I've got to go to him." Louisa looked from Andrew to her mother. "You've got to let me go."

"Louisa . . . ," Helen said softly.

"Please." Louisa's gaze shot back to Andrew. "When he's better, he says he'll be sent back to his ship."

"You've got school."

"I could miss a few days. A week or so wouldn't matter. My grades are good. I could catch up whatever I miss."

Andrew rubbed his jaw. "You couldn't travel alone, Louisa. You're too young."

"Then one of you could go with me. Or Grandma Greyson or Grandma or Grandpa Henning." Louisa's voice rose with each name.

"Darling," Helen began, "you've never even met—"

"I'll die if you don't let me go. I'll just die if I can't be with him when he needs me."

Andrew was tempted to say she was being overdramatic. Wisely, he bit back the words.

Louisa waved the paper in the air. "He could *die* the next time. If Ben had a sweetheart, wouldn't you want him to see her if he was wounded? Especially if you couldn't go to him."

His daughter's question hit its mark. Ben glanced at Helen again and saw the glimmer of tears in her eyes. After drawing a deep breath, he asked, "Do you know the date the ship is to arrive?"

"No. Not for sure." She looked at the V-Mail. "Maybe it's there already. Can we find out? How do we find out? I don't even know how badly he's injured. It must be bad if they're shipping him back to the States. They don't do that for anything minor, do they?"

"There might be a different reason."

"I've got to know how he is, Dad. I've got to." She seemed close to hysterics.

"Louisa." He spoke softly, steadily. "I think you should go to your room and lie down. Be calm. Pray. Your mother and I must talk about this alone. I can't say now if you'll be able to see this young man in San Francisco or not. But I will promise to do whatever I can to learn where he is and the state of his health. That will have to be enough for now."

"But, Dad—"

"That will have to be enough for now."

Crestfallen, she nodded. A tiny sob escaped her throat as she moved past Andrew and disappeared into her bedroom, closing the door behind her.

"We never should have let her correspond with that boy." Helen turned and went back into the kitchen.

Andrew followed her. "Could we have stopped her?"

"We could have tried." She gripped the edge of the sink and stared out the window above it.

"He is a young man serving his country. He needed to hear from someone at home."

"Oh, Andrew. What are we going to do?"

"Let's find out the young man's condition first. He may not even be allowed visitors."

She faced him. "He was able to write to her."

"He might have dictated the letter to a nurse or to a friend."

Helen was silent a long while before saying, “It’s been so long since we had a letter from Ben.”

“If anything was wrong, we’d have heard.” He’d meant the words to comfort them both. It didn’t work for him. He doubted it worked for her either.

Chapter 19

Two days after her abrupt departure, Ashley had called Ben to apologize for it. But she hadn't seen him in person since then and blamed that for the nervous tumble in her stomach as she drove toward the Henning farm on Saturday afternoon, towing the horse trailer behind her truck. Ben being Ben, he welcomed her with his usual easy smile, not even a hint of condemnation in his eyes. Nor pity either, she realized, and the tension in her stomach eased.

"I've got the paddock ready for your latest rescues," he said as the two of them walked to the back of the trailer. "And the new stables should be finished before bad weather hits."

"I can't believe how much you've accomplished since the open house."

"Motivation lit a fire under me."

She returned his smile, thankful that he hadn't brought up her brother or asked how she and her mother were doing. She sensed he would take her lead in that regard, and she was content to leave it be for now.

She lifted the latch and opened the trailer door. "The store scheduled me every day next week. It kind of surprised me. I've known other people who were pretty much ignored after they gave notice, but that's not true for me."

"Proves they value you."

"I suppose." She led the first horse out of the trailer.

Ben followed with the second. "Only these two? I thought you'd bring the other one as well. The one you got the day we first met. Scooter?"

"I left Scooter at home. I didn't want to rob Remington of all her company."

"Softie."

"I know." She felt her mood lighten with each passing moment. Was it Ben or his farm that worked that particular magic upon her?

He stepped back and took a good look at the gelding at the end of the lead. "These guys are nothing like those two." He glanced toward the paddock holding the rescues that had been so severely malnourished.

"I know." Ashley stroked the gelding's neck. "They were unwanted and planned for slaughter, but at least they weren't abused."

"Have you named them?"

"Not yet."

Ben and Ashley turned at the same time and fell into step, leading the horses to the designated pasture. Once the gate was open, they removed halters and leads and set the animals free. The first one, a bay with a large blaze on his face, felt good enough to crow-hop, toss his head, and kick up his heels before running along the fence line for about ten yards or so.

Watching the horse, Ashley laughed, the last of her worries chased away by the sight.

"Come with me to the barn." Ben motioned with his head in that direction. "I've got something to show you."

"Okay."

For the second time within minutes, she fell into step beside him. Neither spoke, but it wasn't an uncomfortable silence. In fact, when Ashley glanced in his direction, she saw that he wore a smile, as if he knew a secret. What was he up to?

She didn't have long to wait for the answer to her silent question. Ben stopped a couple of steps inside the barn and waved with his arm to the right. "What do you think?"

Her gaze followed his motion to the tack room. Only the open door revealed that it was no longer the tack room. The once open studs had been hidden behind finished, painted walls. Curtains framed the small window that let in natural light. A desk, chair, and two file cabinets filled a good portion of the space, yet it wasn't too crowded.

"What's this?" she asked, moving to the doorway.

"The barn manager's office, of course."

"The barn manager's—" She faced him. "You mean, *my* office?"

"In another nine days, yes. By then I should have the baseboard heat installed so you won't freeze this winter and a ceiling fan so you won't cook in the summer." His grin returned as he repeated, "So, what do you think?"

I think you're the nicest man I ever met. Her heart skipped a beat as she looked into his amazing blue eyes.

His expression changed suddenly. Turned serious.

Unsettled by it, she faced the office again. "It's wonderful. Really wonderful. I didn't expect anything like it."

"Did you think I'd make you work outside eight hours a day? In the cold and rain or whatever?" He chuckled. "I realize you love the horses and are willing to do whatever they need, but I'm not heartless."

"I know you're not, Ben," she said softly.

His heart quickened. She usually called him by his last name. He liked that she'd called him Ben this time, and it caused Grandpa Grant's words of advice to whisper in his memory: *"She's a nice girl . . . The two of you have a lot in common . . . You enjoy her company . . . You're at ease with her."*

It was true. It was all true. She was nice. They had lots in common. He always enjoyed being with her.

"I don't want you believing you don't deserve more, that you don't deserve love and a family."

What did Ben think he deserved? Had he closed himself off from love at the same time he was guarding his sobriety and strengthening his faith?

"Remember, we can become so busy doing good things for God that we miss the best things He intends for us."

It hit him in a flash. He would like something more than friendship with Ashley. Or at least a shot at it. But would she want the same? He'd shared parts of his past with her, but he'd never given her the full picture. He'd never told her about the accident, about Craig. He'd never told her that his experience with equine therapy had been part of a recovery program. He'd never told her about the years he'd been lost in an alcohol haze far more often than he'd been sober. How would she feel about him once she knew? Especially given her experiences with her brother.

I don't want to lose her friendship. Did that make him a coward? Maybe. For now, he would have to take it one day at a time.

"How about something cool to drink?" he suggested.

Her shoulders rose and fell on a breath before she turned toward him. A tentative smile curved her mouth. "Sounds good. Thanks."

As the two of them left the barn and walked toward the house, questions whirled in Ben's head. Questions about how Ashley was feeling, *really* feeling, about her brother. Questions about how her mother was dealing with her son's legal predicament. But he didn't want to rush anything. Eventually they would have to talk about it—about everything. Even if they were destined to be nothing more than friends, she still deserved the truth, the whole truth. But the moment wasn't right yet.

He got them each a soda, and they sat on the porch. Dusty joined them, lying near Ben's feet, muzzle flat on the floor but eyes watchful. Occasionally his tail *thwapped* against the wood slats.

Ben grinned, thankful for something to say that had nothing to do with himself or Ashley's family. "I think Dusty's asking why you didn't bring his friends."

"Sorry, boy." Ashley bent over and gave the dog's hindquarters a pat. "Next time."

"You're planning to bring them to work with you, right?"

She looked up, eyes widening slightly. "I hadn't thought about it."

"They're obedient. I see no reason why not."

"You're sure? You're already doing so much more than I expected."

"It's a farm. Dogs are part of the mix." He turned his gaze toward the barn, enjoying the golden haze that had settled over the scene as afternoon waned. "We'll lock them all up once we've got clients here, if we need to."

She laughed softly. "You're quite the boss, Henning. I'm going to like working for you."

"Working *with* me," he said softly, averting his eyes lest she see more than he was ready for her to see.

Monday, March 5, 1944

It took more than a week for Andrew to track down the whereabouts of Petty Officer Third Class Samuel Valentine. Andrew even made a call to his congressman before he managed to get the answers he needed.

The remaining question was what he did next.

"You aren't seriously thinking of taking Louisa to California." Helen stood near the kitchen sink, hands on her hips, eyes wide with disbelief.

He raked a hand through his hair. "Actually, I think I might."

"Andrew . . ."

"I've prayed about it, Helen, and I think this is the right thing to do. The young man has no family to go to see him. Both of his parents are dead, and he has no siblings. That's one of the reasons he needed someone to write to him."

"But you know Louisa's nature. She already thinks she's in love with him. Meeting him in person, while he's wounded and vulnerable and weak, will only stir up more of those romantic notions in her head."

It was tempting to remind Helen that she'd once been seventeen with a head full of romantic notions. She hadn't wanted to wait for him to graduate from the university. She'd even suggested that they elope.

His wife drew a deep breath and released it. "You've made up your mind."

He nodded.

"How soon?"

"We'll leave on Saturday."

"Well, then, you'll go knowing I think you're wrong."

"If I must." He took a couple of steps toward her. "But you'll forgive me. Right?"

She sighed. "I suppose I have no other option."

He took her in his arms and rested his chin on the top of her head.

"But it might take me awhile," she whispered.

He chuckled. "Fair enough."

Silence filled the kitchen. For a short while the two remained where they were, locked in an embrace, two against the world, united even while disagreeing on the matter of their daughter. But eventually Helen took a step back and lifted her head to meet Andrew's gaze. "You'd better go and tell Louisa. She'll want to start packing immediately."

"I'll have to find where I put the suitcases."

"Under the bed in our room."

"Are you sure?"

"I'm sure. I move them every time I dust mop."

He gave her a nod before turning on his heel and walking down the hall to the girls' bedroom. He rapped softly. "Louisa."

Silence.

"May I come in?"

"Yes."

He opened the door. His eldest daughter was on her bed, a pile of letters on the bedspread in front of her. She cast him a sullen glance before lowering her gaze to the letters again. For a second or two he wondered if he should have listened to Helen. Was he making the wrong decision? But the doubts passed quickly. He still believed this was the right thing to do, for the boy as well as his daughter.

"I have located Samuel Valentine," he said.

Louisa's countenance changed at once. "How is he?" She hopped to her feet at the side of the bed.

"His wounds are not life threatening, but it is doubtful he'll be sent back into service, despite what he told you in his letter."

"Where is he?"

"In a hospital in San Francisco."

"Can I . . . Can I go to see him?"

Andrew remembered when Louisa had asked, if it were Ben who was injured, wouldn't Andrew want him to be able to see his sweetheart? Thankfully, as of Ben's most recent letter, his eldest son was well and uninjured. And if Ben's silence regarding the opposite sex was any indication, there was no sweetheart either.

"Dad? Can I see him?"

He nodded. "We'll go on Saturday. I bought the train tickets this morning."

"Dad!" She let out a squeal such as only a teenaged girl could manage and threw her arms around his neck, squeezing tight. "Thank you!"

Please, God. Don't let this be a mistake.

She released her hold on him. "I wish I could buy a new dress. I'd so like Samuel to see me for the first time in something new instead of one of my old school dresses. Could I buy something new?"

"Don't press your luck, Louisa. This trip is going to cost enough."

"Oh, all right. Maybe Grandma Greyson can help me make something. There should be time."

Andrew knew many things about farming, a fair amount about raising daughters, but next to nothing about sewing. Better to withdraw now, before he put his foot in it. "You'll have to talk to your mother and grandmother about that."

"Okay. I will."

He gave her a parting smile before leaving the bedroom, praying as he went for the days ahead.

Chapter 20

Ben strolled beside his grandfather on a path that wound through the retirement community. For the past week, since realizing he would like something more than simple friendship with Ashley, he'd kept silent about his feelings. But finally, he'd known he needed some wise counsel, the type his grandfather never failed to give him.

While they walked, Ben told Grandpa Grant everything—about Ashley and her reaction to her brother, about what Ben felt for her and what he feared, about everything. Then silence ensued until they settled onto a park bench to watch a couple of swans paddling in the pond.

"You will have to share your story, my boy, as you said. I know there's a risk that your history might frighten her away, but I don't see how you can put it off. It wouldn't be honest. Especially not now. This must be her decision."

"I know." Ben leaned forward, arms braced on his thighs. He watched the midday light play across the water. The trees at the far side of the pond had turned to gold and red, the change of seasons painted across the landscape.

"She's quit her job to come to work for you. Am I correct about that?"

"Yes. Today's her last day at the store."

"That complicates things even more."

He nodded. Would she hold that against him? She'd quit her job. She'd risked her financial stability. Would she feel betrayed by his revelation? Would it end any chance he had of seeing if their friendship might become something more?

"Don't waste time on what-ifs and if-onlys, Ben. They don't change a thing."

"I know, Grandpa. But it's hard to tune them out sometimes."

His grandfather draped an arm over Ben's shoulders, and the two returned to silently watching the pair of swans.

It was after ten on Friday evening, Ashley's last day of work in the store. She felt mixed emotions as she pushed open the door and exited the building for the last time as an employee. All day, coworkers had been telling her they were going to miss her. It had surprised her how much their words meant. After all, it wasn't like she'd ever hung out with them. She wasn't the type to go out for a beer after a shift ended, although she'd been invited plenty of times to join them, especially early on in her employment.

"Don't be a stranger!" a woman named Maria called to her from several parking spaces away.

"I won't." Ashley waved, then unlocked her truck and slid onto the seat behind the wheel. But she didn't start the engine right away. She took a moment to let her body relax.

It had been a rough week, as expected. Long hours at the store would be good for her checking account, but she'd fallen behind on life itself. Her dogs and horses had been fed and watered but not much else. Her sink had more than one meal's worth of dirty dishes in it, waiting to be washed. She'd only spoken to her mom once, and that conversation hadn't gone well. The strain of wondering about Dylan—where he was, how he was surviving—was wearing on them both. And whether or not she cared to admit it, she'd missed seeing Ben. She hadn't even talked to him on the phone. Her own fault. She'd told him she was scheduled to work every day this week. In fact, when she'd told him goodbye last Saturday, she'd added, "See you on the fourteenth." Why would he call when she'd sounded like she didn't want him to?

"Did I want him to?" she asked into the silence of the cab.

Yes, she supposed she had wanted it. But it didn't matter now. She would see him on Monday. That was the day she would settle into her new job as a barn manager. *Barn manager.* The two words sounded great together. She would work with horses every day—and get paid to do it. Her uniform would be jeans and boots. Life didn't get much better than that. In fact, she should pinch herself to see if it was true. How'd she get this blessed?

"Thank You, God," she said, recognizing that He was the reason for her blessings.

With a smile, she turned the key in the ignition and drove her truck out of the parking lot, headed for home and a good night's sleep once her chores were done.

Pastor Trent opened the side door of the church before Ben reached it. "Thanks for coming. Sorry for calling you this time of night."

"It's all right. Sounded serious."

Trent motioned with his head. "He's in my office. Passed out." He turned.

Ben followed him. "What happened?"

"I was working late and heard breaking glass. I found him trying to get into the coffee bar. Looking for money, I guess."

"Did you call the police?"

"Not yet."

"Should have been your first call."

"I know."

"Do you know who he is?"

"No. I've never seen him before. I hoped you could talk to him, perhaps learn his name and the reason for his circumstances."

"Depends how drunk he is. It's a waste of time to try to glean information if the alcohol is in control. He won't understand what I say if he's high."

Trent opened the door to his office. The man in question—it was hard to tell his age from where Ben stood, especially given his unkempt appearance—lay on the leather sofa, baseball cap pulled low on his forehead, one foot on the floor, the other draped over the arm of the couch. He snored softly. Trent moved toward the sofa and nudged the man's foot with the toe of his shoe. No response. "I suppose you're right about calling the police." He sat on a nearby chair. "I shouldn't have bothered you at this time of night. I know you work with these men, and I thought . . . Well, I don't know what I thought."

"You're a man of compassion who always wants to help others." Ben took a different chair. "But sometimes the real kindness is to let the chips fall where they may. He broke into the church, Trent, and then he was trying to get to the cash registers in the coffee bar. That sounds like attempted robbery to me. I don't believe letting him sleep it off on your couch is the best option."

Trent sighed. "Neither do I." He stood and went to the phone.

While the pastor made the call, Ben stared at the man on the sofa. He could see now that he was young. Early twenties, more than likely. A stupid young man much like Ben had been not all that long ago. Judging by the smell of him, he'd had no access to a shower stall or bath for a while. His cheeks seemed gaunt. Was he as hungry as he looked? Had he been choosing booze or drugs over food when he managed to get some money? Probably.

By the mercy of God, Ben had found his way out of that life. He could only pray that this young man would do the same.

"The police are on their way," Trent said. "They asked if he had a weapon, but I didn't know. I never saw one. I suppose if I had seen one, he wouldn't be sleeping it off in my office right now."

A groan from the direction of the sofa drew Trent's and Ben's gazes back to the intruder. The fellow rubbed his face, opened his bleary eyes, muttered a curse, then pushed himself upright. He looked like he wanted to bolt from the sofa but hadn't the energy to do so.

"Don't try it," Ben said in a level voice. "I'm in better shape than you are. You'll never make it to the door."

He tried to glare at Ben, but his eyes couldn't quite focus, making the look ineffective.

"My name's Ben. What's yours?"

The only reply was a string of curse words.

"I doubt that's your name."

There was a long silence, then, "Dylan."

A knot formed in Ben's gut. Was it possible? "Dylan what?" he forced himself to ask, dreading the answer.

"None of your business. That's what."

"Maybe not. But it will be the police's business, and if I'm not mistaken, that's them at the door right now."

This time Dylan did push to his feet, but Ben stretched out his arm, causing him to fall back on the sofa. Before Dylan could right himself a second time, the police officers were entering Trent's office. Ben moved out of the way to let the cops do their jobs. Dylan clammed up, saying only one thing when an officer asked him a question: "I want a lawyer." After that he remained mute.

Ben knew he wouldn't hear the kid's last name after that. But he didn't need to hear it. He knew. Despite the fellow's disheveled, haggard appearance, Ben had seen a resemblance to Ashley. Something around the eyes and the cut of the jaw. This had to be Ashley's brother—and Ben was going to have to tell her about Dylan's arrest . . . and his own part in it.

Sunday, March 12, 1944

It was ten o'clock on Sunday morning when Andrew and Louisa arrived at the naval hospital in San Francisco. Andrew had learned enough about Samuel's injuries to believe it would be all right for his daughter to see the young man. However, as a nurse led them down a dimly lit corridor, he began to doubt the decision. Even if Samuel's injuries weren't frightening, could the same be said of the other men in the ward?

"It's all right, Dad," Louisa said softly. "I know. I'll be fine." Something in her eyes told him she'd read his mind. Moreover, what she'd said was true. She would be fine. She was prepared for whatever was beyond that doorway, despite her tender years.

Quick glances into the wards they passed proved the hospital—built to hold five hundred beds—was as overcrowded as Andrew had been told to expect. The medical staff now cared for over thirteen hundred wounded officers and enlisted men. He wondered how the doctors and nurses managed. And this was only one hospital in one city.

The stern-faced nurse stopped and faced them. "Remember, please. Keep your voices down. Try not to disturb the other patients. Someone will let you know when you must leave."

"We understand," Andrew answered. "Thank you."

With a crisp nod, the nurse opened the door and took them into the ward. Andrew tried not to look anywhere but at the nurse's back. Still, he saw legs in slings above the narrow beds and heads wrapped in white bandages.

Samuel was in the last bed on the right. His face was covered in cuts, and there was a patch over his left eye; the right eye was closed for now. His left arm lay wrapped in a cast from wrist to above his elbow, and that hand was bandaged as well. Andrew knew the young man had lost a couple of fingers above the middle joints and wasn't yet out of danger of losing his whole hand.

Louisa cast a questioning glance up at him. Andrew nodded, and she moved to the side of the bed. "Samuel?"

No response.

She drew a chair close to the bed and sat on it, leaning in close to the patient. "Samuel, it's Louisa. Louisa Henning."

He stirred, but it took what seemed a long while before he opened his eye.

Louisa smiled.

At first he was quiet. But finally, he said, "You're even prettier than your picture."

"And you don't look much at all like yours." There was tenderness in her teasing tone.

He grunted. "No, I don't suppose I do."

Louisa looked toward the foot of the bed. "This is my father, Andrew Henning."

"It's a pleasure to meet you, sir." There was pain in the young man's voice, a pain he tried to disguise.

"And you, Samuel."

"I appreciate you bringing Louisa to meet me."

A lump in Andrew's throat stopped him from speaking. He settled for a nod.

Samuel's gaze lingered on Andrew only a few moments more before it returned to Louisa. "Tell me your news. What of school?" His head sank deeper against the pillow.

Louisa took hold of his right hand. "I'll graduate at the end of May. But you know that. I'm doing well with my studies or else my parents would never have let me make this trip."

"And the farm. Tell me about the farm. The way you do in your letters." His eye closed. "I've always loved reading about your farm."

For the first time, Louisa looked a little uncertain. But she squared her shoulders and began. "It's spring, so Dad and Oscar have been preparing for planting. They've plowed the ground already, and the air is rich with the scent of just-turned earth. My mother and I have been getting the garden ready too. It's very large. We hardly have any yard left, but we eat well in the summer, so it's worth it. We have all kinds of fresh fruits and vegetables. And what we cannot eat fresh, we preserve so we'll have food in the winter."

Eye still closed, Samuel said, "You're making me hungry."

Louisa laughed softly. "Don't you have good food in the navy?"

"Tolerable."

"Then when you are well, you'll have to come to Idaho and enjoy one of my mother's dinners. She's the best cook in all of Ada County."

At last he looked at her again. "I'd like that very much."

Andrew saw Louisa squeeze Samuel's fingers, her smile blossoming into something womanly, erasing any sign of girlishness. It startled Andrew. He knew she was growing up, but he wasn't prepared for his little girl to be gone for good.

Chapter 21

The melody of her mom's ringtone yanked Ashley from a sound sleep. She reached for the phone on the nightstand and managed to swipe to answer on the first try. "Morning, Mom," she mumbled.

"Dylan's been arrested."

Ashley's heart hiccupped. "Where was he?"

"Right here in Boise."

"When?" She sat up, then pushed her hair back from her face.

"Last night."

Ashley drew a slow breath. "What did he do, Mom? How did he get caught?"

"I don't know yet. I'm on my way to the jail now."

"Is he getting bail?"

Her mom ignored the question, instead asking one of her own. "Will you meet me there?"

Everything inside Ashley wanted to refuse. But she couldn't. For her mom's sake. Not Dylan's. "I'll meet you. I'll be there as soon as I can. I'll have to take care of the dogs and horses first, but then I'll come. Don't worry."

After ending the call, Ashley shoved aside the bedcovers and got up. She dressed in haste and hurried to take care of her chores. After the animals were fed and watered, she returned to the house for a quick shower. A cup of coffee and a slice of buttered toast served as breakfast before she raced out the door a second time.

It wasn't her first time to drive to the jail because of her brother. She knew exactly where to go. What she hadn't expected was to find Ben Henning sitting in the waiting area beside her mom. The sight of him stopped her cold.

Her mom noticed her first. Cheeks streaked with tears, she rushed to embrace Ashley. Ben stood too. Ashley saw him over her mom's shoulder. His expression was grim, his eyes worried. Questions tumbled in her head, but they seemed stuck in her throat.

Her mom drew a breath before taking a step back. "They won't let me see Dylan yet. I don't know when they will."

Ashley wasn't surprised, although she didn't say so. Her gaze returned to Ben, who had taken a couple of steps toward the two women.

"I got here a few minutes ago," he said, as if she'd asked a question. "I introduced myself to your mother after I guessed who she was. You two look a lot alike."

"Why are you . . . ? How did you . . . ?"

He gave his head a slow shake, and she guessed he preferred to explain out of her mom's hearing. Whatever. She wasn't sure she would understand, even after he explained. It was too bizarre.

She put an arm around her mom's shoulders. "Let's sit down."

"Okay."

The minute hand completed a slow, torturous circle around

the clock. People came and went, police officers in uniform and lawyers in expensive suits among them. But it was the relatives Ashley noticed most. Relatives wearing bored faces, sad faces, frightened faces, angry faces. Some were tear streaked like her mom's. Others were frozen, feelings locked inside. Much like her own, no doubt.

Ben finally stood again. "Why don't I check to see what's happening?"

"Mom." Ashley turned toward her mother as soon as he'd moved away. "It could be hours before you can see Dylan. Let me take you some place for breakfast."

"I'm not hungry."

"You can't go without eating. You need your strength. Heaven knows the next few days aren't going to be easy."

Her mom shook her head. "I'm staying here. I can't miss the opportunity to see him when it comes."

"We don't even know if they've filed charges yet. It could be hours."

Ben returned and, as if in response to her comment, said, "It's Saturday. Nothing is going to happen until Monday."

"Not until Monday?" her mom whispered.

"And . . ." He gave his head a slow shake. "Except for an attorney, he doesn't want any visitors."

Her mom's shoulders slumped. "But we aren't visitors. We're his family."

"That may be true, Mrs. Showalter, but that's his choice. No visitors." He was silent a short while, compassion written on his face. Finally, he added, "I don't think you'd want to see him anyway. He was plenty hammered when he was arrested. Chances are he's still in bad shape. Better to wait."

Surprise caused Ashley to sit up straighter. "Did they tell you that at the desk?" she asked in a low voice.

"No." He sat in the chair next to her.

"Then how do you know he was drunk?" It was a dumb question. Of course Dylan had been drunk. Still . . .

Ben glanced at her mom, then back at Ashley. "I was there when he was arrested."

"Ben . . . I don't understand."

"He broke into the church last night. Pastor Trent called me. I . . . I got there before the police. When I learned his name was Dylan, I guessed he might be your brother. He resembles you and your mom."

"You should have called me."

"It was late. After midnight by the time the police took him away. And he didn't give his last name, so I didn't know anything for sure. I didn't want to worry you needlessly if I'd guessed wrong."

She supposed he was right, but it bothered her all the same.

"I came to the jail this morning, still hoping I was wrong about the young man being your brother. Your mom was alone in the waiting area, so I introduced myself and asked if she was Dylan's mom. Not much later, you got here."

"It had to be your church he tried to rob." Ashley lowered her gaze to her hands, clenched in her lap. "Small world." She released a humorless laugh.

"Small world," he echoed.

Ben wanted desperately to wipe away the wounded expression on Ashley's face. She tried to act as if she didn't care what happened to her brother, as if her only concern was for their mother, but he didn't believe it. She cared about Dylan too. Perhaps reluctantly, but she still cared. He thought about what he'd put his own family through, and it shamed him still. He knew he was a different man today. God had changed him. God continued to change him. Still, he remembered what he'd done. How could he forget it?

He leaned slightly toward her. "Ashley."

She met his gaze again.

"Your mom should go home and rest."

She nodded.

"But if you'd like, I could meet you somewhere later. We could talk. About what happened last night." He had far more than that to tell her, but he would begin there.

She nodded again, although he wasn't certain she comprehended. Her attention was focused on her mom. "Let's get you home, Mom."

"But I—"

"No visitors, he said. There's no point in staying. We'll see him on Monday."

Ben stood and took a step back, not wanting to intrude, yet wanting to be available if needed.

Mrs. Showalter—looking beaten and lethargic—allowed her daughter to draw her up from the chair. Ashley put one arm around her mom's back and guided her out of the waiting area with only a brief glance in Ben's direction. He remained where he was. If she wanted to meet with him later, she would call.

He looked one last time toward the front desk, wishing there was a way he could force a face-to-face with Dylan Showalter. Not that it would do any good. He'd told Ashley the truth about the state her brother had been in last night, and it was doubtful he was up to reasoning about his addictions this morning. Maybe he wouldn't ever be ready. Some people never got to the place of letting go and letting God.

With a sigh, Ben walked out of the jail, but when he left the parking lot, rather than turning toward the farm, he drove to one of his favorite places on the river. He walked to a little-used bench surrounded by cottonwoods and watched the water as it flowed swiftly past him.

"How do I help her, Lord? How do I help them? Is this why you brought us together? Is it about them and not about me and Ashley?"

The ways of the Lord were not his ways. The thoughts of the Lord were not his thoughts. He knew this.

He cared about Ashley. This he knew for sure. But how would she respond when she knew it was Ben who had told the pastor to call the police? And he would have to tell her. He would also have to tell her *why* Trent had called him. He should have found a way before now.

Ben pulled out his phone and opened the messaging app. He tapped on Ashley's name, causing the string of text messages they'd exchanged to appear. He poised his thumbs to begin typing, then closed the app and slipped his phone back into his pocket. This wasn't a time for texting. He needed to be patient, to wait for her to make the next move. If she didn't contact him today or tomorrow, then they would have to talk it through when she showed up for work on Monday.

"God, give me wisdom and the right words. Please."

Of all of the churches in the Boise area, why did Dylan have to try to rob the church Ben and his grandfather attended? That was just one of the questions that repeated in Ashley's head during the long, torturous weekend. Another was why, oh why, had the pastor called Ben so that he'd been present to see her brother taken away in handcuffs? She felt ashamed on her family's behalf for her friend—and new employer—to have seen it for himself.

Several times on Saturday and again on Sunday, she'd nearly called him, nearly taken him up on the invitation to talk. But she couldn't quite bring herself to do it. She stayed with her mom, except for a few quick trips home to care for the two horses. The dogs she brought back to her mom's house.

For some reason it didn't occur to her until Sunday evening that she couldn't show up for her first day of work at the Harmony Barn until after her brother's appearance before the judge. Her mom would need her more than ever then. Her gut told her Ben had thought of it already and wouldn't be surprised. Still, she chose to text rather than call. She was afraid the kindness and understanding in his voice would make her burst into tears.

Ashley: I'll be late to the barn tomorrow. I need to stay with Mom until I know about Dylan.

She didn't have to wait long for his reply.

Ben: No worries. Would you like me to come to court? I can arrange it.

Her heart skipped a beat as she realized how very much she would like his strong presence at her side. Then again . . .

Ashley: No. But thanks. I'll see you at the farm as soon as possible tomorrow.

She waited a short while to see if he would respond again. When no new message appeared, she set her phone on the bedside stand and returned to the living room. The television was on. Ashley went to the sofa and sat beside her mom.

"What are you watching?"

Her mom shook her head. "Nothing. I don't know. Some new show, I think." She looked at Ashley. "The noise is better than silence."

"Maybe you should go to bed. You'll want to be rested for . . . tomorrow."

"Oh, honey. I won't sleep, even if I do go to bed."

She took her mom's hand. "We'll get through this."

"Dylan's going to prison this time."

"Probably."

"The things they say happen to men in prison." Her mom's voice caught. "How can I bear it?"

"He'll be okay. Maybe . . ." Ashley hesitated, then made herself continue. "Maybe this will be what he needs to finally get clean and sober. For good."

Her mom lowered her head. Her shoulders shook as she began to cry again, though she made no sound. Perhaps there were no sounds left inside of her.

Friday, March 17, 1944

The train raced north on Friday morning, carrying Andrew and his daughter toward home.

He and Louisa had visited Samuel Valentine every day that week, staying as long as the hospital—and the stern-faced nurse—allowed. The rest of the time they had explored the city of San Francisco. They'd even managed to get tickets to a road show of the hit Broadway musical *Oklahoma!* That was an experience Andrew wouldn't soon forget. The only thing that would have made it better was if Helen could have been with them.

"Dad."

He looked over at Louisa, seated beside the window. "Yes."

"Do you think Samuel will come to see me when he's released?"

"He said he would."

"I know, but I think he's afraid of how I'll feel if he loses his hand or he doesn't get full sight back in his eye."

"How *will* you feel, Louisa?"

Her eyes widened. "I won't care. I love him."

"Has he told you he loves you?"

"Not in so many words. But in a hundred little ways, yes." A tiny frown furrowed her brow. "You like him, don't you? You would agree to let us marry?"

Andrew felt cornered by the question. "I do like him, but I would have to know him better than I do now before I could give you my blessing for marriage."

"Dad, sometimes you're terribly old-fashioned." She turned her gaze toward the passing countryside.

He almost laughed. He didn't feel old most of the time. He was strong and in good health and still in his thirties. But there were moments when his children could make him feel ancient. This was one of those times. Not the first and undoubtedly not the last.

"Louisa, listen." He took her hand in his. "I may seem old-fashioned, but I do know a thing or two about being in love. And I know that marriage can be hard, even when two people know each other well. Even when they start out in love."

"Like you and Mom."

"Yes."

She faced him again. "I know Samuel better than I know any of the boys I've gone to school with my entire life. I may even know him better than my own brothers. Or you." Her voice rose steadily. "We've shared everything in our letters. Our experiences. Our feelings. Everything."

"Calm yourself, Louisa."

"Sorry."

"If Samuel comes to Idaho, your mother and I will make him welcome. Just know that we expect you not to rush into anything."

Chapter 22

Dusty's bark alerted Ben to Ashley's arrival shortly after one o'clock. He walked away from the chicken coop where he'd finished a few modifications in preparation for the chickens he planned to buy soon. But he stopped before he got too close to her truck, sensing it was better to let her make the first move. At last, the truck door swung open, and Ashley dropped to the ground. When she stepped into view, she found Ben with her eyes and sent him a quick smile that faded almost at once.

It was clear the morning hadn't gone well.

Drawing a breath, he returned her brief smile and gave her a short wave. That seemed to be enough to put her in motion. She walked toward him, stopping about three yards away. "Sorry I'm so late."

"Not a problem."

"It's not the sort of employee I mean to be."

"I didn't think it was. Life happens. To all of us."

She nodded, her gaze dropping to the ground for a few moments.

Despite having guessed the answer, he asked, "How did it go?"

"About as expected. No bail. He has a public defender."

"What was his plea?"

"Not guilty."

Ben nodded.

"Which everyone knows is a lie."

"It's standard procedure, from what I understand. Now they'll start negotiating a deal with the DA, trying to get lesser charges, maybe less jail time."

"Oh, Ben." She seemed to crumple from the inside out.

He reached her in two strides, gathering her in his arms, pressing her close to his chest. She turned her face against his shirt and wept, sobs torn from some place primal. His heart broke at the sound. "I'm sorry, Ashley." He pressed his cheek against the top of her head. "I'm so sorry."

Her fingers gripped his shirt.

"Shhh." He moved his head, allowing his mouth to brush across her hair. He caught a whiff of her fruit-scented shampoo. He'd give just about anything to help stop her pain. Just about anything.

"Ben," she whispered, drawing her head back to look up at him.

Kissing her in that moment was as natural as breathing, and Ben thought he could have stood there forever, holding her close, his mouth upon hers, drinking in her sweetness. He wished he could stay forever. The longer he kissed her, the longer he could avoid the harder conversation that awaited them.

But, of course, the time arrived when he had to break the kiss and withdraw. Not far. Only far enough that the two of them could look at each other. A mixture of emotions swirled in her beautiful eyes. Turquoise colored, he realized. More green than blue, and yet not truly green. Her dark lashes were thick. How had he not realized before how beautiful she was?

"I've wanted to do that for weeks." Strangely, he hadn't known it until he said it.

A smile flickered at the corners of her mouth, although a touch of sadness lingered in her eyes. "I'm not sure it's a good idea."

"Complicated. Right?"

"Ben, I like you. But I'm not sure—"

"We won't know unless we try."

"The timing is bad."

Knowing what he needed to tell her, he said, "You're right. It's bad timing. In fact, we should talk. Let's go sit down."

"Okay." Her expression changed to one of bemusement.

On the porch, they settled onto a couple of chairs.

Ashley flipped her hair over her shoulder, leaned back, and released a sigh. "Sorry for breaking down like that."

"You've been staying strong for your mom. Something has to give every once in a while."

"You had a unique way of making me forget it for a minute or two." There was that sad-sweet smile of hers again.

Oh, how he would prefer to take her in his arms again and kiss her until they both forgot everything else. He thought she might want that too. But he couldn't give in to that desire.

"Ashley, I need you to know what happened on Friday night."

The smile vanished as she squared her shoulders, as if bracing for the worst. "All right."

"When your brother broke into the church, he was completely

wasted. To the point of passing out. Trent didn't really stop the robbery. He just got there in time to see Dylan collapse in mid-progress. Trent saw how bad off your brother was, and he called me for help. Dylan was still unconscious when I got there. I asked Trent if he'd called the cops. He hadn't, and I told him he should." He hesitated to see if this would get any reaction beyond her immediate nod. It didn't. Apparently, she wasn't bothered that he was the one who'd set Dylan's arrest in motion. That was something. "It was while we were waiting for the police that I learned his name was Dylan and began to suspect who he was."

She pushed loose strands of hair away from her face. "Why is it important that you tell me all of that?"

"I guess it isn't. But what is important is why Trent called me to help with your brother."

"You're the pastor's friend." She shrugged. "I get it."

"It's more than that, Ashley. It's because I've done a lot of work with guys like Dylan. Recovery work."

This caused her eyebrows to arch. "You have?"

"I have."

"Why?"

"For lots of reasons." He drew in a breath and pressed on. "One is that it helped keep me focused on my own sobriety."

She paled. "Your what?"

"My recovery. I was like your brother for a lot of years, Ashley. I started drinking as a teenager, and my life spiraled out of control until I finally reached the point of admitting I was an alcoholic. It was Jesus who turned my life around. Faith in Jesus, working the steps of recovery, and the love of my grandparents got me sober. Ever since I've done what I could to help others find it too."

"You aren't anything like Dylan," she whispered.

"Maybe not today." He reached as if to touch her shoulder.

She drew back from him.

There was a buzzing in Ashley's ears that made it hard to concentrate. Or maybe she simply couldn't believe what Ben had said. He'd worked with guys like Dylan to help keep his own sobriety. He was an alcoholic or had been an alcoholic or something like that.

Did he lie to me? No, but he fooled me. Somehow. Somehow he fooled me.

She rubbed her forehead with the pads of her fingers. She'd quit her job. Her secure but low-paying job. She'd quit to go to work for Ben Henning, and now he'd told her he used to have a drinking problem, that he'd worked with people like her brother to help keep himself sober. In other words, he might not stay sober. He could fall off the wagon. Just like her brother had done time and again.

"I'd like to help Dylan," Ben said, as if he'd read her thoughts, "if there's any way that I can."

"He'll be in prison."

"If he is, he'll need help there too."

She rose from her chair, holding up a hand between them. "Don't say anything else. I need to . . . I need to think."

She walked off the porch and headed for the paddocks. Paisley, the black-and-white paint, was the first horse she came to. She looked the gelding in the eyes, then buried her face against his neck. Why had she let Ben kiss her like that? Why had her heart thrummed in response? He was supposed to be a friend. Only a friend.

"I've wanted to do that for weeks." His voice whispered in her memory, causing her pulse to race again.

No. No. No. She wouldn't fall under his spell. He'd fooled her, making him the same as Paul. He'd manipulated her, making him the same as Dylan.

Be fair. It isn't the same. Look at Ben. Look at his life. Look at the way he lives now. The rest is in the past.

She drew in a deep breath. Was addiction ever in the past? Even he had said working with others helped in his own recovery. Did she dare trust him?

Paisley snorted and bobbed his head.

Ashley drew back and moved to look the horse in the eyes again. "I'm working for him as of today. He's given me a chance to do what I want to do. It's a step in the right direction for my future. But it *won't* become anything else. It can't be personal." She brushed her lips with her fingertips. "That was the absolute last time he'll kiss me. He'll have to understand that. I'll make sure that he does."

Monday, March 20, 1944

Andrew's first thought upon hearing the news that eight hundred US Flying Fortresses had bombed Berlin in a daylight raid had been about Ben. The reports stated that the flight in and out had taken nine hours and that losses for the USAAF had been high. It could be weeks before they had a letter from their son that would tell them if he'd been part of the mission. Ben wrote regularly, but the mail could be agonizingly slow. Whenever Andrew saw an automobile on the road, headed toward the farm, he felt a catch in his breath, wondering if it might be the delivery of a telegram with news that would break the family's heart.

"He will be fine, my friend," Hirsch Finkel said as the two men stared at the map on Hirsch's wall. "I feel it in my old bones."

"I hope your old bones are reliable prognosticators."

Hirsch chuckled over the comment. "Come. Sit. Ida has made us some tea."

Andrew had never cared much for tea, but he wouldn't insult his neighbor by refusing. He knew it was Hirsch's way of trying to take his mind off of Ben.

"Tell me about Louisa's friend. When is he expected to arrive?"

He stared into the teacup for a short while before answering. "We're not exactly sure. He thinks he'll be released from the hospital in the next week or so, according to his telegram. It came as quite a surprise that it happened this soon, but Louisa is overjoyed. Especially because Samuel means to come straight here. She was afraid he wouldn't."

"Too bad they did not release him while you were in San Francisco. He could have returned to Idaho with you."

Andrew didn't know if that would have been better or not. He worried about his daughter's heart, worried that she might rush into something for which she wasn't ready.

"It is good he did not lose his hand. Ja?"

"Yes. We're thankful to God for that."

"And his eye?"

"He didn't say. Right now, our main concern is where to put him when he gets here. Louisa doesn't want him to have to share the attic room with Oscar and Andy. She thinks that would be a fate worse than death."

"My friend, I know the answer to your dilemma."

He looked up.

"Louisa's young man will stay with us. We have a room. It will be his as long as he wants it."

"But you don't—"

"Let us do this, Andrew. Let us help a young man who has fought for liberty in this world. He has made sacrifices enough. His hand. His eye. Let us give him our thanks in this small way." Hirsch's voice broke at the end.

"All right," Andrew answered softly. "If that's what you want."

"We do."

The topic turned to farming while Andrew leisurely finished his tea, then he bid his neighbor a good day and returned home. When he entered the house, he found Louisa helping Helen with dinner preparations.

"Louisa," he said as he hung his jacket on a peg, "I have solved the problem of what to do with Mr. Valentine when he comes. The Finkels have invited him to stay with them."

The girl's eyes widened. "But he's coming to see *me*. He won't want to stay there."

"It's only across the road, Louisa," Helen said, irritation in her voice.

Andrew stepped into the kitchen and put his hand on his daughter's shoulder. "Better with the Finkels than in the barn."

"Dad!"

"Well, you don't want him to room with your brothers, and if not with our neighbors, then the barn is the only other option."

Louisa released a dramatic sigh. "Okay, I guess staying with the Finkels is the best choice."

"It was very kind of them to offer Samuel a room. You might be a little grateful."

"Yes, Dad." She nodded. "It was kind of them."

"Perhaps you should tell them so."

"I will. I promise."

"Good." He kissed the crown of her head.

Helen turned from the stove. "I'm glad that's settled. Louisa, please tell your brothers and sister to get washed up for dinner."

"Okay."

After Louisa was gone, Helen moved closer to Andrew while wiping her hands on a towel. "Have we made a mistake, allowing that young man to come?"

"No."

"Are you sure?"

"He seems a decent fellow, Helen."

"She's so young. And so determined to marry him. No matter what."

He put his arm around his wife and drew her close. "We remember what it's like to be young and in love."

"But we didn't rush into marriage." She looked up at him. "We waited until you got your degree and found a job."

Andrew refrained from reminding his wife what had happened soon after their wedding, beginning with the stock-market crash. The road they'd traveled in the early years of marriage had been difficult, full of surprises and more than a little heartache. They could advise

Louisa. They could counsel her. They could offer caution. But in the end, they couldn't live their daughter's life. She would have to live it for herself. Same as for all of their children.

His thoughts turned once again to Ben, somewhere in the European theater.

"Do you suppose he's all right?" Helen whispered, reading his thoughts.

"All we can do is pray and wait."

Chapter 23

While drinking his second cup of coffee the next morning, Ben stared out the kitchen window, watching Ashley as she fed the rescue horses in the farthest pasture from the house. He'd felt the dread fall off his shoulders this morning when her truck arrived, towing the horse trailer behind it. Having the final mare in that pasture made him a little more confident about Ashley staying in the position of barn manager. He hadn't been any too sure after her reaction to his revelation.

When she'd returned to the porch yesterday, she'd thanked Ben for telling her his history, then had made it clear theirs was to be a business relationship only going forward. She hadn't mentioned the kiss, but her meaning had been clear. He'd been wise enough to agree to her condition, although he had to believe—based on her response to his kiss—there was hope for more, given time.

"She's afraid," he said aloud as he rinsed out the mug. Now all he needed to know was how to relieve that fear. For now, he hadn't a clue what to do except to prove himself dependable, to be kind, to be patient. He needed to be a good employer and a trusted friend.

He turned from the sink and stepped to the kitchen table

where Andrew Henning's Bible lay open to 1 Corinthians. Ben had spent time this morning reminding himself what love meant. True Christian love. Unselfish love. The kind that put another person first. He knew what *he* wanted, but what did Ashley want? That's all that mattered for now.

Drawing a deep breath, he went to the front door where he put on a light jacket, just enough warmth against the crisp October morning air. Then he slapped a baseball cap onto his head and opened the door. Dusty darted outside ahead of him and ran toward the barn. In the time Ben had been away from the window, Ashley had disappeared from sight. He assumed she'd gone to her office now that all the horses were fed. Dusty, no doubt, planned to join her two dogs.

As Ben stepped down from the porch, the crunch of tires on gravel caused him to stop and turn his gaze toward the driveway. Recognizing Emily Cooper's black Ford truck, he changed direction, feeling guilty that he'd forgotten he arranged for her to come by that morning.

"Hey, Emily."

"Hey, Ben." She dropped to the ground and closed the truck door. "How goes it?"

"Good."

"Gorgeous morning."

"Sure is."

Her gaze swept the barnyard and fields. "You've been a busy man since the open house. Is that where you're putting the new stables?" She motioned with a tip of her head toward the cleared and leveled area beyond the barn.

"Yeah. The crew'll start construction next week. There'll be an indoor arena too. I think I told you that."

"You did."

They started walking toward the barn.

Emily asked, "But you still don't plan to have your first sessions until February?"

"Nothing official. At least not riding sessions. I'd rather not rush it. Do you agree?"

"Yes. You'll have plenty to keep you busy until then. Volunteers to train. Tack to get ready. More advertising. There's a lot to be done."

They reached the barn, and he opened the small door to take them inside. "Ashley," he called.

She stepped into the doorway of her office. Her expression revealed nothing.

"You remember Emily. I think I forgot to tell you she was coming this morning."

"Yes, you did forget. Hi, Emily. Good to see you again."

"You too. Ben told me you've got a few more horses on the place. Any with riding potential?"

"You mean from the rescues?" Ashley glanced at Ben, then quickly away. "One of them, maybe. Let me grab my jacket, and I'll show her to you."

A few moments later, the three of them headed outside on their way to the farthest paddock. The dogs ran ahead of them, racing and tumbling over one another in their excitement. Ashley smiled at the dogs' antics, and Ben felt his spirits lighten when he saw it. He shortened his stride and allowed the women to move on ahead of him. Neither of them seemed to notice his absence as they slipped between rails to enter the pasture, making their way to where the horses grazed. Ben stopped at the fence and leaned his arms on the top rail. He couldn't hear their conversation, but he sensed that talking to someone who loved horses as much as she did would brighten Ashley's spirits. He smiled to himself, thankful for that. Thankful for anything that would put her more at ease.

"You must be in seventh heaven," Emily said after she'd inspected the three newest arrivals at the farm.

"Sorry?"

"Getting to work here all the time instead of just volunteering."

"Oh." She looked at the horses, then let her gaze sweep over the land before looking at Emily again. "Yes. I guess that's a good way to describe it."

"You plan to take on more rescues, don't you?"

"Definitely. There's plenty of room for them here. I didn't have anywhere close to enough space at my place. Four horses maxed me out."

Emily grinned. "I'll bet you've always loved horses."

"For as long as I can remember."

"Me too."

Ashley nodded.

"Did you compete when you were younger? Barrel racing or anything like that?"

"No. I wasn't ever into that kind of thing. And I didn't have a trailer until I was out on my own, so all of my riding as a teen was done in or near the pasture I rented, unless I could bum a ride from somebody else. What about you?"

"I loved to jump when I was young." Emily turned her back to the horses. "My dream was to be in the Olympics one day, but reality set in early. We didn't have the money to buy a horse of Olympic caliber nor to get me the kind of training I would need." She shrugged. "I was disappointed for a while, and then I realized I didn't need to be in the show ring to enjoy my horses."

"What got you into equine therapy?"

"I stumbled upon it, actually. There was a fancy-dress fundraiser, and a friend told me about the event because it had to do with horses. I was intrigued, so I decided to check it out. Before I knew it, I was volunteering for a barn in Ontario. Eventually I became a certified instructor."

"I'm surprised you haven't started a program of your own."

Emily laughed. "No, thanks. I didn't have the setup for that. Besides, I don't want the headache and paperwork. I'd rather be working with the horses and helping people. Management isn't my thing." She looked across the pasture. "Seems to be Ben's thing. I've never known anybody more focused and organized than he is."

Ashley's gaze went in the same direction, but Ben was no longer where she'd last seen him. Despite herself, she felt a sting of disappointment.

"What made you decide to work for him?" Emily asked.

"I was an unhappy girl when I got my first horse. A gelding named Gus. He rescued me. I'd like to help make that happen for others. This seemed like the best way to do that." Her words served as another reminder of why she wanted to keep working for the Harmony Barn—for Ben.

"Looks like you're going to be doing that. I plan to start training sessions with our volunteers in a couple of weeks."

"We'll be ready. Me and the horses, I mean."

Tuesday, April 4, 1944

Samuel Valentine arrived in Idaho on Louisa's eighteenth birthday. Before leaving the house for the train depot, Andrew overheard Louisa telling her younger sister that Samuel coming on her birthday was a sign. It meant they were destined to be together. Francine, eleven years old and not the least interested in boys, told Louisa that she was stupid. The remark had made Andrew smile, despite his concern for his oldest daughter.

Samuel's appearance had improved since the last time Andrew saw him. No patch covered his eye, and the cuts on his face were mostly healed, although there would be some scarring. The cast had been removed from his left arm. His missing fingers were disguised beneath a glove. He moved with a slight limp, one others might not notice if they weren't looking for it.

On the depot platform, Andrew shook the younger man's hand. "You're looking good, Samuel. Very good."

"Thank you, sir. I'm feeling better too. It's good of you to allow me to come." His gaze flicked to Louisa, then back again.

Andrew took a step back. "I'd like you to meet my wife, Helen Henning."

"Mrs. Henning. A pleasure." Samuel tipped his head to her.

"Welcome to Idaho," Helen said.

Samuel smiled briefly, then turned toward Louisa. "It's good to see you again."

"You too." She blushed and lowered her gaze, apparently over-taken by a sudden shyness.

Taking pity on her, Andrew motioned toward the end of the plat-form. "Our automobile is parked over that way. Do you have any other luggage?"

"No, sir. Only this." He picked up the duffel bag that he'd dropped near his right foot upon meeting them.

"Then we'll be on our way." Andrew hooked arms with his wife and led the way, leaving Samuel and Louisa to follow behind.

At the car, Helen insisted that Samuel ride up front with Andrew while she rode in the back with Louisa. "It's more comfortable and you can see everything better." Andrew assumed his wife would also prefer not to have to keep looking over her shoulder throughout the drive back to the farm to see what the young couple was doing.

It turned out that Samuel appreciated the offer. A city boy from the East, he took unexpected interest in the passing countryside. He asked numerous—and intelligent—questions about crops, irrigation, and livestock. Andrew found himself liking the young man even more than he had already.

"That's our farm up ahead on the right," he said when the house and barn came into view. "And since we're short on bedrooms, our neighbors across the road have opened their home to you."

"I hate putting anybody out."

"You're not. The Finkels are delighted to host one of our brave fighting men. You'll understand why after you meet them." He slowed the automobile and turned into the driveway. "It's past lunchtime. I imagine you're hungry."

"I wouldn't mind eating, sir."

"Good. I'm hungry too. Come on inside, and we'll see what there is to eat."

Chapter 24

The last day of October arrived with gray skies and much colder temperatures, making it the perfect day for Ashley to sit at the desk in her office in order to finish the final chapter of the book she'd been reading. After turning the last page, she closed the cover, her heart aching yet filled with joy at the same time. The stories of traumatized kids finding healing through interactions with horses had brought her to tears a number of times. She was so thankful Ben had loaned the book to her, and so thankful she'd finally read it, even if it had taken her too long to do so.

Reaching for a tissue, she dabbed her eyes. Speed raised his head from the floor and looked at her with something akin to sympathy.

"I'm fine," she told the border collie.

The dog lowered his head to the floor once again, this time with a groan.

Ashley got up from the chair and left her office, reaching for her jacket as she passed the coatrack near the door. No horses were in the stalls. If not for the creaking caused by the persistent wind, all would have been silent. The construction crew was gone today. Ashley didn't know why they'd taken the day off—Halloween wasn't an official holiday, after all—but the absence of noise from the direction of the new stables and arena made her feel abandoned. Ben was gone from the farm today as well, and she felt his absence even more than the lack of pounding hammers and shouts from the workers. Strange, since they'd interacted so little over the past couple of weeks, even when he was there.

The ache in her chest intensified. An ache that had nothing to do with the poignant book she'd finished and everything to do with the wall she'd put up between herself and Ben. He'd honored that wall, as she'd demanded. Trouble was it hadn't made her feel any better. She missed the way they'd been before he'd kissed her. Before he'd told her about his past.

That thought circled her around to her brother. He'd finally allowed their mother to see him at the jail, once in person, a few times via video conference. Mom had invited Ashley to join one of those sessions. She'd declined. Dylan might have allowed it. Ashley wasn't ready yet.

Giving her head a shake, she opened the barn door, Speed following at her heels. The wind tried to push her back inside. She leaned into it and closed the door behind her. Now that she was outside, she heard a few other sounds—the clucking of hens coming from the direction of the coop, a whicker from one of the horses. She turned toward the nearest pasture and saw Dusty and Jack running through the grass at the far end near a row of trees.

"How come you're not with them?" she asked Speed. As if in answer, the border collie darted away from her in pursuit of his canine friends.

Ashley laughed softly.

The crunch of tires on gravel drew her around, and she watched the familiar old Buick roll to a stop near the front door of the house. A moment later Grant Henning got out from behind the wheel. He squinted as he looked around. A smile replaced the squint when he saw her.

"Ashley!" He waved.

"Mr. Henning." She walked toward him. "It's nice to see you."

"It's been too long, young lady. I was rather hoping you would join us at church again."

"Sorry. I've meant to. I really have. Things in my life got a bit . . . crazy."

"Life can do that."

She nodded, then said, "Ben isn't here. I don't know when he'll be back."

"Actually, Ashley, I was hoping you would give me a tour. Let me see the changes my grandson's made to the place since the open house."

"Me? Shouldn't Ben show you around?"

"I'd rather have a pretty girl for a tour guide. Come on. Humor me. I'm here and Ben's not." He offered his elbow, along with a grin.

She was helpless against that grin. It was so very like Ben's. The one that seemed to take hold of her heart even when she didn't want it to. "Okay." She placed her fingertips into the crook of his arm. "We'll start with the barn."

They moved at an unhurried pace. Grant Henning didn't say much as they checked out the barn; the stables and arena that were currently under construction; the chicken coop, newly populated; the new paddocks with their fresh white fences; and the horses grazing therein. Mostly he nodded and made an *ummm* sound every so often to let her know he was listening. When they'd seen it all, he invited her to sit with him on the porch.

"Thank you for showing me around." He lowered himself onto one of the chairs. "I'm amazed by all that's been accomplished since the last time I was here. Simply amazed."

"Your grandson's very focused on the end goal."

"Indeed." The older man's gaze moved from Ashley to the land, and a faraway look entered his blue eyes. "My granddad, Andrew Henning, loved this farm. He worked it into his sixties, but when he started to have health issues, the farm came to me. My dad loved the place too. It was supposed to be his, but in the end, the farm skipped that generation and came to me. I was the one who had a passion for farming above all else. Then it skipped another generation before it went to our Ben."

Our Ben. The words caused a frisson in her stomach.

"Grandpa Andrew was a man with a deep personal faith in God. His faith got him through many rough patches in life. The Great Depression. Raising five kids, three of them adopted. World War II." He fell silent for a short while, then cleared his throat and continued. "He told me that we're put on this earth, first of all, to come to know God through Jesus, and after that to discover His purpose for us so we can fulfill that purpose for all we're worth right up until we step into eternity." He met her gaze again. "I believe Ben has found his purpose with this equine therapy business."

"I think you're right," she said softly.

"But he followed a very difficult path to get to there."

"He told me."

"I wonder if he told you everything." The older man's eyes seemed to look beyond the farmland into the past. "It began with the foolishness of youth. He and his best friend Craig got drunk, and then Ben got behind the wheel. There was an accident. They could have both died. It was a miracle they didn't. Sadly, Craig ended up in a wheelchair, and Ben ended up saddled with a guilt that he tried to assuage with more alcohol."

Ashley felt her heart break a little over this latest revelation.

"My wife and I feared he would be lost for good. We prayed against that end for a long, long time. But the day came that he encountered the love of Christ, and he was changed by it. Immediately in some ways. Slowly in others. But changed forever. He's a good man. One of the best."

I know. Her throat was too tight to say it aloud.

"Well." He put his hands on the chair arms and pushed himself to his feet. "I'd best be on my way. Thanks again for the tour. And please. Think about joining us for church again soon. You are a pleasant addition to our after-church lunches."

Before Ashley could answer him, a black SUV turned into the driveway and drove up to the house. She moved to the edge of the porch and watched as the driver, a middle-aged man with a receding hairline, got out. He held a clipboard beneath his left arm and a pen in his right hand.

"May I help you?" she asked, moving to the top of the steps.

"Not really. I'm here to do an appraisal." His gaze flicked to the dogs on the porch behind her. "Do I have to worry about being bitten?"

"An appraisal?" Maybe Ben was taking out a loan. But why would he do that after the successful fund-raiser earlier in the month?

"Yes, miss. An appraisal."

"Who hired you?" she asked, still unsure.

The man glanced at the papers on his clipboard. "The attorney representing a Wendy Henning."

She heard Grant suck in a breath as he stepped to her side. She looked at him.

The older man's expression was stern. "I'm sorry, but Wendy Henning is not the owner of this property. She has no authority to hire you to do an appraisal."

"Really?" He looked at the papers again. "My boss's note says I need to get this done ASAP because of a hearing."

Grant's voice dropped to a whisper. The resolve left his face. His body seemed to sag. "A hearing." He slowly returned to the porch chair and sat down.

Feeling suddenly protective of her friend, Ashley stepped toward the stranger and his clipboard. "I'm the manager here. Why don't you give me your business card, and I'll make sure the owner calls you when he returns. His name is Ben Henning. But until he gives the okay, I can't let you have access to the farm."

The man opened his mouth as if to argue, then closed it again before reaching into his pocket and pulling out a business card. Ashley took it from him. Then she stood there, not moving an inch until he got back into his SUV and drove away. Only after the automobile was on the road did she hurry back to the porch.

"Mr. Henning, are you all right?" She sat beside him.

"I'm not sure, Ashley. I'm really not sure."

Ben grinned when he saw his grandfather's car parked near the house. What a nice surprise. He drove his truck to the carport and got out. Before he could walk far, Ashley came to meet him.

"Ben, somebody came by awhile ago. Something about an appraisal that your mom's attorney ordered on the farm. Whatever, it seemed to really upset your grandfather."

Ben's stomach clenched, sickening him. He didn't wait for her to say anything more. "Thanks." He strode quickly toward the front porch. "Grandpa?"

Grandpa Grant looked up. "We were wrong to think it was an idle threat. It seems she was serious."

"Grandpa, she won't succeed. And how'd she even come up with the money to hire an attorney? That's what I'd like to know."

"You know your mother. She seems to always find a way. I gave her six hundred dollars over a month ago myself."

Ben's gut churned. If hiring an attorney or trying to get an appraisal was what she used that money for . . .

"I wish I knew what I did to make her want to hurt me this way."

Ben sank onto the chair next to his grandfather. "It's about the money, Grandpa. Not hurting you."

A humorless smile crossed his grandfather's lips. There and gone.

"I'll call my attorney in the morning. I'll find out what we can do to nip this in the bud."

"Your grandmother and I spent many an evening analyzing your mom's growing-up years and second-guessing all of our parenting decisions. We asked her so many times to tell us what hurt her, what made her so angry. But trying to talk only seemed to make her more angry." He looked at Ben, pain in his eyes.

Ben reached to take hold of his grandfather's hand, knowing that nothing he said would help what the older man felt. He settled for a simple, "Love you, Grandpa."

"Love you, too, son."

Hours later, his grandfather and Ashley both having returned to their own homes, Ben sat at the kitchen table with Andrew Henning's Bible before him. He'd tried praying, but his thoughts were scattered and his heart heavy. Forming words in his head had been next to impossible. And so he opened the Bible, looking for something—anything—that might provide answers or comfort or, better yet, both.

He wasn't aware how long he'd read before he came across Andrew's penciled scrawl on the back of the 1 Samuel title page.

> Father, for these sons I have prayed. They are dedicated to You. I leave them in Your care, and like Hannah, my heart delights in the Lord. No matter what lies ahead, I will bow in worship. (1 Samuel 1:27–2:1) December 1, 1944

His eyes moved to the designated verses, then back to Andrew's declaration of trust. It was as if he heard God whisper to him, "Dedicate it to Me. Leave it in My care, and then worship Me." In response, he felt his grip loosen. His grip on this farm and its future. His grip on anger toward his mom. His grip on his growing feelings for Ashley. Even his grip on the guilt he held on to about Craig.

"For these things I have prayed," he said into the silent room. "They are dedicated to You, Lord, and I leave them in Your care. Amen."

When he opened his eyes, he knew he was different, even if the circumstances weren't. Even if they never were.

Saturday, April 8, 1944

Dear Ben,

I pray this letter finds you well wherever you are. It has been weeks since we received your last letter. It takes them so long to reach us, and often they arrive in bunches. The delay always makes us impatient for news.

We suppose that you have been involved in the bombing raids over Berlin, and we pray that you have come back unharmed every time. Time and again, your mother and I have placed you into the hands of your Heavenly Father, trusting you to His gracious care.

Everyone stateside seems to believe that Italy will soon be ours, and France not long after. There is hope that the end of the war is in sight. Many say Germany has already lost, only they haven't the good sense to admit it. Your mother and I try to take heart from that belief.

Oscar remains anxious to join the fight. I worry about the anger that has settled into his heart. He seems so set on getting revenge. I try to tell him the war isn't about revenge. Or at least it shouldn't be. But he doesn't hear me.

Louisa's young sailor, Samuel Valentine, is here in Kuna. He was released from the hospital earlier this week and is staying across the road with the Finkels. Samuel and Hirsch have formed a strong bond in only a few days. I like the fellow too. As for your sister, if things continue as they are now, I expect she and Samuel will soon be engaged. I will have no objection, as I feared I might when their romance first began. Because of his injuries (as I told you in another letter, he lost two of his fingers, but his hand was saved), Samuel won't be returning to the navy.

His parents are deceased, and he has no other immediate family. Only some distant cousins. Perhaps he will seek employment here rather than return to the East. Perhaps he will even choose to become a farmer. Whatever might keep him in Idaho would make me glad. I cannot bear to think of Louisa moving too far away. It is hard enough having you gone from our midst.

Write soon, Ben. Your mother and I are always anxious to hear from you.

Your beloved father

Chapter 25

Papers and bills were strewn across the kitchen table, and Ben was determined this would be the last time the table served as his desk and his laptop as his only computer. He'd been putting it off for too long. Later today he would buy a desk and filing cabinet and convert one of the bedrooms into the official office for the Harmony Barn. Ashley had her barn-manager office. He should have one of his own.

He pulled an invoice toward him. With a grunt, he began to write in the checkbook ledger. Of all of the expenses for this fledgling nonprofit, the insurance was among the worst. At least when he bought hay, he knew it would be put to good use. Insurance was necessary but not tangible. Or at least that's how it seemed to him.

Half an hour later, the last check had been written. He picked up the file box from the floor and put the various papers and invoices away. Thankful that chore was finished, he headed outdoors for a breath of fresh air.

Ben and Emily had concluded their first training session

with a group of Harmony Barn volunteers earlier that morning. Now everyone was gone and the barnyard was quiet. Ashley hadn't been able to make the session because of something to do with her mom. Ben hadn't pressed for details lest it bring up something unpleasant.

Dusty ran off the porch, looking for something to chase. The dog had grown used to having company during the week when Ashley was there with Speed and Jack. On the weekends, the yellow Lab seemed lost without the other dogs. Ben felt kind of the same way when Ashley wasn't on the property.

"Come on, boy. Let's walk."

He headed first toward the new stables and indoor arena. It wasn't finished yet but would be soon. The outdoor arena, however, was ready for use. In fact, that's where he and Emily had met with the volunteers that morning, despite the cold November air that had required most of them to bundle up in coats, hats, and gloves.

Ben marveled at how much the farm had changed in a few months' time. Surely God was in the details, for he couldn't see any other way all this could have happened so fast. The therapy sessions would soon be a reality. Yet there was still a lot to be done before the Harmony Barn was fully operational.

Dusty ran off, but Ben was too deep in thought to pay much attention. He didn't have to worry. The dog seemed to know the exact boundaries of the forty acres and never strayed beyond them—perhaps because he'd walked the fence line with his master many times.

Ben headed toward the paddocks next, pausing at the first fence. Inside the pasture, Paisley and Sundowner grazed on the short clumps of grass. The dun noticed Ben first. With a snort, he walked over, hoping for a treat. Ben rubbed the gelding's head. "Sorry, boy. My pockets are empty."

Between the two of them, Ben and Ashley had managed the feeding and care for the horses, but it had occurred to him this morning that they couldn't count on it always being that way. Horses could get sick or injured. For that matter, he or Ashley could get sick. They needed more than volunteers to help during sessions. They needed volunteers willing and able to step in with daily chores. And as they increased the number of horses they kept at the Harmony Barn, the need for volunteers would increase as well.

Sundowner gave Ben's shoulder an impatient nudge. He laughed softly and moved on to the next paddock, Dreamer's and Thunder's current home. The two had become quite the friends over the past weeks. Seeing them together made him grin—Dreamer so diminutive and Thunder so tall and stately. The pair paid him no mind as they stood together, braced against the chilly wind.

The next paddock held three of Ashley's rescue horses. Scooter stood at the far end of the pasture near a long row of poplars that served as a windbreak. Penny and JoJo were near the hay box, perhaps as hopeful for their evening feeding as Sundowner had been for a treat. "Sorry," he called to them. "It isn't time yet."

Dusty's persistent barking penetrated Ben's thoughts. He looked for the dog, finally discovering him not too far from Scooter. By the sound of him, Dusty had something up one of the trees. But then Ben saw something larger than a squirrel move from behind one tree to another. Perhaps it was someone from the irrigation district, walking along the easement. Nonetheless,

Ben decided to check it out. He slipped through the paddock rails and headed across the pasture. He'd almost reached the dog when a head covered in a dark knitted cap peeked out from between a couple of tree trunks. The kid's eyes widened a second before he disappeared again.

"Dusty, quiet. Sit."

The dog obeyed.

Raising his voice slightly, he said, "It's okay. Dusty won't hurt you. It's safe to come out."

Nothing happened right away. No movement at all. But finally the same head leaned out from behind the tree.

"It's okay," Ben repeated, his voice lowered again.

The boy who stepped into full view was maybe eight or nine years old, judging by his size. "I wasn't doin' nothin' wrong."

"Of course not. You're not on private property over there."

"I just wanted to see your old horse." His gaze flicked in Scooter's direction.

"Scooter's not so old. Probably not even as old as you are."

The boy stood a little straighter. "I'm ten."

That surprised Ben. He looked younger. "My name's Ben. What's yours?"

Again there was a lengthy wait before he answered, "Kurt."

"Where do you live, Kurt?"

The boy hung his head. "No place."

Ben took a few strides toward the fence line. "No place?"

"We're stayin' with friends of my mom."

"Oh." Something in Kurt's manner told Ben not to press for names. "Well, do you think it'd be all right with your mom if I introduced you to Scooter? She wouldn't mind you getting close to the horse if I was here. Right?"

"She wouldn't care. She doesn't care about nothin'."

He heard anger and pain in the boy's voice and felt compassion well in his chest. "Come on, then." He motioned for the boy to slip through the fence and join him.

Kurt's expression revealed the battle going on inside his head—the desire to get closer to the horse, the reluctance to accept Ben's invitation. Whether that was because Ben was a stranger or for another reason, Ben wasn't sure.

"Maybe another time, then." He reached for Dusty's collar.

"No. Wait. I'm coming."

Ben motioned for Dusty to stay, then watched as Kurt made his way into the pasture. "You stay here with my dog," he said when the boy reached him. "His name's Dusty. I'll go get Scooter." He was thankful it was the palomino who was nearby. The mare loved attention whenever she could get it. He pulled baling twine from his pocket as he approached the horse and looped it around her neck to use as a lead. "Come over here, girl. You need to meet somebody."

Kurt's eyes widened as man and horse approached him, but he didn't back away. However, he did put a hand on Dusty's neck, as if to draw courage from the dog.

Ben stopped Scooter with better than a yard to go. "She's a nice, quiet horse. She loves to have her head scratched, especially right here behind her ears. My friend Ashley got her this summer. Scooter's owners didn't want her anymore, and I guess they were going to—" He stopped himself before he said the word *slaughterhouse*. "They were going to send her away."

"Like my dad sent us away." Kurt's expression turned inward. "He didn't want us either."

Ben felt another catch in his chest. He knew what it was like to be unwanted by a parent. For an instant, he felt no older than Kurt, felt the sting of rejection in a personal way once again. He cleared his throat, then said, "Come over here. Move slowly but with confidence. Right here beside me. That's it. Now reach your hand like this. Palm up. Nice and flat. Let her give you a good sniff."

As if she'd practiced this action on command, Scooter brought her mouth down against the boy's open hand, bumping it gently and wiggling her lips against his skin. Then she huffed.

Kurt grinned.

Ben did too. *Way to go, Scooter.*

"That was cool."

"I agree. Cool."

This was how it was meant to be at the Harmony Barn. A boy and a horse. An easing of tension or anger or hurt or fear. A blossoming of hope.

This was their future.

Ashley stood at the paddock fence, watching Ben with the little boy, certain they were unaware of her presence. They remained totally focused on the horse. She couldn't hear the exchange between them, but something about the scene stirred her heart.

As he turned toward the gate where she stood, Ben lifted his gaze. Even from a distance, she saw a look of surprise, followed quickly by a smile and a wave. She remembered what his grandfather had told her about the young man he'd been compared to the man he was today. Did she have to be afraid of the feelings he'd stirred to life with his kiss? The question made her heart skip. Unable to help it, she lifted her hand to wave back, continuing to watch as they walked across the pasture.

"Hey, Ashley," Ben said when he and the boy got closer to the gate. "Didn't expect to see you today."

"I didn't expect to be here. I left something in the office yesterday that I needed."

He didn't ask what. Instead, he glanced down to his right. "This is Kurt. He and his mom are staying down the road with friends. We're about to go talk to her about him helping us with the horses sometimes. Want to join us?"

Something in his eyes told her much more than he'd said aloud. It seemed important that she agree. "Okay."

Ben opened the gate, pausing a moment to show the boy what he was doing and stressing the importance that all gates on the property be fastened so the horses wouldn't get loose. He was such a natural with people. Both adults and children. Everybody felt comfortable with him, Ashley included. Despite all of the reasons she didn't want to be.

"Lead the way, Kurt," Ben said.

The boy set off, and Ben fell into step beside him. Ashley followed right behind.

After they'd left the driveway and were walking beside the road, Ben said, "You didn't tell me your last name."

"Jackson."

"What's the name of the family where you're staying? Your mom's friends. Maybe I know them."

Kurt sent him a sour glance.

Ben shrugged. "Okay." He turned his gaze down the road again.

"Wallace. His name's Ron. You know him?"

"You know, maybe I met him at the open house we had here last month. The name sounds a little familiar."

"I don't like him much. He's kinda grumpy."

"I'm sorry about that."

"His wife's okay. Her name's Julie. She tries to keep Mom from cryin' so much."

Listening to them, Ashley's thoughts flashed back to the weeks after her father had died. Her mother had been inconsolable, and Ashley had often felt in the way. So she'd poured out her pain to their neighbor's pony, and the stodgy little horse had seemed to understand and give comfort back in return.

Kurt pointed. "That's their place."

Unlike most other houses on this country road, the Wallace home was fairly new. It didn't look to be part of a working farm either. No barn. No chicken coop or pasture. Ashley suspected the section of land the home was built on had been sold off by one of the neighbors, probably to raise needed cash. Sadly, it wasn't an uncommon occurrence.

Kurt took them to a side door.

"We'll wait here." Ben stopped at the bottom of the steps. "You get your mom."

"Okay." The boy's expression was grim once again as he opened the door and disappeared into the house.

"He's an unhappy little guy," Ashley said softly.

"Yeah. I'm hoping we can help change that."

The door opened again, and a young woman, somewhere close to Ashley's age, appeared on the stoop. "May I help you?" Her face was wan, her brown hair caught with a tie at the nape. Kurt stood right behind her.

Ben put a foot on the bottom step. "Mrs. Jackson, I'm Ben

Henning. I've got a place down the road a bit. It's called the Harmony Barn. Maybe you've seen the sign. I met Kurt this morning while he was out exploring, and he took a liking to one of our horses."

She glanced behind her. "What did you do?"

"No, wait," Ben interrupted. "He's not in any trouble. He didn't do anything wrong. I asked him to bring me to meet you because I was hoping he might be able to help around the barn on occasion. You know. After school or weekends. Whenever it was okay with you. He'd always be with an adult."

Kurt's mom looked at Ben, then Ashley. Assessing them, no doubt. Trying to decide if they could be trusted.

"Miss Showalter here is our barn manager." He looked over his shoulder at her and smiled "She sees to the care and training of the horses."

Ashley felt that warm smile all the way down to her toes.

He looked back at the boy's mom. "We'd love to have Kurt come over sometimes."

"That's kind of you, but I wouldn't want him to be in your way."

"Mom," Kurt whispered.

"Mrs. Jackson—"

"Call me Tracee."

Ben nodded. "Tracee, I promise you. He won't be in our way. Working with kids and horses is what our place is all about."

She frowned. "I don't think I understand."

Ben gave her a quick summary of the way the Harmony Barn would operate once it was open.

"I couldn't pay you anything," Tracee said when he fell silent.

"Sorry. I guess I didn't make that clear. Nobody will be kept from participating because of an inability to pay." He leaned slightly to the side so he could look at Kurt. "Besides, this will just be one neighbor hanging out with another."

Ashley could have sworn she saw a weight come off of Tracee's shoulders. A hint of a smile curved the corners of her mouth. "I suppose it would be all right, then."

"Good." Ben straightened and removed his foot from the step. "Maybe you and Kurt could come over tomorrow to have a look around. I go to church in the morning and then have lunch with my grandfather. So let's say anytime after two o'clock. Would that work?"

"It would work, Mr. . . . I'm sorry. What was your name again?"

"Ben. Ben Henning."

Tracee reached for her son's hand. "We'll see you tomorrow."

Tuesday, July 4, 1944

In mid-April, as had happened numerous times before, the Hennings received several letters from Ben on the same day. In one of them, he warned his parents not to expect regular communication from him, adding that if they didn't hear for a while, they shouldn't be concerned.

They were concerned anyway.

The country celebrated when the Allied forces occupied Rome at last. The celebration was more muted when they learned of the successful Normandy invasion. How could it be otherwise when the death toll was so high? Less than two weeks after that, the bombing of Japan began with a raid on the island of Kyushu. Surely, most believed, the end of the war on both fronts would happen soon.

Samuel Valentine, now an employee of the hardware store in Kuna, warned others not to get their hopes up. The war wouldn't be over by fall. Probably not even by the start of the new year. "It'll happen," he said. "We're gonna win. But it'll be bloody getting there. Our boys are gonna have to fight for every inch they gain."

That wasn't the sort of talk Andrew wanted to listen to, even if he believed it to be true.

However, it wasn't the war or Ben's safety or even Frani's birthday that occupied Andrew's thoughts on this Independence Day morning. Instead, he cared only that he wouldn't stumble over his own feet and make a fool of himself as he walked Louisa down the aisle of the church on her wedding day.

"Oh, Dad," she whispered to him as they stood in the small narthex of the church. "I'm so happy."

He glanced down at her, standing at his side, her arm looped through his. For an instant, he saw the small, hungry orphan she'd once been. He remembered her dirty face, her tangled blond hair, and her large blue eyes. He remembered the way she'd tucked herself tight against her older brother while at the same time trying to protect and shelter her younger brother.

Where had the years gone? When had she turned into this self-assured young lady? The white satin gown clung to her lithe figure, and her face was aglow behind the gauzy veil. He marveled at what Helen and Mother Greyson had managed to create. While wedding gowns weren't rationed, it still wasn't easy to come by fabric such as this. Or maybe it was the bride who made it all so beautiful.

The first notes of the "Wedding March" reached his ears. "Are you ready?" he asked softly.

She looked down at the bouquet of pink roses in her hands. The flower stems had been wrapped in lace, the delicate material held closed with a brooch of his mother's. *"Something old,"* he'd heard his mother say when she'd given the jewelry to her granddaughter.

After a moment, Louisa glanced up again and nodded. They stepped forward in unison, right feet first, as they'd practiced often in the past week. He saw the smiles of their friends, standing now in the rows of pews. There had been so many reasons for sorrow in this small, close-knit community in recent years. It was good to have a reason to rejoice.

He looked ahead and saw Samuel's expression. One of awe, adoration, and perhaps a little bit of fear. There was no doubt the young man loved Louisa and was determined to make her happy. Still, they would have difficult times, as all couples did. *When* trials came, the Good Book said. That was a promise to all mankind. When, not if. But when people put the Lord first in their lives, they prevailed through the best and worst of times.

Andrew and Louisa paused beside the front pew, long enough for the bride to lift her veil and kiss her mother's cheek. Helen had tears in her eyes but managed not to let them fall. At least not right then. They moved on and stopped, at last, before the pastor.

"Who gives this woman to be married to this man?"

In a strong voice, Andrew answered, "Her mother and I do."

Louisa lifted her veil a second time so that she could kiss his cheek. "I love you, Dad."

"I love you too."

With that, he passed her hand to Samuel. It seemed that something sharp pricked his heart as he did so. Strange, how joy could be mingled with an equal dose of melancholy.

God, be with them. Bless their union. Strengthen them in the hard places. Teach them to rejoice in everyday beauties. And draw them ever closer to Yourself.

Chapter 26

Ashley awakened in the wee hours of the morning. Her first thought was about her brother. His sentencing was expected to happen soon, and she had yet to comply with her mom's request to go to see him.

The idea filled her with resentment.

"Please, honey. You need to do this," her mom had said last night. "He needs to see his sister." That request had kept her awake past her usual bedtime, wrestling between guilt and frustration. And apparently it hadn't let her sleep very long either.

She rolled onto her side, staring at the glow of the digital clock on her nightstand. Three thirty. Was her brother awake right now? Probably not. He was likely sound asleep, free of remorse.

Her anger flared. *Why? Why must I always be the one to do something for Dylan? He did this to himself. Why can't he do something for me for once?*

The instant the thought formed, she felt shame. More than that, she felt something stir in her spirit. A sense that if she allowed the bitter feelings that consumed her to remain unchecked, if she continued to nurse resentment and distrust, she would lose something of great value. Perhaps it was crazy—she had no personal experience to draw upon—but she thought it might be God trying to speak to her.

And if she was honest with herself, He'd been speaking to her for a while. She just hadn't wanted to listen.

"I'm not the one who needs help." Wasn't that what she'd tossed out to Ben the other day? It wasn't her who needed fixing, right?

She'd been saying that for so long, she'd almost begun to believe it.

Almost . . .

Overwhelmed by the feelings swirling through her, she closed her eyes. "God," she whispered. "I'm tired of feeling this way. Help me. If You have something to tell me . . . I'm listening."

Five hours later, she drove into Boise, her stomach churning. She wasn't sure of the reason. Was it anticipation or uncertainty? All she knew was that something had begun to change in her heart that morning, and it seemed very important that she allow God to finish what He'd started. Would she find her answers today in church? She hoped so. She'd certainly felt led to come.

The parking lot was filled with cars when she arrived. She pulled into the first open space she came to. As she dropped to the ground, she drew in a quick breath.

"Ashley?"

She turned at the sound of Ben's voice, her pulse accelerating. "Hi."

"You didn't tell me you'd be here today."

"I didn't know for sure until this morning." She gave him a swift smile. "But here I am."

He tilted his head toward the building. "Come on, then. We're both running late."

Before they reached the front doors, Ashley heard singing coming from the sanctuary. She didn't recognize the song. She wasn't familiar with a lot of Christian worship music yet, although she'd started listening to one of the local Christian channels in recent weeks.

There were still a few people lingering in the large entry hall. Some sipping coffee. Some standing outside the bookstore. Two men seated near a stone fireplace, leaning toward each other, obviously in prayer. Something about the scene calmed her.

The sanctuary was dimly lit, except for the stage where the worship team performed. "This way," Ben said, just loud enough for her to hear him above the music. He stepped in front of her and led the way to his grandfather. When they arrived, the older man's eyes were closed as he sang. There were two vacant chairs beside him. "Those must be for us." Ben stopped in front of the farthest one, giving Ashley the one between the two men.

Grant Henning opened his eyes, saw her, and smiled. Then, ever so briefly, he took her hand in his and squeezed it. His welcoming gesture warmed her, like that first sip of hot coffee on a chilly winter morning.

And somewhere, deep inside, she felt God welcoming her in a similar fashion.

Ben had been surprised when he saw Ashley getting out of her truck in the parking lot. She'd never committed to returning to his church, despite saying how much she'd liked her first visit. He hadn't pressed her, despite how much he'd wished to do so. He knew better than that. While the wall she'd erected between them didn't feel quite as impenetrable today as it had three weeks earlier, it was still there. Patience was his best friend for now. Nonetheless, he took it as a good sign that she was in church, of her own volition, standing between him and his grandfather.

He closed his eyes and joined the singing, praise welling inside of him.

It wasn't easy, but Ben managed to keep his attention focused on the service instead of Ashley. Right up until the closing worship song. That's when he realized Ashley was crying. She didn't make a sound, and her head was bowed, hiding her face. And yet he knew. What should he do? Before he could find an answer to his own question, he saw his grandfather's arm go around her shoulders. A moment later she turned and hid her face against the older man's chest. Grandpa said something near her ear. She nodded but didn't pull away.

Whatever it is You're doing at this moment, God, whatever the reason for her tears, open Ashley's heart and her mind to You. Even if she never wants me, help her to fall more in love with You and to find her comfort in Your presence.

Part of him wanted to take back the prayer. Not all of it. Just the "*even if she never wants me*" part. Ashley needed Jesus as everyone did. But Ben wanted her to need him too. He wanted her to fall in love with him. Still, there was no taking back the prayer. He sensed it was as much for himself as for her.

Ashley pulled up the collar of her coat as Remington picked her way along the trail. It was rutted in places and littered with various sizes of lava rock, but neither horse or rider minded. The desert was a good place to think, and they weren't in a hurry. All was quiet except for the whistling wind. She let the buckskin have her head. Remington was smart enough to follow the trail with little guidance. As for the dogs, they were in canine heaven as they chased each other through the sagebrush.

It was Ashley's experience at church that morning that consumed her thoughts. She didn't know what equated to a miracle, but that's what she would call what happened. She'd gone to church, hoping that God would finish changing her heart, and that was exactly what had happened. In those blessed moments, she'd shed fear and anger the same way she shed her coat after entering a warm house. The years and years of resentment she'd felt toward Dylan had dissipated. Fallen away. Gone. Healed. And with it had gone fear and distrust. The experience had left her shaken, relieved, and in tears.

She lifted her eyes. Clouds were blowing in, threatening a storm. For some reason, the weather made her think of Halloweens with her dad and Dylan. Dad had always been the one who walked with them around the neighborhood while they filled their little pumpkin buckets with miniature candies. She remembered the taste of Butterfingers and Milky Ways on her tongue, and the way her dad would take a few for himself. "Don't tell your mom we all ate candy before we got home," he'd warned with a grin. Of course, her mom had known. How could she not, given the smear of chocolate often left on someone's chin? But it had been a fun game, all the same.

Pictures of the family filled her mind. So much joy. So much laughter. Ashley had adored her little brother at that age, and he'd adored her right back.

I forgive you, Dylan.

Her heart thrummed.

I forgive everything. I'm not angry anymore. Not anymore.

Wednesday, November 1, 1944

On the first day of the new school term, Oscar left the house along with the two younger children, but he didn't return with them when school let out. Andrew wasn't concerned at first. He assumed the boy, a senior in high school that year, was involved in some extracurricular activity. That changed when Oscar still hadn't returned by nightfall. Nor the next day. Nor the next.

Andrew and Helen searched high and low. They called or visited everyone who might possibly know where Oscar had gone. To no avail. But it didn't take long for Andrew to suspect what must have happened. His son had grown tired of waiting to come of age. By whatever means necessary, Oscar had gone off to join the war effort.

Their worst fears were confirmed weeks later when they received a letter.

Dear Mom and Dad,

By the time you get this letter, I will be at sea with the navy, somewhere in the Pacific. Please don't try to bring me home. I didn't lie about my age, only that I had permission to join up. I could get in real trouble if they found out I forged Dad's signature, but I am asking you not to say anything. I didn't want to miss out on the fighting. The war is coming to an end, and I want a chance to serve my country before it is all over.

I was in Farragut, Idaho, for boot camp. It was lots harder than Samuel made it sound when he told me about it. Days were long and full of marching, calisthenics, drills, pulling oars into a boat, loading heavy shells into a gun, and other kinds of training. Every night I fell into bed exhausted, and then, on too many nights, the chief petty officer would wake us up, shouting words he would not dare say in front of Mom. A lot of them are words I never heard before.

There were times I wanted to quit, tell them the truth, and come home. Plenty of the boys got homesick, even the ones lots older than me. But we all managed to stick it out.

Everything I own now can be packed into a sea bag, and it all has to be packed in a particular order. Mom, you would not believe how good I am at it. When we are moving, my sleeping gear gets rolled up inside a hammock and wrapped around my sea bag. Then I whip the whole thing over my shoulder and march off. It is efficient.

I hope I will be a good sailor. Ben always wanted to be in the air. I always wanted to go to sea. I guess we aren't land lovers like you, Dad. We loved growing up on the farm, but there is this big world out here, waiting for us.

I love you, Mom and Dad. I know that is not something I ever said much, but I do. You made a man of me, and I hope I will make you proud by the way I serve my country. Tell Louisa, Samuel, Frani, and Andy I love them too. And say hello to the Finkels too.

Oscar

"What do we do, Andrew?" Helen asked, her cheeks streaked with tears.

"We do as he asked. We let him serve."

"But he's only seventeen."

He took her hand. "He is at sea now. He is of age to serve."

"But he forged your permission."

"Helen, I don't think we should force him to come home disgraced." Emotion choked his voice. "I think we must let him be. No matter . . . no matter what may come."

His wife stepped into his embrace, the two taking comfort from each other.

Chapter 27

Just as Ashley turned her truck into Ben's driveway on Monday morning, he was going the opposite way in his truck. They stopped next to each other and lowered their windows at the same time.

"I'll be gone most of the day on a job," he told her.

She hoped her disappointment didn't show. She had so much she wanted to tell him, not to mention one big favor to ask. "Okay."

"Do you mind looking after Dusty?"

"Of course not."

He grinned. "Good. I left the front door unlocked, just in case. Glad I won't have to drive back to let him out."

"Me too." She returned his smile.

"I'll try to be back before you leave. If not, just put Dusty inside again before you go home."

"Okay."

He glanced out the windshield and back again. "Have a good day, Ashley."

"You too."

He drove on.

After parking her pickup, she let Dusty out of the house and watched as the three dogs wiggled and sniffed and wagged their exuberant hellos. Then she headed for the hay shed. Before long she was wheeling feed toward the paddocks. The horses whinnied and snorted. Impatient sounds that made her smile.

"All right. All right. I'm coming."

A short while later, as she dropped hay into the last of the feed boxes, she heard the sounds of a vehicle slowing on the road. She turned, expecting to see the work crew arriving. They were only a day or two away from completion of the stables and indoor arena. Instead, it was a car, one that looked vaguely familiar. She left the wheelbarrow beside the fence and walked to greet the visitor.

The driver wasn't just any visitor. Ashley recognized Wendy Henning as soon as she stepped from the vehicle. "Ms. Henning," she said as she drew closer.

The woman turned, her expression sour. "Where's Ben?"

"He isn't here today. He had a job to do."

"Why are you here?"

Ashley hesitated a moment. "I work here."

"You *work* here? Doing what?" Wendy Henning's gaze was dismissive at best.

"I'm the barn manager. I take care of the horses."

"And you get *paid* for that?" She looked away. "I knew he was a fool when it came to money."

Ashley's temper flared. She fought to keep it out of her voice. "Your son isn't a fool, Ms. Henning. He's a man with a vision."

"I wouldn't expect a woman who's sleeping with him to say anything else."

She drew back. "I'm *not* sleeping with Ben."

"What's the matter?" His mom's eyebrows went up. "Not good enough for you? Not rich enough, maybe."

Ashley realized the other woman was baiting her, that no matter what she said, it would be turned against her. A fast retreat seemed the best option. "Excuse me. I've got work to do." She turned on her heel.

"Wait up."

She drew in a steadying breath before turning around again.

"Tell him that he won."

Ashley tried not to let on that she understood what that meant. Ben had shared a little about his mother's threats the day after the appraiser had come to the farm. Grandpa Grant, according to Ben's attorney, wasn't in any real danger of being found incompetent. There was too much evidence to the contrary and more than one medical professional willing to attest to that fact. Still, Ben had been afraid his mother would press on to the bitter end out of spite.

"Tell him I quit. I'd fight for it, but then the attorneys would take it all anyway."

Somehow Ashley kept from smiling. "I'll tell him." But after Ben's mom got back into her car and drove away, Ashley did a happy dance right in the middle of the barnyard. She waved her arms up high and shouted, "Thank You, Jesus!" For the first time, she understood what others felt when they did the same.

Still grinning, she turned and headed for her office in the barn. As she stepped through the doorway, she saw something on her desk. A box, wrapped in shiny silver paper and decorated with a pearlescent ribbon and bow. Her heart gave a little flutter as she stepped toward it. A square envelope was slipped beneath the ribbon. She opened it and removed the card.

For Ashley. May you be blessed. Ben and Grant.

Wondering what they'd given her, she slid the ribbon from the package and removed the paper. Inside was a box that held a Bible, the leather a dark-burgundy color. She took it from the box and pressed it against her chest. Tears welled unexpectedly. The Bible she'd been reading since becoming a follower of Christ was one she'd found in a secondhand store. She'd never owned a brand-new one, and she was profoundly moved that this was what the two men had given her.

She sank onto her chair, set the Bible on the desk, and carefully opened it to the middle, pressing gently on each side. Then she began slowly working her way, a few pages at a time, toward the front and back covers. Her dad, a great lover of books, had taught her this method when she was no more than five or six years old. "Do it this way," he'd said, "and you'll break in a book without ever ruining its spine." She'd never forgotten the lesson, and she never acquired a new bound book without taking the time needed to prepare it for reading. It seemed all the more important because this was a Bible.

A short while later she came to an attached ribbon marker, folded between two pages. She stopped long enough to straighten it between index finger and thumb, and that's when she saw a small sticky note had been added to the page. *Remember this, Ashley,* had been scrawled in black ink onto the pale-yellow paper, along with an arrow pointing upward. Her gaze slid to the verse above the note.

"For I know the plans I have for you," says the Lord. *"They are plans for good and not for disaster, to give you a future and a hope."*

The words seemed to coil around her heart and warm her soul.

Traffic was heavy as Ben drove along the freeway at three o'clock that afternoon. He'd completed the repairs he was hired to do in record time. Determined to get home before Ashley left for the day, he hadn't even taken time to eat lunch, as evidenced by the audible growl from his belly as he took the freeway exit and turned onto Meridian Road.

More than once during the day, he'd thought about calling Ashley. Not that he had a reason to, other than wanting to hear her voice. Sometimes he second-guessed his decisions when it came to her. One moment he believed firmly that he needed to give her time to find her way. Others he feared his hesitation, his patience, would allow her to walk away from him for good, that he would never have a chance to change her mind, to win her heart.

When he turned into the driveway, a weight lifted off his chest. Her pickup was still parked near the barn. There were also several other vehicles that belonged to the construction crew. And it was the foreman, Jerry Castle, who walked toward Ben as soon as he'd stepped out of his truck.

"Good news, Ben," the man said. "We're finished."

"Really? I thought it was going to be another day or two."

"Nope. We're done." He looked toward the new stables. "We're packing up our gear now and doing the last of the cleanup. Want to have a look?"

"Sure."

The two men fell into step.

After they'd walked past the barn, Ben noticed Ashley in the outdoor arena with Paisley. She rode the paint in slow circles, guiding the horse more with the pressure of her legs than the reins. Everything in Ben wanted to change direction and go to her. He forced himself to stick with Jerry.

As soon as they entered the stables, Ben knew Ashley had been there before him. Probably for the better part of the day. Tack had been moved to the room near the main entrance. Lead ropes were fastened to hooks near each stall door.

But it was the observation room, where parents and others could sit and watch in comfort, that caught Ben's full attention. Chairs had been arranged, some near the glass that separated them from the indoor arena, others in small groupings around the room. Cushions had been placed on a number of the chairs. A couple of area rugs softened and warmed the concrete floor. A bookshelf had been lined with books for all levels of readers. Posters of horses had been pinned to the wall, filling much of the available space. In the bathroom in the far corner, the air was scented with something fresh and minty. Seeing the reeds in a small green bottle on a shelf, he suspected that was the source. He chuckled to himself. It would be several months before this building, this observation room, was in full use, and yet Ashley had already made it the most welcoming place on the farm.

He turned toward the doorway where Jerry stood silently. "It's even better than I imagined it would be."

"You have Ashley to thank for all of these finishing touches."

"I know. I could tell."

"I'm glad I got to work on this project. I'd never heard of equine therapy before. Ashley explained what you plan to do here. I told my sister about it, and you may hear from her. I think she's gonna want to volunteer or donate or something."

"Whatever it is she chooses to do, it'll be appreciated."

"I'll tell her that too." Jerry pushed off the doorjamb. "Do you have any questions for me? Or did you see anything we need to take a second look at?"

Ben shook his head. "I don't think so."

"Okay, then." Jerry tugged on his cap. "I'll help the guys finish cleaning up. You let us know if anything comes up."

"I will. Thanks, Jerry. I'll be sure and let your boss know how pleased I am with the work you all did."

Jerry grinned and nodded before stepping out of view.

Ben gave the observation room one last look before heading outside again. His gaze went straight to the big arena. Ashley was no longer riding. She'd dismounted and was now brushing Paisley, the saddle and blanket resting on the top rail of the fencing. The brush stopped in midsweep when she saw him.

"You got back earlier than expected," she called to him.

"Yeah."

"Your mother was here to see you."

His stomach sank at the news. "Was she in one of her moods?"

"Yes." Ashley nodded, but the smile remained. "But she had good news."

That surprised him. "Good news?"

"Good for you and your grandfather. *She* wasn't too happy about it."

He closed the distance, stopping on the opposite side of the fence, eager to hear the rest.

"She said to tell you that you won. She said she would have fought you for the farm, but even after she won the attorneys would take everything anyway."

Ben released a breath. "I didn't doubt we would win, but I was afraid it would take longer than this before it was over."

"I think God answered your prayers."

If it weren't for the stupid fence between them, he would have kissed her. "You're right. He did."

"I got your gift," Ashley added. "Yours and your grandfather's. Thank you. It was very thoughtful."

"We thought you might like it."

Her cheeks and nose were red from the cold. Tendrils of hair had escaped her ponytail, giving her a delightfully disheveled appearance. But there was something else that drew his notice. She looked more . . . more at ease than he'd seen her in a long while.

"Did you write that note in Jeremiah?"

"What note?"

She smiled. "I thought it must be Grant's handwriting instead of yours."

"What did it say?"

She quoted the verse to him.

"Ah. It's a good one for all of us to remember."

"I'm going to try to memorize a new verse every week. Maybe you can share a list of favorites sometime."

"I'll do that."

They were silent for a long while, simply standing there, looking into each other's eyes. For the second time, he wished the fence wasn't standing between them. In another moment, he might have climbed over it. But then she lowered her gaze to the brush in her hand.

He tried to think of something else to say. Anything else to say. Finally he settled on a neutral topic, something he hadn't told her yet. "Kurt and his mom came to see me yesterday afternoon. Like she said they would. She's going to let Kurt come over a couple of days a week. Wednesdays after school and Saturday mornings."

"Is he your first client?"

He shrugged. "Sort of."

"Then we should have a file for him, shouldn't we?"

"Yes." He grinned. He couldn't help it. Whenever she said "we," it made him happy.

Ashley untied the loose knot in the lead rope and started walking toward the arena exit. Ben kept pace on his side of the fence. By the time they reached the gate, he'd sensed a change in her mood. He held the gate open for her and Paisley. They started through, but she stopped suddenly, her expression serious. "I need to ask a favor," she said softly.

"Sure. Anything."

"You don't know what it is."

He waited.

"I want to see my brother. It would help if you went with me."

Friday, December 22, 1944

His morning chores completed, Andrew's gaze scanned the newspaper headlines.

Yanks Stop German Drive 40 Miles inside Belgium
Nazi Forces Half across Luxembourg in Ardennes Drive
German Command Claims Bridgeheads on Ourthe River
Factors behind Nazi Surprise Thrust Analyzed by Reporter

With a knot forming in his belly, he began to read the longest article. He stopped when he came to the quote of a first army staff officer who said "the biggest battle of the war and the greatest slaughter man has ever known" was likely before the German counteroffensive was completed.

"God, protect Ben. Only You know if he's providing air support for all of those soldiers on the ground. He probably is. Help him to help them. Help him to save lives. Bring this war to an end, Father. In Your great mercy, bring it to an end. Keep Oscar safe in the Pacific until it's over and he can come home."

"What did you say?" Helen stepped into the kitchen.

He laid the newspaper on the table. "I was praying for Ben and Oscar's safety. And for all the boys fighting."

"How bad is the news today?"

"Probably worse than they want us to know," he answered grimly.

His wife came to stand beside his chair. He leaned his head against her side while his right arm went around her waist.

"Maybe we'll get some letters today," he said, as much for himself as for Helen.

She leaned over and kissed the top of his head before moving away. "I hope so. It always feels an eternity between them." She dampened a cloth and began to wipe the countertop, although she'd already cleaned the kitchen after getting the younger children fed and off to school.

"Mom? Dad?" Louisa called. A second later the front door closed against the bitter December wind.

"We're in here." Andrew folded the paper, putting the worst of the headlines facedown on the table.

His daughter entered the kitchen, cheeks pink and eyes bright. "I've got a surprise." Her smile told them it was a good one.

"What is it?" Helen asked.

"You're going to be grandparents." Clapping her hands, Louisa hopped up and down a few times—looking like the teenager she was.

"Grandparents?" Helen looked at Andrew, joy wiping away the worry in a flash. In the next moment mother and daughter were hugging and laughing.

His wife didn't seem to mind that she would become a grandmother while she was still in her thirties. Look at her. She barely looked more than a teenager herself. Weren't grandmothers supposed to have broad laps and gray hair? For that matter, weren't grandfathers supposed to walk with a bit of a stoop?

"Dad?"

He stood and went to Louisa, embracing her as her mother had done. "When's the happy occasion?"

"Around the fourth of July."

Andrew laughed. "Well, why not? We already celebrate Frani's birthday and your wedding anniversary on that day. Why not add another reason for joy to the mix?"

Chapter 28

Ashley's heart raced as she waited for her brother to be brought to the visiting area. It had taken days for the visit to happen. She wasn't sure if the delay had to do with the application process or jail rules or Dylan's own reluctance to see her. Her mom possibly knew since Ashley had left the arrangements up to her, but she hadn't asked. It was all she could do to keep up her courage to see Dylan, to say the things she wanted to say.

A sound drew her gaze toward the door. Her brother entered, dressed in jail garb. Six weeks had made a drastic difference in his appearance. He'd lost weight since the day she'd seen him outside of her home, and he looked older than his actual years. Much older. At least his eyes were clear. There was no haze of drugs in their depth.

Once Dylan was seated opposite her, beyond the plexiglass, Ashley said, "It's good to see you."

"Is it?" His voice sounded part listless, part resentful.

She swallowed. "Yes."

"You haven't come with Mom before this."

"I couldn't. I was angry with you."

"When aren't you angry with me, Ash?"

It was a fair question, but not the reason for her visit. "I wanted to see you to tell you that, no matter what, I love you. You're my brother. I'll always love you."

"Great."

"And I forgive you."

He swore beneath his breath.

Had she expected this to be easy? No. And yet her brother's response hurt anyway. "I was remembering the other day, how Dad took us trick-or-treating, and then he'd sneak some of our candy for himself, pretending we wouldn't see him. We laughed so hard. Do you remember that?"

"Sure, I remember."

"He used to tell me to always look after you 'cause you were my little brother. I wish I'd done a better job of it."

Dylan's sullen expression eased a little. "You were a kid. You did the best you could."

"Maybe."

"You couldn't control me. Neither could Mom. I sure didn't make it easy on you."

"No. We couldn't control you. But I wish—" She broke off, tears filling her eyes.

"Don't cry. All Mom does is cry when she sees me, both here or during one of our video visits."

Ashley sniffed and dried her eyes with a tissue. "You're right. I'll stop." She drew a deep breath and let it out on a sigh. "And I'll change the subject. That should help. Besides, I want to tell you what's happened to me and why I'm so determined not to go on blaming you and being angry with you."

"What happened? You find God or something?" He spoke dismissively.

"I didn't have to find Him. He was there all the time. Waiting for me." She smiled. "Will you let me tell you what's happened to me?"

"Okay. You've got about ten more minutes. Go ahead."

In the waiting area, Ben occupied his time by answering some texts and emails on his phone. But even with distractions, his thoughts were never far from Ashley and her brother. Visits with prisoners were kept short, yet the wait felt long. He hoped it was going well. He hoped Dylan would listen to Ashley. Whatever happened, he knew God was in the midst of the situation.

The opening of a door at the opposite end of the room drew his attention from his phone screen. An older man and woman exited first. Ashley followed right behind them. Ben stood and waited for her to walk to him.

"How was it?"

"Okay." She shrugged. "I think."

He couldn't help it. He put his arm around her shoulders. It pleased him that she didn't pull away.

"He says he won't be here much longer. His sentencing will happen soon. But I asked him if he would add you to his visitor's list."

"You did?" He drew his head back so he could meet her gaze.

She nodded.

"And?"

"And he agreed. I think he's scared. He pretends not to be,

but he is. Anyway, his attorney said it would help his case if he was willing to work with someone on recovery."

Ben cleared his throat. "So he knows my name."

"Yes."

"Does he also know I was there the night he was arrested? That I'm the same guy."

"I don't think so."

"You'd better give me the name of his attorney. My first visit better be with him."

Ashley nodded. "Whatever you need. I'll get the attorney's information from Mom."

"Great." He removed his arm from around her shoulders. "You know I'll do whatever I can to help."

"Yes, Ben. I know you will."

He searched her eyes, wondering if she'd meant that to sound the way it did.

"We'd better go," she said softly. "I don't want my boss to think I'm shirking my work."

"No." He gave her a gentle smile. "That wouldn't do."

Neither of them said anything during the drive to the farm. Ben could tell she needed to be left to her own thoughts. It wasn't until the truck turned into the driveway that she broke the silence.

"Ben, I'm sorry I reacted the way I did when you told me you were in recovery."

He glanced to his right as he braked to a halt. "I understood why."

"You only understand some of it. It wasn't all about Dylan."

"I'm listening if you want to tell me."

She released a sigh. "There was a guy I dated awhile back. Paul. I wasn't in love with him or even serious, but I thought maybe we might get serious in time. He was smart, professional, successful. In fact, there were times I wondered why he chose to date someone like me."

Ben didn't wonder why. He could have told her a hundred reasons why any man would want to be with her.

"I never talked about Dylan's problems with anybody, but eventually I decided he ought to know the truth about my family. The whole truth. So I told him everything."

Jealousy tweaked Ben's chest. He knew that didn't make a lot of sense, but he recognized the feeling.

"It seemed safe to tell him about it. Dylan had been sober for a while. Long enough that I was beginning to have hope for him to stay that way." Ashley's gaze turned out the front windshield. "A few months later I came home from work and found Paul and Dylan in my place. They were drunk. The both of them. They'd been partying together."

"Ashley," Ben whispered.

She raised a hand to stop him from saying more, but her gaze remained on the land beyond the glass. "Even before I told Paul about Dylan, he knew that I didn't drink and didn't like to be around anyone who did. In all that time, I never saw him take a drink of anything alcoholic. Not beer. Not wine. Not anything. And I certainly never smelled anything on his breath or saw his eyes look unfocused. I never saw any signs at all. He fooled me. *Me!*" Now she looked at Ben. "Paul got drunk with my brother, even after all that I told him about the hurt and the pain. And when I caught them at it, he thought it was funny."

No wonder she'd reacted the way she had when Ben told her about his past. No wonder she had trust issues.

"I've been scared ever since that night. Scared that someone else would fool me. That I would be too blind to see what was staring me right in the face."

"You don't have to be afraid of me."

She was silent for what seemed a very long time. "I believe you, Ben. I'm thankful that you want to try to help Dylan. And I'm . . . I'm glad you're my friend."

She didn't say it, but Ben heard the silent *But* all the same. He was going to have to be patient awhile longer.

Monday, January 29, 1945

A foot of snow lay on the ground, and the temperature on that blustery January day hovered just above freezing. But inside the barn, where the still air smelled of animals and hay, it felt considerably warmer.

Andrew leaned his forearms on the stall railing and watched as Frani brushed the yearling filly she'd named Sunrise in honor of the time of her birth. For this moment, he was able to push aside thoughts of the landing on Luzon in the Philippines. For this moment, he was able to cease wondering if Oscar had been part of that task force.

Frani stepped in front of the filly and pressed forehead to forehead. "You're so pretty," she said to the horse, loud enough for her dad to hear too.

And so are you, he thought, feeling as if time had slipped through his fingers. Frani had acquired a girlish figure in recent months, a fact he'd been loath to admit to anyone, least of all himself. His youngest daughter was twelve and a half. How much longer before boys were hanging around, the way Ben's college friends had come to the farm hoping to catch Louisa's attention? Not long enough to suit him.

"Hey, Dad." Frani looked at him.

"Hmm."

"Do you suppose we could make a riding arena up near the road in the spring? I'd like to work with Jewel more. It's fun to ride around, but I think I'd like to do more. You know, maybe some trick riding like they do in rodeos."

"Trick riding?" He straightened away from the stall. He knew his daughter loved horses, but he didn't like the sound of that.

"It doesn't have to be dangerous, Dad."

Good. Because he was sick to death of all things dangerous.

Almost of its own volition, his hand went to the breast pocket of his coat where he'd placed Oscar's latest letter.

Dear Dad,

One of the guys told me that fathers like to get letters just to them sometimes, so I thought this should be one of those letters. Of course, I know you will show it to Mom, so I want her to know I love her. I don't know how long it will take this letter to get to you. I'm sending it through a friend who is bound for the States. It won't be going through any censor that way, which means maybe I can say more than I have in other letters. Not that I plan to say anything I shouldn't. You know, loose lips sink ships. I know I don't write often enough. Sorry about that. It's hard when you've got to think about every word you put on paper.

The ship I'm on has fought some tough battles since I came on board. It is scarier than I thought it would be. I've seen enemy planes not just drop bombs but fly into ships, almost like it was on purpose. You see those things coming, but there is nothing you can do but keep fighting and keep praying. As to that, I've learned a lot about prayer since I joined the navy. You might not believe me, but it's true. Faith gets to be more important when you see things exploding around you and metal tearing into flesh.

I think a lot about Ben these days. I used to envy him, getting to go off at the start of the war and fly those planes and be right in the thick of it. But I guess all I was thinking about was getting even. Or maybe I wanted the glory. Turns out, there isn't a lot of glory when it comes to the fighting. It is more sweat and fear than anything else.

Dad, I'm not sorry I joined the navy. I don't want you thinking I am. I'm glad to be here. We didn't have any choice but to respond after we were attacked at Pearl Harbor, and I'm proud to fight for America. But I finally realized there isn't a guarantee that I'll make it home. I've seen more than a few good men die already. Young and old. Doesn't make a difference. They go if a bullet or a bomb has their name on it.

General MacArthur kept his promise to return to the Philippines. I know because I was there at Leyte with him. And I want to be there when the general steps foot on the Island of Japan too. But there's other places we're going to have to take back from the enemy first, and from what I've seen, I don't think they are going to let any of it go easy. So I am plenty aware that I might not make it to Japan, let alone make it home.

I guess more than anything I wish I let you and Mom know how much I love you when I was there to tell you in person. I've been thinking how young you both were when you made a home for me and Ben and Louisa. You didn't have to do that, but you did. You loved us, even when we weren't so lovable. I'm one of the lucky ones. I realize that now more than ever. If anything happens to me, if I don't get to come home again, I want that to be what you remember most. That I know how lucky I am.

Oscar

"Dad?"

Andrew blinked away thoughts of the letter—and was surprised to find Frani now out of the stall and standing before him, her expression somber.

"Are you okay?"

"Yeah. I'm fine."

"I think about them too," she said as she slipped her arms around his waist.

"I know you do, baby." He leaned down and kissed the top of her head. "I know you do."

Chapter 29

Early the following Wednesday morning, Ashley stood in her bathroom, staring at her reflection in the mirror, wondering if others thought she looked any different. She felt so different on the inside that she wanted others to see it. She hoped they could. Sadly, neither her mom nor brother had noticed a change. Not so far, anyway. But then, Dylan had only seen her on the other side of plexiglass in a less-than-congenial setting, and the lunch with her mom on Monday had been brief because of an appointment.

"But I want them to see it," she whispered. "I want them to see how God's set me free."

Each morning it seemed that she awoke with a little more hope and a little more joy and a lot more freedom.

Her phone pinged, letting her know she had a text message. It was from a guy she knew in the rescue network.

Eddie Walker: Urgent. Need help with horses. Owyhee County. Can u come with trailer?

She knew without asking that Ben would say yes, but she dialed him quickly.

"Hey, Ashley."

"Sorry to call you so early. I'm needed for a rescue. I might not be to the barn for several hours. Maybe not until this afternoon. Is that okay?"

"Of course it is. Do you need me to come along?"

She would have loved for him to come along. She treasured the time she spent with him. She treasured it more with each passing day. But she also knew he had another commitment that morning with a counselor. "No, I can manage. I won't be alone. Whatever's going on, we can handle it."

"Call me if that changes."

"I will."

After ending the call, she smiled, enjoying the feeling that had flowed through her at the sound of his voice. Then her eyes widened. She'd been thinking that she awoke each day with a little more hope. Suddenly she realized what she hoped for. She hoped for Ben. She hoped for a future with him. She wanted to call him back, to tell him what she'd discovered, but she couldn't. It would have to wait. According to Eddie, the situation was urgent.

She replied to the text and soon learned her destination. Then she rushed through her morning chores, hooked the trailer to her pickup, and headed south, her dogs riding shotgun.

It took better than an hour to reach the location. The ranch, if it could be called that, was rundown. Sun-bleached buildings tilted to the side, fencing ready to topple in many places. A sign near the highway advertised "Horse Training." If what Ashley found there was "training," she would eat her hat. Someone had been using a whip on the horses without mercy.

"Is the guy responsible in jail?" she asked Eddie as the two of them stood at the corral fence.

"I'd like to think so. But probably it'll just be a fine."

An unrelenting, cold wind whistled across the sagebrush-covered desert, sending dust devils churning across the land.

Ashley turned up the collar of her coat. "So does he own these horses?"

"Not these five." Eddie pointed. "They're the ones we're taking with us. And I hope their owners sue the heck out of this jerk. I'd do worse to him if I got my hands on him."

She nodded, strong emotions making it hard to speak.

"I'm taking three with me," Eddie continued. "Those two, the big bays, they're going with you. The owner said they're yours to do with as you please. You can keep or sell as long as they don't go to a kill pen. But they're ruined for what the owner intended, and he would never be able to sell them the way they are now."

"Ruined?"

"You'll see. Scared of their own shadows. Not sure anybody will ever be able to ride them again. And don't make any sudden moves. They spook easy. May not be much fun to get them into the trailers."

Eddie was right. It wasn't fun. It took over an hour to coax the five frightened horses into the two trailers. By the time they were ready to pull out of the depressing place, Ashley was chilled to the bone.

Eddie stuck an arm out the window of his truck to wave goodbye as he turned right onto the highway. Ashley waved back, prepared to turn left. But she decided to send a quick text to Ben before beginning the long drive back to the farm.

Ashley: Starting drive back. Should be there around 11:30. Bringing two horses with me.

After hitting Send, she dropped the phone into the console,

checked the deserted highway for traffic, and turned left. The wind pushed against the truck with full force, and she felt the two horses dance nervously in the trailer. One of them whinnied its complaint.

"Easy, boys. It'll be better once you're to your new home."

She reached for the knob on the radio, hoping to find some music to drown out the lonely whistle of the wind. Mostly she found static. With a sigh, she settled for silence. Another wind gust hit the truck and trailer, and she tightened her grip on the steering wheel. One of the dogs whimpered.

"Have a little faith, fellas." She glanced to see which one had made the sound.

As her gaze returned to the road, she saw a porcupine waddle into her lane. She cringed, certain she would hit it. But instead of the *thunk* of a small body colliding with a tire, she felt an even stronger gust of wind push the truck and trailer sideways. Panic rose in her chest as she fought to keep the truck upright. In the next instant, they seemed to be airborne, the seat belt cutting into her chest and shoulder. A grinding sound roared in her ears, then pain exploded in her head before blackness overtook her.

As soon as Ben received Ashley's text message, he moved horses around so that the new arrivals would have a paddock to themselves. He put hay in the wheelbarrow, although he kept it outside the pasture, not sure if the horses should eat right away or not. That would be up to Ashley.

Since she'd gotten such an early start, Ben knew she would be hungry when she arrived at the farm. Normally she brought her own sack lunch and most always ate it in her office. But even if she'd remembered to pack a lunch that morning, he decided she was going to eat something hot and filling. He wouldn't take no for an answer today.

At eleven thirty, he had soup on the stove and toasted French bread warm in the oven. It was still there at noon with no sign of Ashley. After another fifteen minutes, he texted her, asking for her ETA. No answer. Which, if she was driving, was for the best.

By twelve thirty, he'd grown anxious. He called her phone, but it went to voice mail.

At the tone, he said, "Ashley, it's Ben. Just wondering when you thought you'd be here. It's already twelve thirty. Give me a call. Okay?"

Ashley stretched her arm as far as possible, but she couldn't reach her phone. It lay against the passenger door, quiet now. It had turned in circles when it buzzed from an incoming call.

With a groan, she touched the top of her head. The pain seemed worse, even though the flow of blood had stopped. Her hair and scalp were sticky now. She wasn't sure how long she'd been there or how many times she'd wafted in and out of consciousness.

From what she could tell, the truck was on its side in a ravine. Her seat belt had held her in place so she hadn't fallen to the other side of the cab, but it was also her seat belt that continued to hold her captive. She was unable to reach the buckle with her right hand, and to complicate things, her left arm had been injured. There was no strength in it. Not even enough to move it.

Speed and Jack both seemed to be okay. Banged up a bit, perhaps, but able to move about. Jack had stayed in the cab with her, but at some point, Speed had crawled out through the now missing back window. The wind whistled through the opening, and she shivered, feeling the chill. Miraculously, the horse trailer was upright—she could turn her head enough to see that—and the two horses inside were quiet for now. All she could do was pray they were unharmed. As if they hadn't been through enough already.

"God, help us," she moaned as her eyes drifted closed once again.

Wednesday, April 4, 1945

The Henning family gathered on the farm to celebrate Louisa's nineteenth birthday. There were nine of them gathered around the table that day. Andrew and Helen. Andrew's parents and Mother Greyson. Louisa and Samuel. Frani and Andy Jr.

Looking at his oldest daughter, six months pregnant, her face glowing with happiness, Andrew felt a surge of thanksgiving. They were not all here. They were not all protected from the perils of war. But God had brought them safe thus far.

A verse from Joshua, which had become such an anchor for him in these past few years, replayed in his mind. *"For ye have not passed this way heretofore."* No, they hadn't passed this way before, but God not only knew the way, He was the way. God was both walking with them and He waited at the destination, wherever it was.

"Do you know what I learned in school today?" Frani said, intruding on his thoughts.

He expected her to tell them all something about horses, since that was her usual topic of conversation. She didn't.

"When the United States' First Army crossed over the Rhine River last month, it was the first invading army to do that since the days of Napoleon. Isn't that something? And maybe Ben was there to see it."

"If he saw it," Andy intruded, "it woulda been from the air."

"You don't know that." Frani poked her brother in the shoulder.

"Children," Helen cautioned softly.

His youngest daughter's comment couldn't help but turn Andrew's thoughts in the direction of his sons. They had received letters from Ben on a more regular basis this year. The same couldn't be said of Oscar. It seemed forever since the last one had come.

Louisa touched the back of his hand. "Do you know what Ben wrote to me?"

He shook his head.

"He said he can't picture me getting ready to be a mother 'cause I'll always be a snot-nosed kid to him. Can you believe that? I'm going to make him pay for it when he gets home."

Everyone laughed. Everyone but Andrew. His thoughts had drifted to the closing paragraph of Ben's most recent letter.

> Not sure I ever said this in a letter, but I'll be honest. I haven't always believed I would make it home outside of a pine box. Not given the percentage of bombers that fail to come back from missions. But I'm not feeling that way these days. I think the end is in sight, and I think I'll be coming home again. But I won't be the same kid who left Idaho. I don't know that I'll ever be the same.

"We have not passed this way heretofore," he said beneath his breath. "But God has."

"What did you say, Dad?"

He looked at Louisa and smiled. "Nothing, dear. I was just talking to myself."

Chapter 30

Ben was afraid Ashley might keep all of her contact numbers on her phone. That's what he did. Relief rushed through him when he saw the address book on her desk. It was filled with names and numbers and notes about how she knew each person. People in the equine rescue network had all been entered in a particular color, making it easier for Ben to work his way through them. It took calls to eight different numbers, but finally he found someone who knew where Ashley had gone that morning. Once he knew that, it wasn't long before he was on his way with a Thermos of hot chocolate, some snack bars, and several blankets on the seat beside him.

He'd made one more call before he left the farm. He'd called his grandfather and asked him to pray. It was the older man's prayers—and the prayers of whoever Grandpa Grant had told next—that kept Ben's fear at bay. He was sure of it.

He managed to keep his speed from going too much over the limit. He didn't want to get stopped. Not because of a ticket but because it would slow him down even more. Strong gusts of wind buffeted the truck as dark clouds began to fill the skies, making midday feel like dusk.

He added his own prayers to those of his grandfather. He prayed for Ashley to be kept safe, wherever she was. He prayed that he would see her around the next bend in the road. He prayed that she would know how important she was in his life.

More important than even he'd known up until that moment.

His gaze dropped to the speedometer. If he'd estimated right, he should be within thirty miles of Ashley's original destination. He looked up again, scanning the rolling desert that surrounded him. Sagebrush and lava rock. Mountains to the south. River gorge to the north. And not much else. Not another vehicle in sight. No buildings. Nothing.

His truck went over a swell in the road. At the top of the rise, a gust hit him so hard the right tires left the asphalt and threw up dirt and gravel. Even as he corrected, his heart seemed to lurch with equal force. If the wind hit a horse trailer like that . . .

He pressed his foot down hard on the accelerator.

Ashley came to again, this time to the feel of Jack's tongue on her cheek. He whimpered as he settled back against the other door.

"I'm okay, boy."

A lie. Her head throbbed. Her side hurt from where the seat belt pressed into her. Her arm pounded. She was cold, and her mouth was dry. Beyond the windshield, it had grown darker. Had night fallen or was it only the coming storm? She couldn't be sure. A thump sounded. She managed to lift and turn her head enough that she saw Speed, standing on the truck's bumper, staring in at her through the windshield.

"I'm okay," she repeated, so softly she wasn't sure she made any sound at all.

Was it possible she was going to die like this? The accident didn't seem to have been all that serious, and yet there she was, suspended in the air, trapped by a seat belt, the cold working its way into her bones. Perhaps she *would* die like this. It made her sad to think of those things that had gone undone or unsaid or both. She would like to tell her mom how much she appreciated her. She would like to tell Dylan one more time how much she loved him. Yes, she was sad. But she wasn't afraid. She wished she could tell everyone she knew that she wasn't afraid to die, and the reason why. It would surprise those who knew her best. It even surprised her.

She tried one more time to find the buckle. If she could press the latch and free herself, she could crawl out of the truck. But the buckle didn't seem to be there. It had disappeared somewhere into the seat or behind her body.

"Stay awake," she told herself. "Keep alert."

She tried to remember one of the Bible verses she'd read over the past week. She'd highlighted so many. Time and again, something had spoken to her heart. And yet now, when she was certain they might bring her comfort, her mind was blank.

"Grandpa Grant would be able to quote them to me. So would Ben."

Ben. He'd come to mean so very much to her. Despite her fears and determination to resist him, he'd won her heart. He'd won it with his generous and compassionate nature. He'd won it with his smile. He'd won it with the way he loved people, loved those less fortunate. He'd won it with the way he'd changed his life and now wanted to help others change theirs with the use of horses. He'd won it with the way he loved God.

"Ben," she said, her eyes closing, despite how hard she tried to keep them open.

"I'm here, Ashley. I'm here."

She didn't open her eyes, certain it was her mind playing tricks on her.

"Ashley, stay with me."

An arm came around her neck, supporting her head. Another around her waist. The relief was instant, and she relaxed into the embrace.

"Hold on, honey. We're going to get you out of here."

She opened her eyes. He was there. He was real. She hadn't imagined him after all. "Ben."

"Where are you hurt?" he asked, his lips close to her ear.

"Just my left arm, I think. I can't move it. And my head. It was bleeding."

"Help is coming. I don't want to move you until the EMTs are here. They'll know the best way to free you without causing you more pain or risking further injury."

"Are the horses okay?"

"They look fine. Restless but okay. The trailer stayed upright."

"Speed and Jack?" She closed her eyes again.

"They're fine too. A few bruises and scratches. That's all."

She felt herself slipping into unconsciousness again. "I'm glad you found me."

"Me too." His mouth was near her ear. "I love you, Ashley. You're found for good. I'm never letting you go."

V-E Day 1945

Early on that morning in May, Andrew was turning out the cows to pasture when he saw his oldest daughter and her husband pull their old Model T Ford into the driveway. He wondered what had brought them to the farm at this early hour, but he returned his attention to the cows, guiding them around the corner of the barn. A few minutes later, Helen's loud cry sent alarm shooting through him. He took off running toward the house, the cows forgotten.

His wife saw him coming and hurried toward him, her cheeks streaked with tears.

O God, not one of the boys.

"Andrew, it's over." Her words hardly made sense to him. "The war in Germany is over. Ben will be coming home."

He couldn't take in her words. It was almost as if they were in another language.

"It's over in Europe, Dad. Germany has surrendered. Unconditionally."

"Over?" he echoed, still hardly able to comprehend.

"It's in the news," Samuel said. "President Truman's gonna do a broadcast at seven o'clock. We wanted to come here and listen to it with you."

"We'd better go in. It's almost time."

He allowed himself to be drawn into the house. Once there, he turned on the radio, listening to the static as he adjusted the knob. Frani and Andy soon joined them, breakfast and school forgotten. They hadn't long to wait before the president of the United States was introduced. Silence gripped the room.

"This is a solemn but glorious hour," Truman began. "I wish that Franklin D. Roosevelt had lived to see this day. General Eisenhower informs me that the forces of Germany have surrendered to the

United Nations. The flags of freedom fly all over Europe. For this victory, we join in offering our thanks to the Providence which has guided and sustained us through the dark days of adversity and into light."

Immediately after the brief address, no one moved. Even the children seemed to understand the momentous nature of this day, this hour. The war in Europe was over at last.

As had been so often the case of late, Andrew's mind went to the book of Joshua. This time he remembered Joshua's address to the eastern tribes before he sent them to their homeland and their families, cautioning them to remember to serve the Lord God and to keep Him first in their hearts. *May we all do the same, Father. And may we provide comfort to everyone who lost a loved one during this war.*

"Do you suppose the Finkels know?" Samuel asked, breaking the silence. Without waiting for an answer, he got to his feet. "I'm going to tell them. Then we all need to go into town to celebrate."

Helen looked at him with wide eyes. "Celebrate? It's barely seven in the morning."

"Who cares?" Samuel hurried out the door.

Andrew shoved away the thoughts of loss and heartache. "Samuel's right. We need to celebrate today." He stood, his gaze sweeping over the family gathered with him. "Get ready, everybody. We're going to town."

Chapter 31

"Ashley Showalter, you get back into that bed."

She didn't look up at her mom until she'd finished pulling on her right boot—not easy to do one-handed. "I can't stand to stay down another minute. Two days of rest is enough. There's nothing seriously wrong with me."

"Your arm has a bad sprain, and you hit your head and needed stitches. I wouldn't call that nothing serious."

"Mom." She reached for her other boot and began tugging it on. "I'm fine. I appreciate all you've done for me, but I'm going to go crazy if I don't go to work."

"Ben told me you don't have to go in until you're completely healed."

"They're having another training session for volunteers tomorrow. I want to make sure everything is ready with the horses. Plus I need to see to my new rescues."

"You know Ben's taken care of everything."

Ashley stood. "Yes, I know. But I need to see to the horses myself." She walked to where her mom stood in the doorway, stopping long enough to kiss her cheek. "I love you, and I love that you've spoiled me rotten since I left the ER. But it's time for you to go home and sleep in your own bed. I'm perfectly able to get along now."

Her mom opened her mouth as if to argue further. Then, after releasing a sigh, she closed it again. Her eyes said she knew when she'd lost the battle.

Ashley smiled as she leaned in to kiss her mom's cheek a second time. "Thank you. For everything. Not just your help since the accident. For everything."

"Be sure you tell Ben this wasn't my idea."

"I will. I promise."

An hour later, breakfast eaten and her chores finished, Ashley got into the rental car that had been delivered the day before. It was harder than expected to fasten her seat belt with only one hand, but she managed it—unlike on the day of the accident. She also felt a little too close to the ground in the midsize vehicle. It would be good to get her truck back, despite having to come up with the high deductible. The insurance company hadn't considered the truck totaled. She wasn't sure if that was good or bad and decided to worry about it later.

"Hold on, guys," she told the dogs in the back seat before pulling out of the driveway.

She arrived at the farm as Ben was walking toward the house. When he saw her, he changed directions. His smile caused her pulse to quicken, her heart to beat erratically. She'd seen him only once since the day of the accident. He'd come to her home, bringing a large bouquet of flowers for her and a box of chocolates for her mom. But saying anything personal had been difficult with her mom hovering in the background. So they'd talked about the damage to the truck and the miracle of the trailer not flipping onto its side and who had towed the horses to the farm and how the horses were getting along now.

There were things about the accident, both before and after it happened, that she still couldn't make sense of. But one thing she *did* remember. She remembered when he'd said, *"I love you, Ashley."* She remembered those words and the feel of his arms as he'd cradled her, but she couldn't hardly believe either of them.

Ben opened the car door. "I wasn't expecting you today."

"I don't do well stuck in bed."

"Bad patient, huh?"

"Very bad. Just ask my mom."

He opened the back door to let Jack and Speed out. Then he offered his hand to help Ashley from behind the wheel. She wasn't sure she needed the help, but she did want to hold his hand. She took it and allowed him to draw her up and out. Her pulse quickened even more as the seconds passed and he didn't let go.

"Ashley."

"Hmm?"

"Did I happen to tell you how scared I was when you didn't show up when you were supposed to?"

"I don't think so."

A gust of wind hit her back and pushed her closer to him. She found herself staring at his throat.

"Well, I'm telling you now."

She tilted her head back.

"There's a whole lot more I want to tell you about how I feel." There was no sign of a smile on his lips now.

Her heart thrummed in response. "And there's a whole lot more I'd like to hear."

At last the corners of his mouth curved into a slow smile, and the look warmed her better than a blazing fire.

Ben had been patient long enough. Weeks of patience. He gently drew Ashley tight against him and claimed her lips with his own. If a picture was worth a thousand words, he hoped his kiss was worth a million. Yet there were a few words that still needed to be spoken aloud, now when he was certain she could hear him, and when the kiss ended, he said them. "I love you, Ms. Showalter."

"I love you, too, Mr. Henning." She smiled and her eyes glittered with unshed tears.

"Let's get you inside out of the cold."

"Is it cold?"

"Yes." Although, truth be told, he didn't feel it either. He swept her up into his arms and started carrying her toward the house.

"Now what?" she asked as he stepped onto the porch.

"Now we start planning a life together."

"You're a man who loves to make plans, aren't you?"

He chuckled as he opened the door. "Some more than others, Ashley. Some more than others."

Wednesday, August 15, 1945

The Western Union telegram that came in June told Andrew and Helen that Oscar was missing in action. It hadn't been unexpected. At least not by Andrew. The battle for Okinawa had lasted for two and a half months that spring. Close to forty thousand Americans had been wounded in the fighting, and almost thirteen thousand Americans had lost their lives, many during relentless *kamikaze* attacks by the Japanese. Finally, after weeks of wondering, they received a second telegram. Oscar Tandy Henning, age eighteen, was never coming home.

For Andrew, the arrival of V-J Day was bittersweet. While others rejoiced in the streets, much the same as they'd done on V-E Day, he mourned the personal cost as he climbed the ladder to the loft in the barn and dropped to his knees.

"Naked came I out of my mother's womb, and naked shall I return thither: The LORD gave, and the LORD hath taken away; blessed be the name of the LORD."

He choked back a sob as another verse from Job came to his mind.

"Wherefore is light given to him that is in misery, and life unto the bitter in soul; Which long for death, but it cometh not."

He didn't long for actual death. He had a wife, four more children, a son-in-law, and a grandchild. There were plenty of reasons for joy. Plenty of reasons to live. And yet there was a pain in his heart unlike any he'd felt before, knowing that Oscar would never grow older. He would always be a boy in Andrew's memory. He remembered well that night he'd added Oscar's name in his Bible, the moment he'd counted the towheaded boy as one of the arrows in the Henning family quiver. Imagining life without him seemed impossible.

Andrew stayed on his knees, head bowed, eyes closed, heart

heavy for a long, long while. But eventually he recalled the familiar words of Joshua once again.

"Choose this day whom ye will serve."

He drew in a long breath as he lifted his head and his eyes, then whispered, "'But as for me and my house, we will serve the Lord.'" With that he stood, somehow knowing that God would sustain them in their time of grief and through whatever else lay before them in their earthly journey.

Epilogue

It was one of those early March days in southwestern Idaho that said winter was truly over. The sky was blue, and the sun was warm upon Ashley's head and back. Warm enough that she'd shucked off her jacket some time before.

From where she stood, she saw Ben and a little girl named Isabella approaching Thunder in the round pen. Isabella, according to her mother, had stopped speaking almost a year before. Her mother had been in a long-term abusive relationship, and although they had escaped the nightmare many months earlier, the six-year-old girl still refused to speak. The referring counselor hoped equine therapy might do what other treatment had not.

When the pair got close to the horse, they stopped. Ben hunkered down, making himself the same height as the girl. He talked to her for a while, then reached out an arm to Thunder. The big black horse sniffed Ben's hand as he took a step closer. Isabella pressed herself against Ben's side but didn't back away. Her eyes widened as she mirrored her instructor's action, reaching out her own arm. As if trained to do so, the gelding sniffed her hand too. Then he huffed and bobbed his head.

Ashley was learning—everyone who worked or volunteered at the Harmony Barn was learning—that miracles could be found in little things such as the courage to let a horse sniff a hand. Miracles could be seen in that moment when a hurting child or confused adult let a horse get close in a way that no human being was allowed. She was learning that miracles came in different sizes, both large and small. Large, like the phone call Ben had received yesterday from Craig Foster—the one where he learned his old friend planned to visit the Harmony Barn tomorrow. Small, like a smile, the way Isabella was smiling at Thunder right now.

After a long while Ben stood. Isabella slipped her hand into his, a trusting action on its own, and he walked her back to her mother. The two adults spoke briefly, then mother and child returned to their car, the session over.

After watching them go, Ben turned toward Ashley. Her pulse quickened as their gazes met. His smile caused joy to spiral through her, a now-familiar reaction. That morning she'd read a Bible verse that she was certain would be her new favorite. *"Then the Lord God said, 'It is not good for the man to be alone; I will make him a helper suitable for him.'"* Her gaze lowered to the engagement ring on her finger. She was that suitable helper for Ben, and he was the same for her. God had made them for each other.

She lifted her eyes again and saw that he had rapidly closed the distance between them. "Isabella's getting better," she said to him.

"You saw?"

"I saw."

"She's started to trust me."

Ashley moved into his arms as naturally as the taking of her next breath. "It's easy to trust you, Ben."

"Almost as easy as it is for me to love you." His gaze lowered to her mouth.

Her breath caught in anticipation of the kiss she knew would follow. As familiar as his kisses had become to her, she never tired of the thrill that moved through her at the first touch of his lips upon hers.

When he drew back, just far enough that they could look into each other's eyes again, he said, his voice husky, "I love you, Ashley. Forever."

"Cross your heart?" she whispered in return.

His smile was slow and sexy. "Cross my heart."

This was one of those good plans God had promised in Jeremiah, she realized as another wave of warmth swirled through her. Good plans that gave them a future and a hope.

"We have horses to feed, Henning," she said, and it was her voice that sounded husky now.

He grinned as he slipped an arm behind her back, and together they headed around the side of the barn, walking into their future side by side.

A Note from the Author

Dear Friends:

My mother used to tell me that my first word was *horse* rather than *mommy*. Similar to Ashley, I didn't come from a family who owned horses. I saved up and worked to buy my first horse at the age of fifteen. And although I haven't been a horse owner for far too many years, I did pass my love of horses to my daughters and to at least one of my granddaughters.

When the idea for *Cross My Heart* came to me, I knew I would be drawing on the experiences of my granddaughter Shayla, who has rescued a number of horses over the years as well as been involved in the training of wild mustangs so that they can find good homes.

The best part of writing this book came with the research on equine therapy. I read a number of wonderful books on the subject and visited an amazing therapy program located in southwest Idaho. If you love horses and want to help people, I suggest you look into programs you might have in your area. Perhaps you'll find yourself involved in something really worthwhile.

As I write this note, I'm at work on the third book in the Legacy of Faith series. In it you will meet another of Ben's (*Cross My Heart*) and Jessica's (*Who I Am with You*) cousins, and you will enter a new stage in the lives of Andrew and Helen Henning. I look forward to sharing this story when the time arrives.

Blessings,
Robin Lee Hatcher

Discussion Questions

1. Which character did you most relate to and why?
2. Ashley's experiences with her brother's addictions made her withdraw from many relationships. Have you ever allowed past experiences to keep you from living life fully?
3. Despite being a strong Christian, Ben still carried a lot of guilt. Have you found it difficult to let go of guilt over past sins or mistakes? How did you overcome it?
4. Wendy Henning was not a loving daughter or mother. Her family never understood why she behaved as she did. Have you been called to love someone who behaves in an unlovable way? Have you had someone behave in a less than kind manner toward you, but you never got answers about why they behaved that way? How have you dealt with it?
5. Equine therapy plays an important role in *Cross My Heart*. Did you have knowledge of equine therapy in any form before reading this book? What has been your own experience with horses?

6. Andrew's family was embroiled in World War II throughout this novel. Did you learn anything new about that war from these characters? Were you surprised by decisions made by Ben, Louisa, or Oscar? If so, what and why?
7. Andrew found comfort in the book of Joshua during the war years. What passages of Scripture have helped you through difficult times in life? How has God used those verses to strengthen or comfort you?
8. Andrew's Bible becomes a source of comfort and instruction for his descendants. Do you write in your Bible? What will your descendants find therein to encourage them even after you're gone?

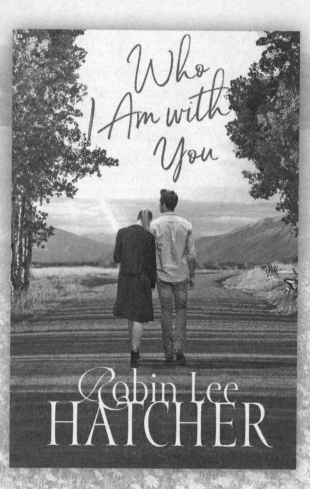

About the Author

Robin Lee Hatcher is the author of eighty novels and novellas with over five million copies of her books in print. She is known for her heartwarming and emotionally charged stories of faith, courage, and love. Her numerous awards include the RITA Award, the Carol Award, the Christy Award, the HOLT Medallion, the National Reader's Choice Award, and the Faith, Hope & Love Reader's Choice Award. Robin is also the recipient of prestigious Lifetime Achievement Awards from both American Christian Fiction Writers and Romance Writers of America. When not writing, she enjoys being with her family, spending time in the beautiful Idaho outdoors, Bible art journaling, reading books that make her cry, watching romantic movies, and decorative planning. Robin makes her home on the outskirts of Boise, sharing it with a demanding Papillon dog and a persnickety tuxedo cat.

For more information, visit robinleehatcher.com
Facebook: robinleehatcher
Twitter: @robinleehatcher